Heaven is for Heroes

By

PJ Sharon

HEAVEN IS FOR HEROES

Acknowledgements

I must, of course, start with Carol LaCoss who taught me all I know about misplaced modifiers and proper sentence structure. Thanks Carol. I'm still learning, so keep your red pen handy. I would also like to acknowledge my wonderful critique partners, my beta readers, and the vast network of friends and associates I've met through the CT chapter of RWA. You guys are awesome.

Since the onset of this journey, a host of clients, friends and family have encouraged and supported me. Thank you for cheering me on. You know who you are and I love you all!

I'd like to add a special thanks to my husband, Addy, who created the book jacket, handled all the formatting issues, and is my constant technical support in more ways than I can count. You are an amazing man, and I am the luckiest girl in the world.

Dedication

I would like to dedicate this book to all of the men and women who serve in the Armed Forces.

And to the families who love them.

CHAPTER 1

The crack of gun fire exploded in the air…once…twice…three times. I flinched with each pop, the smell of gunpowder thick in the warm mist raining down over the cemetery. The crowd around me faded into a mass of black suits, women in dark coats with their high heels sinking into the sodden grass, umbrellas overhead, and a sea of Marines in their dress blue uniforms. I clung to my mother in the folding chair beside me.

The military had it wrong. They'd made a mistake. Or maybe someone was covering up—lying. But why would they? My insides shifted and tightened. If it was a lie, Mom would never be able to live with the truth. I wasn't sure if I could either.

An eerie silence fell and then was broken by the sound of a bugle blaring out the soulful notes of Taps, the signal for the end of a long day for a Marine…or the end of his life. My grandfather saluted his comrades, his face stony and expressionless, deep lines etched between his brows and around his mouth--the only evidence of his sorrow. The weariness in his eyes spoke louder than words. He had buried too many young men.

The canopy above us kept the rain off, but my face was wet with tears. Two Marines lifted the

American flag from my brother's coffin, moving
with mechanical precision. In their shiny black
shoes and perfectly starched uniforms, they
stretched the edges taut and began folding and
creasing, folding and creasing, until the stripes
disappeared into a compact triangle with just the
white stars showing against the navy background.
One of the folders and creasers, nearly faceless
beneath his round white hat with its polished black
visor, presented the triangle of flag to my mother,
who clutched it to her chest and released another
shuddering sob. I gripped her shoulders tighter as
she collapsed against me.

 I scanned the crowd, tuning out the final
words of Father O'Keefe as he committed Levi's
soul to God and his body to the earth. Friends,
family, neighbors and military personnel
surrounded the scene, rows deep. I recognized my
friends from school, half the senior class turning out
to show their support. Katie, Samantha and Penny
from Somerville, all stood up front, crying openly
and holding hands. The pain in their eyes reflected
what my heart refused to let in. I felt hollow and
cold, almost dead inside. A terrible numbness
resided in my limbs, as if I'd fallen asleep in a snow
bank and my body had frozen. My eyes darted
through the faces, each expression as painful as the
last.

So much love, so much sadness, so much grief. Whether they knew him or not, people turned out to mourn the death of a young hometown soldier. A Connecticut boy killed in combat. My brother...my brother Levi was dead. My mind let the thought in, trying it on as if maybe I could send it back if it didn't fit. The casket, the scent of roses, what Daddy would have called 'angel's tears' falling from the heavens, gently caressing the broken hearts of the mourners—it felt surreal. I wanted to believe it was a bad dream, a made for TV movie that my family and I were playing in as extras. My mother shuddered in my arms, the scent of her strawberry shampoo waking me to the reality--this wasn't a dream or a movie. This was real life—and real death. But I couldn't let myself know it fully, because then everything would be different.

The faces blurred. I closed my eyes, my ears disconnected from the words of the priest, and I felt myself gasp for breath. Tears spilled down my cheeks. Then my lungs expanded. I was still alive—still breathing. My heart resumed beating. I opened my eyes and swiped at my cheeks, sniffling to gain control. I searched deeper into the crowd, wanting only to see one person.

Then I spotted him, standing shoulder to shoulder with several other Marines in the third row. He was the only man in uniform who stood round shouldered and slouched, a sign he was leaning on the crutches that held him upright. I couldn't see his eyes beneath his hat, but his face was pale and his lips were drawn in a straight, tight line. I shivered in spite of the balmy, June air, the dampness seeping into my bones and chilling me to the core.

The service ended. The crowd slowly dispersed, each person laying a single white rose on the casket as they said a final good-bye. One by one, they turned away, faces sad and tear stained. I waited for Alex to approach, but he didn't. He just disappeared into the crowd. I stood and looked through the sea of umbrellas, catching sight of him flanked by two Marines who were assisting him to a nearby black sedan. Awkwardly negotiating his crutches, he hopped on one foot, his right pant leg drawn up and pinned neatly below his knee, the lower part of his leg no longer there to stand on. My stomach twisted and salty tears burned my throat.

"Jordan, I'm so sorry for your loss." Alex's mother stood in front of me, her hand resting on my shoulder. "Levi was...he'll be missed." I looked back to the casket where my mother was standing with her back to me, my grandfather's arm tight around her waist as she broke down again and cried inconsolably.

"Thank you, Mrs. Cooper. It means a lot to us that you and Alex were here today." My eyes followed the black sedan as it pulled away from the curb. "This must be terrible for him."

"The doctors didn't want him to leave the hospital, but you know Alex...." She pushed a stray wet hair off my cheek, her eyes filled with emotion. "They're taking him back now." She glanced at the Government Issue car working its way along the narrow drive of the cemetery, crawling along in the parade of cars. "I'd like to follow and see him get settled in his room again. Tell your mother I'll stop by soon." By this time, my grandfather was leading my mother away from the casket, nearly carrying her toward the limousine that awaited us.

"I'll tell her." My eyes felt hot and puffy like big caterpillars ready to burst. Everyone had gone and Mrs. Cooper turned to leave. A part of me wanted her to stay. She looked so put together, her blond hair neatly pulled up in a twist, an umbrella protecting her from the rain. I envied the calm professionalism that rolled off of her, the black business suit with pin-striped pants and sensible flats that said she was in control. My own hair hung in long strands, wet on my face, darkened by the rain--not its usual sun streaked red and gold pulled into a ponytail. The last thing I felt was put together. I called after her. "Tell Alex I'll be by to see him at the hospital as soon as I can."

"I'm sure he'd like that," Mrs. Cooper stopped and turned, her eyes moving to the coffin one more time. The entire surface of the dark mahogany was covered in white roses, not fully in bloom. The scent clung in the damp air as if they knew the box they lay upon would soon be buried under six feet of dirt. Before Alex's mother walked away, she said, "Again...my deepest sympathies, Jordan." She cleared her throat, hesitating a moment longer. "I know it's hard to imagine, but a year from now, everything will feel differently." Then she was gone.

I stood by the casket alone, my own flower in hand. I felt a moment of crushing silence-- nothing except for the drizzling rain and the distant caw of a crow. Mrs. Cooper was right. It was difficult to imagine how I might feel a year from now. I understood that time faded the pain of loss, but I also knew that grief had a way of scarring a person. I glanced over at my father's headstone, his funeral so far back in my memory it was all but lost. A year from now, things might feel different, but they wouldn't be different. Levi would still be gone, Alex would never have his leg back, and I was pretty certain the scars on my heart would remain raw and painful for a very long time.

I imagined the deep hole beneath the thin layer of green carpet, an abyss about to swallow my brother. He wouldn't have liked this at all. He told me he would rather be cremated, an idea my mother had immediately dismissed. *"Catholics bury their*

*dead so on the last day, they have a body to rise up
into when Christ returns,"* she'd said. I knew Levi
well enough to know he wasn't concerned about the
'last day' as much as he was about being buried in a
box in a deep hole where his body would decay and
his flesh would be eaten by worms.

I shivered again, my sweater growing heavy
with wetness as the drizzle turned to a full-on rain.
Long strands of hair had fallen from my barrette
and stuck to my cheeks. I brushed it off my face and
tucked it behind my ears.

"Oh, Lee, how could you? What have you
done?" My eyes burned as the words fell on the
silence, my voice weakened by sadness and
drowned out by the sound of the rain pattering on
the muddy ground. "I'm sorry I didn't…" But there
was no point in being 'sorry' now. "I'll…miss you,"
I whispered as I laid the final rose on the mound of
flowers. As I let go, it hit me. I would never see him
again. The realization slipped one level deeper into
my consciousness, penetrating my carefully placed
wall of denial. The searing jolt to my heart dragged
a sob from my lips.

Familiar footsteps registered behind me.
"You about ready to go?" My grandfather laid a
large, firm hand on my shoulder.

"Yeah, I guess so." I wiped the tears and
rain from my face. We stood there for another
minute, the two of us saying a silent good-bye, any

promise of a future snuffed out in one horrible tragic event. But I knew that was how Levi had wanted it, probably even planned it. He told me more than once that he didn't belong here in this life, that God had made a mistake. He'd been a reckless daredevil since we were kids, self-destructive in a way that wasn't natural. He'd led me and Alex into more trouble than any kid could possibly find on their own. That's how I knew it was all a lie. The military report had to be wrong. Part of me wanted to let it go and let them be right—to forget what my brother was capable of and blame it all on Alex. But the part of me that knew it wasn't true couldn't let Alex take the blame, even if it meant I had to take as much responsibility as anyone. If I had told someone…things could have been different.

In my mind I could see Levi running headfirst into a bad situation knowing there was a good chance he wouldn't come out alive. His preoccupation with death had been a topic of concern since the first time he cut himself on purpose when he was ten. With every destructive act after that it became clearer—at least to me—that Levi was capable of killing himself. Mom stuck her head in the sand and tried to wish it all away, but I knew what my brother could do the same way I knew that there was no way Alex would have led them into danger. It must have been Levi's idea.

He'd been good at persuading people. The military had the facts wrong. That's all there was to it. "I need to know what really happened," I said, my words coming out stronger than I thought myself capable of.

My grandfather let out a slow breath. "Sometimes it's best to let things be. Your brother died a hero. There is no greater sacrifice than to lay down one's life for a friend. It's a good way to go for a soldier."

My teeth pressed together. "So the truth doesn't matter?"

"It won't change anything. And your mother…" His voice lowered and I heard the sadness creep in. "Your mother needs to believe there is a purpose and a plan in all this." He wrapped a strong arm around my shoulder and led me away from the grave site, my feet resisting even as I leaned into his broad chest.

"I don't get it, Brig. What purpose is there in a twenty year old being put in the ground? Or Alex losing a leg?" My voice carried the sound of defeat. I walked with him towards the limo, dreading the ride back to the house where, no doubt, there would be another crowd to contend with. Exhaustion ran bone deep inside me, fighting with the growing anger that fueled my need for answers. I recognized my grandfather's tone to mean he wouldn't help me dig into the details surrounding Levi's death. He and my mother would be just as happy to believe a lie. If I wanted the truth, I would have to find it myself.

As I climbed into the back of the limo and slid across the seat where my mother was already reaching for my hand, a rush of adrenalin ran through me. The first place I would start was with the one person who was there when it happened. Whether he was ready to talk about it, or not, Alex was going to tell me what I needed to know.

Chapter 2

My quest for answers would have to wait. Despite my six phone calls to the hospital, Alex was still refusing visitors. Besides, I had my hands full at home. Mom stayed in bed for three days while Brig and I took turns bringing food and trying to coax her back to life. As much as I wanted to lie down and disappear beside her, I knew Levi wouldn't have wanted that.

So I got up every morning and went for my usual six mile run around the lake. I ran cross country for Somerville High and was one of the fastest long distance runners in the state, but no matter how fast or how far I ran, I couldn't escape the heaviness in my heart or the constant lump in my throat that had taken up residence ten days ago when two soldiers showed up at our door with the news. Levi was killed in action and Alex had been wounded.

So I ran. School was out for summer but I needed the routine to make me feel normal, some kind of proof my life would go on even if Levi wasn't here. As I took to the trails, I focused on my stride and disappeared into the sensation of soft pine needles underfoot.

I ran past the Coopers' house, one of the largest homes on the lake. The sweeping lawn led up to a large deck surrounded by a rose garden just coming into bloom. A landscaping crew was busy at work, Mr. O'Shea on the mower and his two sons, Jake and Barry armed with weed whackers and hedge trimmers. My muscles pumped harder as the sound of the buzzing equipment faded to a distant hum. It always seemed sad to me that such a big house was occupied by only one person. Mrs. Cooper stayed on alone after her divorce and her son Alex's hasty departure into the military at the end of his senior year of high school. With her busy law practice, it was no wonder we didn't see her much. She had stopped by the house as promised, but Mom refused to see her, screaming loud enough to get the message across that she wanted nothing to do with the Cooper family.

As I ran the path around the lake, each heel strike drew me deeper into the numbness I sought for my soul and farther away from the grief that threatened to paralyze me. I tried to focus on the bright green leaves on the maple trees as they flashed past—anything to keep my mind off my brother and the million questions I had.

Thompson Lake was a community-owned property ten minutes outside of Somerville. A thousand acre lake surrounded by cottages, cabins and a few good sized houses for the full-time residents who enjoyed the whipping winds and heavy snows of winter in the Litchfield hills of Connecticut. One of those residents was my grandfather, retired Brigadier General Alistair Dunn, "Brig" to everyone who knew him. A tall, broad shouldered man with a stubble of white hair on his head and the constitution of a polar bear. The harder the winter, the better he liked it.

His son, Jonathan, was my father. He had died from an aneurism when I was four. We came to live with Brig when I was six and Levi was nine, after a couple of rough years of living in the volatile household of my mother's sister Theresa and her cop husband, Ted, who fought incessantly. I had a vague recollection of Brig showing up and packing us into his car and getting us out of there, but I didn't have any clear memory of why.

The houses on the lake blurred along with the trees and shrubs that lined the trail as I zipped past. My breath came in a steady rhythm, my heart settling into its galloping beat. Shaded by the trees, the warmth of the sun hit me in tiny bursts that cut through the branches of tall pines, oaks and maples. Levi and I used to run the trails together, him leading and me following…always following. Trying to keep up with my big brother had occupied more of my life than I wanted to admit.

Before I could stop them, tears leaked from my eyes and my breathing came in erratic spurts. I

guess I couldn't escape after all. I slowed to a stop
and bent over, my hands on my knees to recover. I
had only run a couple of miles, but I couldn't go on.
Whatever life coursed through me wasn't enough to
propel me forward.

I walked the rest of the way home,
memories of my brother playing over and over in
my mind. The stinging mosquitoes provided a
welcomed distraction from the images that flooded
my brain with the bitter sweetness of good
memories mixed with bad. I swatted at my ear and
the incessant buzzing halted momentarily. Another
bug landed on my arm. An itching sting took hold
and I slapped it, leaving a tiny blood stain behind. I
scratched the rising welt. Levi would have stopped
and watched the mosquito draw blood, waiting for
the little parasite to engorge itself before he splatted
it, just to see the blood stain it left behind.

He did things like that. Dissecting frogs to
watch their beating heart or tormenting one of the
neighborhood cats by wrapping paper booties on its
paws and watching it stumble around until it
worked the elastics off and could escape. I would
cry and tell him how cruel he was and he would just
laugh, trying to convince me and Coop it was all in
fun.

At other times, he could be so soft hearted,
it was like the world's suffering was his own, and
he couldn't tolerate injustice or cruelty. Then his

anger would turn outward and he would say that
God should just destroy the earth and start over. He
would act out in violent fits, although they always
seemed to be aimed at inanimate objects. Rocks
through a window, a baseball bat to his car, or his
fist through a wall, were the only things that
satisfied his temper. Even when he was being mean
to our mother, he knew the limit. Brig would never
allow physical violence, even though he tolerated a
lot--anything but fighting, which seemed
uncharacteristic for a Marine.

My brother wouldn't attack anyone
unprovoked, unless, of course, someone picked on
me. Levi hated bullies and Brig gave him some
slack when it came to defending me. On any given
day, Levi could be a champion for the weak and
helpless, or frighteningly demented and cruel. When
we were little, it scared me. But as we got older and
I understood him better, it just made me sad. He
didn't like his unpredictability any more than
anyone else did. On a really bad day, he fought with
kids in school, assaulted our mother with the
cruelest of insults, or generally wreaked havoc any
way he could.

Then came the cutting. I shuddered at the
unwanted intrusion of an image of the scars that
lined his arm like railroad tracks.

Determined as I was to find the truth
surrounding his death, I wasn't so sure Levi would

want me to. He had sworn me to secrecy time and time again, not wanting to worry our mother or Brig with what he called his "dark side." If they knew, no one ever talked about it. So I kept quiet, too. He promised me it was only once in a while when he needed to feel something—anything beyond his rage. Now a mix of guilt, anger and grief weighed me down to the point I could barely lift my feet to make it up the driveway. Maybe if I'd told someone, he wouldn't have been able to join the Marines and he might still be alive. The thought made my misery complete.

Even the antique shop sign reminded me of Levi—how he and I and Coop would sit across from the sign and see if we could spit all the way from the other side of the driveway and hit it. If I hawked up a good one, I could spit as far as the boys, a talent I was proud of at the time. The memory faded along with the ghosts it conjured. The old farm house that had stood through three generations of Dunns loomed before me, the tree lined gravel driveway an obstacle course of pot holes and puddles.

My grandfather appeared out of his workshop and came into the sunlight. He spent most days there lately, in his barn, building custom ordered furniture--beautiful rockers, dressers, tables and book cases people came from all over to buy.

He stared at me for several moments. "That was a good long run," he said as he squinted into the light. "I walked most of it. Is Mom up yet?" It was a rare Sunday that we missed church, which is how I knew she still wasn't doing well. "No. I was going to go in and check on her, but I'm sure she'd rather see you." He wiped his hands on a rag and stuffed it into the back pocket of his jeans. He was a handsome man, my grandfather, fit and strong, even at the age of seventy. He had an easy smile and his crystal blue eyes had a spark of mischief behind them that made it clear there was always some amount of planning going on in his head.

"I'll make sure she eats something," I said, heading for the front porch. The old rocking chairs, the deacon's bench and the antique Canadian Flyer sled leaning against the house reminded me again it was Sunday, my usual day to work with him in the shop. "Would you mind if I took the day off?"

Something Old, Something New was my Grandma Josie's labor of love, a family antique shop she had revived back in the nineteen seventies. It had a good reputation for servicing the locals year round and any tourists that came up to the lake seasonally. Brig had kept it going after Gram died from cancer just after he retired and before we came to live with him. Another pang of feeling that life was so unfair hit me square in the chest.

I'd been helping in the shop since I was twelve, sweeping floors, cleaning windows, polishing furniture and eventually working the register and taking inventory. Brig and I were more or less partners now and I worked on commission, earning fifteen per cent of anything I sold on my shift, which sometimes added up to big dollars on a busy weekend, but more often than not, barely kept gas in my tank.

He looked up, his bushy brows rising in surprise. "I wasn't expecting to open today anyway. You got big plans?"

"I'm going to see Alex in the hospital."

Whether he likes it or not, I thought.

Brig followed me onto the porch and then leaned on the screen door with one hand before I could open it. He still surprised me at how fast he moved for an old man. "You're not planning to pester that boy, are you?"

I glanced over my shoulder at him, my hand on the door handle, my height closing in on his since I'd grown another two inches this year, making my above average height of five-foot-eight jump to a standing-way-out-in-the-crowd, five-foot-ten. Our eyes met dead on, though he was twice my width and enough taller to be looking down his frequently broken, and very crooked nose at me. "Of course not," I said. "I just thought he could use some company."

18

He lifted his hand and let me proceed, following on my heels. "Just remember he's been through a lot. He isn't likely to be up to answering a bunch of questions. And don't be too upset if he doesn't want to see you. It's hard...for soldiers to have people look on them with pity." A brief look of understanding crossed his face and then disappeared. "We're a proud lot."

"Don't I know it?" My mother said from the arched entry of the living room. She was showered and dressed, although her eyes still looked swollen and red, her nose raw from blowing. "Proud and stubborn, too," she said. Her face couldn't quite manage the amusement that carried in her voice.

She looked surprisingly young without makeup and with her strawberry blond hair pulled back in my trademark pony tail. Other than being shorter and curvier, and her hair a little darker and tamer, she looked like a slightly older version of me in her jeans and sweat shirt--as if she could pass for my sister rather than my mom. Other than the fatigue and dark puffy circles under her eyes, you'd never know she was forty.

"Good to see you up and about, Katherine. Can I fix you girls some lunch?" My grandfather didn't wait for her to answer but headed into the pantry and came back into the kitchen with two cans of soup and a loaf of whole wheat bread. He pulled a bowl of tuna salad from the fridge and started making sandwiches. He wasn't much of a cook, but when he made a meal, he made it with love.

Mom sat down at the table and I put the tea kettle on to boil. "Do you want a cup of tea, Mom?"

"You two need to stop fussing over me. I'll be okay. It's just going to take time." Her voice cracked and she lifted a crumpled tissue to her nose.

"I'm going to see Alex after lunch," I said, hesitantly. "Do you want to come with me?"

Her face hardened. "Why…why would I want to see him? It's his fault this happened. If Levi hadn't gone into that building after him…" Her voice trailed off and she broke down crying again.

Before I could respond, my grandfather spoke. "Katherine, you can't blame the boy. Levi did what he was trained to do. Any soldier worth his salt would have done the same. They were on a mission and they did the best they could with the intelligence they had." He set a steaming bowl of soup and a sandwich in front of my mother. "Blaming Alex won't bring Levi back. You need to let it go."

Acid churned in my stomach. I glared at my grandfather, the question burning on the tip of my tongue. *'You still think the truth won't change anything?'* Instead I gripped my mother's hand, hoping she'd see reason. "I need to see how he's doing. Levi would have wanted us to look out for

Alex now." My own voice threatened to break again and I knew a flood of tears would follow. Her expression grew darker. I gave her fingers a squeeze and let go, hopes of changing her mind lost to her sour expression.

An overwhelming urge to escape shot through me. I needed to get out of the kitchen and into the warm June air. Maybe then I could breathe. Maybe then, the ice that encased my heart would begin to melt. I looked to my grandfather, who was setting a second bowl of soup on the table. "I'm not really hungry," I lied. My stomach rolled in protest of my refusal to eat, but I felt queasy at the thought.

Food seemed a betrayal somehow since Lee would never again taste a sandwich or soup or a steamed hot dog from a Rock Cats game, or his favorite thing in the world, spaghetti and Mom's giant meatballs. I glanced at my mother as she picked around the edge of her sandwich, wondering if she was thinking the same thing. "I'll grab something later," I added.

He nodded and moved the soup and sandwich across the table and sat down. "You tell Alex we're thinking of him."

Abruptly, my mother rose from the table and headed back through the living room, her footsteps pounding up the stairs to her room and the door slamming shut behind her. I sighed and rose from the table, turning off the tea kettle that had started a shrill whistle.

My grandfather shook his head. "You girls sure are fond of stomping your feet and slamming doors. Your grandma used to slam the doors so hard, I'm surprised there's a door knob in this house that still has all its screws." He slurped a spoonful of minestrone. "She'll come around. You know Alex is as much like a son to her as your brother was."

"I hope you're right." The sound of my mother's crying drifted through the old floor boards, echoing softly like a ghostly moan. I looked up at the ceiling, my throat aching for the release of tears my mother had found so effortless. But I could hear Levi's voice, *don't be a cry baby, Jordie.* I swallowed hard, a salty lump catching in my throat.

"Everyone handles grief in their own way, Sunshine. She'll get through this, and so will you. We all will." He exhaled slowly, his eyes cast down. "Its times like this I wish your grandma were here…though I wouldn't want her to have to suffer this loss with the rest of us."

"You must miss her terribly," I said, my heart splintering another fraction. It was clear she had been the love of his life since he hadn't really found anyone else in the ten years he'd been widowed. "I wish I'd known her better and had more time with her."

"Me, too." Brig's eyes had grown misty again and he cleared his throat, straightening his shoulders. "But I'm sure she's up in heaven right now welcoming Levi in through the Pearly Gates." He flashed me a sad smile and set his spoon down, meeting my eyes with that look he got when he wanted me to pay close attention. "You know, wherever your brother is right now, he's at peace."

"I know." I tipped my ear to the ceiling, listening to Mom's fading sobs, "I wish she thought so."

"Don't worry, she'll come around," he said with assurance. "You know, Alex is lucky to have you for a friend." Brig's usually stern features held the tender expression I knew he reserved for the people he cared most about. "He's going to need all the help he can get. Just don't push him, understand?"

I crossed the kitchen and stood behind my grandfather, wrapping my arms around his neck and leaning my chin on his bulky shoulder. The familiar scent of saw dust and lemony wood polish comforted me, and I sighed, "I'll do whatever it takes to help him."

Brig patted my hand. "That's my girl."

After a hot shower and another private round of tears, I threw on jeans and pulled on a tank top, layering it with a button down blouse and tying the ends at my waist. It was cool for a June day. I hadn't noticed it earlier. Noticing anything beyond the memories and images that played on a continual loop in my head took great concentration. I turned away from the sad faced girl in the mirror and wished I wasn't her. She looked desperate and lonely and I hated feeling so weak. Levi's voice popped into my head, *'Life sucks and then you die— get over it.'*

I flopped onto my bed, reaching for the box underneath. Slowly, I lifted the lid and ran a hand over the envelope on top, my heart racing in anticipation. My name and address printed in Levi's neat, left slanted scrawl, stared back at me. His last letter, dated March 23rd, two months after he returned for his second tour in Iraq. The letter told about how he'd spent his twentieth birthday partying with his pals on base and day to day events in the desert—nothing that would give me a clue as to what had happened on that last day. I skipped through the pile and reached for the letter at the bottom.

I needed to start back at the beginning, back when I still knew my brother. Being a Marine had changed him so much. I had thought for the better, but now I wasn't so sure. I took the folded pages out, pressing them flat on the bed. Knowing our hands had touched the same paper made me feel connected to him, and another blanket of lonely grief wrapped around my heart, squeezing until I couldn't breathe.

I picked out the first letter he'd sent me two weeks after enlisting.

Hey Jordie,
So far, Basic pretty much sucks. They keep me ridiculously busy and tired. The food isn't too bad but it's not Mom's. Training is wicked. My feet are killing me and every muscle in my body feels like I've had the crap kicked out of me. I'm getting used to the daily grind but getting up at the crack of midnight is seriously twisted. You know how I like sleeping in. No TV or internet here so nothing to do but eat, sleep, and work. You would probably love it.

It was weird, coming onto the base the first day. I could feel my life changing as the gates closed behind me, like suddenly being marooned on another planet. By day three, I wondered WTF I'd gotten myself into. I'm sick of the DIs screaming in my face and calling me a maggot. It freaks me out. But I figure I'll be okay as long as I follow orders and don't ask questions. It's becoming clear that every stupid thing they make us do ends up having a reason, so there's no sense questioning anything.

I only get a few hours of free time on Sundays to write letters, hang out, or catch some extra sleep, so I'll write when I can, but you know me and good intentions. Mom will be happy to know I'm going to church. It seems like the only time we can get away from the DI's and have an hour to think for ourselves. Most of the guys here seem to lean pretty heavy on their faith to get them through the tough times and the homesickness. I just like the peace and quiet of the chapel where nobody is in my face. I do miss home, though. Especially my bed, my car, and of course, my baby sister. At least Coop is here with me. I know Brig had something to do with keeping us in the same class of cadets. I guess he thinks I'll work harder if I'm competing against my little bro. We're in separate barracks but I get to see him every day in classes and out in the field.

I can see how Brig was right about the Corps making me grow up. Don't tell him I said so though. I'll never hear the end of it. I have no choice here but to take care of myself and 'man up' as the DIs say. Nobody is going to pick up after me or hold my hand in this place. They don't let you off the hook for anything. After the DI made me remake my bed about twenty times, one of the other guys showed me to use some boot straps to hold my sheets and stuff in place so I don't have to mess with making up my rack every day. It's good to know even the Marines have a few short-cuts.

All in all, I'm getting settled okay. I can't help but wonder though, if Juvenile Detention

*wouldn't have been easier. A year in Juvie or
thirteen weeks of Marine hell—it's a toss-up. At
least I'm learning something here. School is hard,
but I'm studying stuff I never did in high school.
The history of the Corps is pretty cool and I'm
learning a lot about weapons. I get to go out on the
rifle range tomorrow. Should be fun.*
  I guess that's all for now. Coop says Hi.
  Love ya like crazy,
  Lee

  I folded the letter and slipped it into the
envelope, bringing it to my nose to see if it smelled
like Lee, a sweet mix of woods, fresh air and some
spicy deodorant. But there was nothing but the
smell of the cedar box I kept them in. The last time
I'd seen him was at Christmas, just before he went
back to Iraq. He said he felt needed there—like him
being there could make a difference.

  I wiped fresh tears off my cheeks and put
the letter back at the bottom of the stack, resisting
the urge to take out and read another one. All of the
letters he'd written from boot camp and then from
Iraq lay, like my brother, dead in a wooden box,
whispering the only words I would ever hear from
him again. I wanted to wrap myself up in the pages
and pages of words—let myself imagine him
hugging me and telling me he loved me one last
time.

I wanted to read the one letter I'd read a hundred times--the one where said he thought Coop and I would probably end up together. But after seeing what happened to Coop, I had no idea how that could happen now, and honestly, I wasn't sure my heart could take another reminder about what we'd all lost and what might have been.

Chapter 3

I pulled the Rabbit into the parking garage at the Veteran's hospital, having gotten lost three times before finally stopping to ask for directions. Levi had asked me to take care of his car while he was gone and I did my best to keep the old VW going. It was like thirty years old, carried multiple dents—war wounds of its own-- and had a couple of hundred thousand miles on it, but it still ran like a champ, thanks to Brig, who often spent more time working on *it* than on making his furniture.

I passed the information desk and went straight up to the third floor where Mrs. Cooper had said Alex's room was. He had been transferred here from Walter Reed hospital three days ago, just in time for Levi's funeral. The smell of antiseptic and sickness filled my nostrils, making my stomach flip flop. I swallowed hard and took a breath, determined not to back out. My heart thumped a swift beat as I closed in on my destination. What could I say that would make Alex feel better about everything that had happened? Nothing, I suspected. I would just have to try not to stare at his leg or cry or make stupid jokes.

My stomach tipped as the reality of his loss hit me again. What could I say? Probably something embarrassing since the last time I'd had a real conversation with him I had made a fool of myself and told him I loved him. I was only fifteen then and by the look on his face (which was seared into my memory), he had not been happy about my big confession—something about bad timing, he'd said. We had only seen each other a couple of times since then, and he seemed to go out of his way not to be alone with me, as if he were avoiding any more of my mortifying declarations.

I rounded a corner and stopped.

"I am not touching that thing! Why can't you people just leave me alone?"

Crap. My knack for bad timing had apparently not improved any. I stood outside the door and listened in on what was obviously a session with the physical therapist.

"Look, Mr. Cooper…Alex, you have to learn to bandage the stump to keep down the swelling. If you want your leg to fit into a prosthesis…"

"I don't want a prosthesis. I don't want anything from you. I just want to get the hell out of here and go home!"

"You can't go home until we get this swelling under control and get you fitted properly…"

"Get out!" The sound of a tray crashing to the floor made me jump. "I said, get out!"

30

A woman--probably in her thirties--wearing scrubs, a white coat and sneakers burst out of the room and then slowed when she saw me. "If you're here to visit Corporal Cooper," she raised her brows and brushed past me, "I hope you brought combat gear."

I sucked in my breath and dove into the icy waters. I froze in the doorway. I wished I could have prepared myself better. He was wearing gym shorts and a green tee shirt and he was swinging his leg—what was left of it—onto the bed. His eyes came up to mine and my eyes went back to his leg. The angry red stump below his knee joint captured my full attention like a train wreck I couldn't ignore. He whipped the blanket across his legs and glared at me. I looked away.

"What are you doing here?" he snapped.

"Nice to see you too," I said, keeping my eyes trained on his. I took another step into the room, fighting the urge to turn and run the other way. Instead, I went straight to the bed and hugged him as hard as I could. After a few seconds, he wrapped his arms around me and hugged me back, a firm embrace that spoke more words than either of us could find to say. I held back my tears, determined to stay strong. When I pulled away, he showed the flicker of a smile. I took it as a sign he didn't want to throw me out. A fresh scar over his right eye and faded bruises on his neck were the only visible injuries apart from his leg.

He had changed so much that I hardly recognized him. His blond hair was sun bleached and cut military short, his jaw and nose sharp angled and hard. Everything about him seemed harder. He was no longer the skinny, six foot-two, computer geek with braces, acne, and glasses—the boy who used to pull my hair and tease me about my freckles. At nineteen, he was a man, his face darkly tanned with a few days' beard growth that took me completely by surprise. I didn't know what I'd expected, but it wasn't this. I heard my pulse pound in my ears before I registered his words.

"Are you going to have a seat or just stand there?"

"Um…yeah. I thought maybe I should wait for an invitation. It didn't sound like you wanted company." I stepped over the mess on the floor and sat in the chair next to the bed. "You were kind of tough on her, don't you think?"

He studied me for a long time and then looked down, the blankets unable to conceal the missing right lower leg and foot. He looked out the window. "I'm just sick of being poked and prodded. When they aren't taking blood, pumping me full of drugs or waking me in the middle of the night to take my temperature, they're harassing me about the

32

stupid leg." His eyes wouldn't meet mine. "I can't wait to get out of this place."

"Maybe if you co-operate a little more, you can get out sooner." I said it in my most cheerful voice.

He wasn't buying in. "They can kiss my…" he caught himself and then a small smile crept over his lips. "Sorry. I'm not used to being around civilians, let alone the company of a pretty girl."

My ears heated up. "Did they teach charm in the Marines, or are you messing with me?"

He looked me up and down, his face darkening with a reddish tinge. "I guess a lot has changed, hasn't it?" An awkward silence settled between us. "You let your hair grow out," he said at last.

I would bet a pink glow had reached my face by now. Being fair skinned and Irish meant I wore embarrassment like a waving red flag. I fiddled with the buttons on my blouse and tucked a curl behind my ear. "There was nobody around pulling my hair, so I figured it was safe to wear it a little longer."

He smiled at that, but kept his focus on his hands. "How's your mom?"

"She's having a tough time. You know how she is…was…about Lee." My voice dropped a notch lower and cracked when I said his name. *I will not cry, I will not cry,* I chanted as I took slow breaths in through my nose.

"Yeah. They were pretty tight." Alex glanced up at me, his pupils large and his eyes a startling green I hadn't remembered, watery and bright like the sea. He had a wistful look on his face as if he had stepped back in time in his mind. "I used to wish she was my mom. Even though she worked hard, she always had dinner on the table or was making pies or cookies or something. Every time I went to your house, she made me feel like part of the family."

I was glad to talk about the past. Our childhood seemed a safe place where we could find common ground and avoid the pieces of ourselves that were so obviously missing. I didn't think either of us was ready to talk about Levi. But then again, reminiscing about my mother doting on my brother like she was always trying to make up for something, didn't offer much appeal either.

"Your mom's cool, too," I said, attempting to shift the topic away from my dysfunctional family life. "She always says hi when she sees me out running." I suddenly wished I hadn't brought up running. It was another reminder that nothing would ever be the same. I couldn't think of one thing to talk about that wouldn't be painful or awkward.

Alex must have felt the shift back to reality too. He let out a slow breath and leaned his head back on the pillow, looking up at the tiled ceiling apparently trying to stay focused on the current conversation. "Yeah, she's friendly to the neighbors at least." A note of sarcasm infused his tone. "After my dad left, Mom buried herself in work, climbing the corporate ladder and all. Let's put it this way, if it weren't for dinners at your house, I would have been living on Hot Pockets and waffles." He flashed a half grin and then looked my way again, his dimple sending a curl of warmth to my belly.

"Hey, do you remember the time Lee and I ran away and hid out in the woods at the fort for like three days? We packed so many leftovers from your fridge that we thought we could last a month."

The three of us had built a fort into the side of a hill down by the river that fed into the lake. It was miles from the house and we were all sworn to secrecy about its location. They were twelve or thirteen at the time, Alex running away from his parents' divorce, Levi running away from whatever part of himself he couldn't seem to escape no matter how far he ran. As usual, I was both conspirator and accomplice, covering for them and worrying about the consequences.

Alex had perked up while telling the story. I tried to keep the mood light. "With you two chow hounds, you were lucky to last the three days. Mom was frantic. She had Brig out searching the woods every day. It was a good thing Lee left a note or she would have had the police on your trail."

"How is the General?" He relaxed and his guard dropped. His face looked softer and younger, the hard edges of manhood smoothed out by memories of his boyhood, more like the Alex I'd known.

My pounding pulse settled and then I looked at the outline of his missing leg again, and my breath caught. I'd almost forgotten for a second. I cleared my throat. "Oh, you know Brig. Same as always. Tough as nails on the outside and soft as mashed potatoes on the inside."

"I doubt there's another person alive that would describe your grandfather as soft in any way. Does he still have those guys over for poker on Friday nights?"

"Not so often anymore. Maybe once a month or so. You'd think they were plotting to take over the war themselves the way they hide out in Brig's workshop until all hours, not wanting to be disturbed."

A flash of something indefinable crossed his face and then it was gone, replaced by a grimace as he shifted his injured leg under the covers.

"Does it hurt much?" *Stupid question.* "I mean should I get a nurse?" I started to stand, but he waved me off.

"No. It's not that bad. It aches some, but mostly it itches. I try to scratch it, but it's weird. It itches below the…never mind. You didn't come here to talk about this." He motioned to the leg as if it were luggage that didn't belong to him.

I looked around at the mess on the floor. "Should I get someone to clean this up?"

"Don't worry about it. Nurse Betty will be by with my pills shortly. She'll take care of it." His voice was filled with bitterness and I couldn't help but think of how much he had changed from the boy I'd known. Alex had always been quiet and shy, uncomfortable with people unless he had a computer in front of him or some electronics gadget he could show off. Once you got past that, there was a goofy kind of sweetness underneath. He was the light to Levi's dark. Bitterness had never been part of his nature. I hoped in time he could get past it. I missed that boy, and wasn't at all sure I knew anything about the man in front of me.

I bent over and picked up the tray, stacking the plastic dishes and utensils on it and setting it on the rolling table nearby. "It's not like a Marine to let someone else pick up after him." When I caught him checking me out as I bent over, he looked away. I felt heat rise in my face and ignored it, determined not to be distracted. "It's also not like a Marine to give up. You should be doing everything you can to get back on your feet." *Crap. Did I really just say that?*

"You're kidding, right?" His face lost any sign of good humor.

"I just meant you should be trying to get better. They do amazing things with prosthetics these days. I was reading up on the internet…"

"I'm not a charity case and I don't want you looking up stuff and trying to convince me to…" His voice rose, his face going pale. "Just forget it, okay?"

"I'm sorry, Coop. I didn't mean to upset you. I just want to help."

"You can't. No one can." He closed his eyes and rested his head on the pillows, his hands running through his short cropped hair.

"Well, I'm here if you need me."

"I don't *want* your pity," he snapped. He turned his back to me, wincing as he settled his leg again.

The silence grew thick in the air between us and I realized just how much had changed. We weren't kids anymore, playing at being grown up, kissing behind the barn, afraid we'd get caught and be in real trouble. Life had turned us into strangers seemingly overnight, both of us losing the essential innocence we'd had as children, stolen by tragedies beyond our control. Maybe it was all we had in common now. A shiver ran through me, whether from the air conditioned room or the realization my brother wouldn't come home and maybe Alex—the Alex I knew--wouldn't either.

I laid a hand on his shoulder, refusing to give up so easily. He didn't pull away. Maybe that was a start. "I can't imagine what you're going through. But I'll never turn my back on you, Coop. No matter what happens. We're friends—more than friends. You and Lee were like brothers, and you and I...well...we're like family. I'm here and I'm not going anywhere."

His body had grown more rigid with every word and I worried he was about to explode, but worse, he exhaled like a deflating balloon, his whole body draining of tension. "Go home, Jordie."

I let my hand fall away and thought about leaving but I was there for answers and I didn't know when I would get the chance or courage to ask again.

"Coop, maybe this isn't the best time, but I'd appreciate it if you could tell me what happened...to you and Lee."

He rolled onto his back and glanced at me, his eyes having lost the sparkle and gone hollow. His face had turned a sallow shade of green, and I saw his Adam's apple jump. I wondered if he might be sick, but instead he stared blankly at the ceiling. After a minute, he said, "I can't talk about it."

I leaned in closer, resting my hand on his arm, trying to get him to look at me—to see I only wanted the truth—I only wanted to help. "Why can't you talk about it?"

His voice took on the tone of a soldier, the color and all of the hardness returning to his face in the span of seconds. "I'm under orders. Besides, there's a lot I can't remember." When he lifted his eyes to me, they held raw emotion more powerful than any words. "I don't remember much past getting my orders that morning. The doctor said it might come back to me, but..." he stopped, his head popping up to confront me. "Wait... is that why you came here? To grill me about how Lee died? So you could hear me tell you it was my fault?" His face contorted with anguish. "Well, I'm sorry...okay...I'm..."

"No, Coop. I didn't mean..."

"Just read the report," he said, the anger draining from his voice, his face returning to its mask. He stared into space, lost and floating somewhere beyond the white walls of the room.

His expression pulled at something deep inside me. I thought that's why I had come, but the truth was I needed to be here for him, for me, for the brother whom we had both lost. "I came to see how my friend was doing," I answered. But I couldn't stop the question that hung in the air. "I just can't help wondering whether the military told us the truth about what happened."

"Why would they lie?" He came back to the moment and met my eyes, his expression pained and serious.

"I don't know. You tell me."

The room got very quiet then, the two of us staring at each other for a tense moment. He looked away first, adjusting himself on the bed, clearly uncomfortable with both the line of questioning and being in his own skin. "I can't help you, Jordie." His voice was tired but icy.

"Maybe when you get home, you'll feel more like talking."

"I won't." He slumped back onto the pillows. "I'm kind of tired. Can you just go?"

It was clear he wasn't going to help me--at least not now. Brig was right. He had been through so much. I shouldn't be harassing the poor guy with stupid questions when he was all messed up like this. A huge wave of guilt washed over me. I felt like a traitor. I should be here helping him to cope with the loss of his leg, the death of his best friend. Instead I was stuck on some idiotic quest for a truth that might not even exist. But I knew down deep inside there was more to the story than we'd been told, and the part of me that loved my brother more than anything needed to know for sure. I stood and headed for the door.

"I'm sorry, Coop. I'll go, but you know I'll be asking you again. I need to know what happened."

He flinched and closed his eyes, his body going so still, I wondered if he was breathing. Then he opened his eyes and drew in a breath, staring me down with a steely resolve that reminded me so much of Levi my heart clutched in my chest. "I told you, I can't help you. If that's the reason you came here today, don't bother coming back." He turned his head to stare out the window, refusing to see the hurt his words had caused. His expression reminded me of sculpted steel, like one of those statues at the war memorials, all the pain hidden by pride. "And Jordie," he turned back to me. "I'm not Coop anymore. I'm Alex Cooper, Corporal, U.S. Marines." He glanced down at his leg. "At least I was until a couple of weeks ago."

My eyes ached from the tears that threatened to spill over and my throat burned as I held them back. "And I guess I'm not Jordie anymore either. Everyone calls me Jordan now. I haven't been Jordie since you and Lee left. I guess we've all grown up." Meeting the eyes of the stranger who stared back at me, I knew how true it was. Our lives were changed irreversibly.

Then I saw a flicker of the boy I knew—the first boy I'd kissed. "No matter what you think has changed, you are who you've always been, Alex--a good friend to me and my brother." I turned away and walked through the door, afraid to look back, my tears held in check by only my wounded pride. "See you around, Marine."

CHAPTER 4

I cried all the way to Vic's Gym, the only place I could think to go where I could kick and scream without drawing attention. I passed Somerville High, cursing the stupid building that had started all the trouble. Levi and Alex had been caught setting fire to the new high school while it was being built. It was pretty clear Levi was the instigator, and Alex, as usual, had been in the wrong place at the wrong time. Brig and Mrs. Cooper had worked out the deal with the courts that the boys, both seniors at the time, could either go to Juvenile Detention for a year, or finish school and join the Marines upon graduation. Like Levi said, Juvie would probably have been easier.

The Rabbit sputtered along past the skating rink, the post office and a row of small buildings. Carver's Plumbing and Supply, Diana's Bakery, and Phil's Diner were all open for business late for a Sunday afternoon. This time of year every business in town stayed open as much as possible with all of the summer residents flocking back to the surrounding lakes and hills. Cars lined the main street and people shuffled from one establishment to the next, their friendly smiles an insult to the desolation I felt in my soul.

I crawled into the parking lot and sat for a long minute, trying to get my emotions under control. Alex's attitude had shaken me up. I should have expected it. I couldn't blame him for being angry, confused, frustrated. Whatever he was feeling, I was pretty sure it was normal. It didn't mean his rejection of my help and refusal to answer my questions didn't both hurt and piss me off. I let out a long sigh and slammed the car door, my gym bag slung over my shoulder as I steadied myself to face the stares, whispers and displays of sympathy I would undoubtedly have to deal with upon entering the gym.

I stopped by the unattended front desk and checked the schedule. Vic would soon be finishing a power yoga class in the main exercise room. I would have joined the next class, but I needed more than a good sweat. I needed to hit something. I headed to the locker room, avoiding eye contact with anyone and everyone, focused on the black rubber floor mats under my feet. I changed into my Gi, the white pants baggy and soft from wear, grabbed my hand and foot gear from my locker, and made a dash for the open gym.

I exchanged solemn nods with well-meaning members who knew me well enough to know I wasn't up for a conversation about the death of my brother. I was sick of hearing people say, "I'm sorry for your loss." The idea that I'd 'lost' my brother seemed ridiculous to me. It insinuated that I'd misplaced him somehow and that he could be found, as if he was only away on some secret mission and would soon return--a possibility I considered every morning when I woke up--until the reality hit me and sank in a notch deeper. Soon, I would have no choice but to believe he was truly gone forever.

I propelled myself past the weight room, a spinning class in progress, and a group of people waiting for the racquetball courts to empty. I'd made it all the way to the arena when I heard a voice call out behind me.

"Hey, Kid. Wait up." Vic caught up and met my long stride. "I won't bother asking how you are. I can only imagine how tough it's been for you and your family. I'm really sorry about Levi."

I slowed down and glanced at Vic who was pulling on a pair of leather gloves as she followed me to the heavy bag in the far corner of the arena past the boxing ring. "Thanks. I'm doing okay. I don't want to talk about it though."

"I get it." I sighed in relief that she wasn't going to press me to talk. Victoria Peterson was a woman in her fifties who stood a few inches shorter than me but outweighed me by thirty pounds of curves and muscle. Her hair was cut short and dyed blonde, spiky tufts sticking up in all directions. I slipped on my padded hand gear and threw a half-hearted round of punches at the heavy bag. Dark eyes stared expectantly at me from the other side of the bag. "Is that all you got?"

I continued to pommel the bag, each strike increasing in force. I found a perverse sense of peace when I hit the bag and felt a recoil of energy run through my body, an effect far more powerful than spilling my guts over feelings I couldn't control or events I couldn't change. The deep emotional pain that left cracks in my heart hovered around me, reverberating off the black leather as I tried to beat it back down. I swiped at the sweat sliding down my cheek and realized it was tears. I stopped to catch my breath and bent over, gasping. "I can't talk about this yet," I said, not sure if I was talking to her or myself. I walked around in circles, hands on hips and shaking out my legs, and then came back for another round. Kickboxing had to be better than seeing a psychiatrist—which is where I would be if I didn't get my head under control.

If I could talk to anyone, it would be Vic. It wasn't like I considered her a second mother to me, but she'd certainly been a good friend, taking me under her wing when Brig first brought me to her gym when I was twelve. He'd caught me and Levi smoking pot and had given me the choice of being shipped to a girl's boarding school or joining the gym and learning martial arts. He said all I needed was some focus and discipline. I spent most of the last five years studying Tae Kwon Do, yoga, Eastern philosophy and all around survival skills from Vic. She could be tough, but fair, and I had learned to appreciate her 'never-give-up' attitude.

"I can understand you not wanting to talk about it, but you never know—it might help." She caught the heavy bag and stopped it from spinning, waiting for me to hit it again. I landed a solid blow that felt as good as I'd hoped it would. I blasted several shots in a row and started my footwork, a dance that had me hopping forward and back on my toes, my right front jab gaining momentum as I planted my weight into the front foot and swung my back leg into a crescent kick. I thought back to the point where Lee and I began growing apart, wondering what there was to say.

Brig sent me off with Vic, but he had other plans for Levi. That summer they had spent nearly every day together fishing, hunting and camping, Brig's attempt to tame the wild side of my brother. He said the Native Americans would send off their adolescent sons and tell them, *"Do not come back until you have killed a bear."* Brig's equivalent was survival training and constant supervision.

Mom went along with Brig's tough love approach like she usually did. Her fragile state of parental stability was especially challenged in those days when Levi caused her no end of grief at every turn and my hormones kicked into whiny overdrive. Lying and sneaking around to see what we could get away with quickly became our favorite pasttime. Mom was easy to fool then, when she worked long hours and slept at odd times, always exhausted and seldom paying close enough attention to me and my brother to keep us in line.

Her main focus always seemed to be earning a paycheck, keeping a clean house and pretending she was Martha Stewart, so the world would not see that her life as a widow and single parent was far less than in perfect control. She and Levi were at constant odds with her hovering and nagging when she *was* around and with him snapping at her and picking fights to push her away.

Lee and I were old enough to fend for ourselves and took advantage of her emotional absence when Brig was traveling. But once Brig was home, getting away with anything was nearly impossible. It was tough sneaking past a man who had fought in four wars and had led special ops teams in a dozen countries in as many years. Brig and Vic were old friends and she had done him a favor by taking me on. Honestly, I don't know what would have become of me if she hadn't. I'm sure following in Lee's footsteps would have led me to certain destruction. My heart pounded in my chest. My ears rang. Then I heard Vic's voice.

"How's your mom dealing with everything?" She leaned her shoulder into the punching bag, keeping it steady as her deep brown eyes met mine, forcing me to focus.

"Like always. She's sleeping a lot and not talking about it." I threw a kick, landing a hard round house high up on the bag and knocking it out of Vic's grasp. She grabbed the leather and recovered.

"So that leaves you taking care of her again. It hardly seems fair."

I pummeled the bag with a combination of kicks and strikes that had my heart racing and my face heating up. "Brig helps. I don't have to do too much." My breath came in gasps as I slammed the bag with another assault—wheel kick—back fist—hook—knee. I jumped in and out, jabbing, kicking, stepping back as if evading an invisible opponent.

"So what else is eating you?" She gave me the look she had that said, *Don't bother covering, I see right through you.*

"I went to see Coop." I stopped dancing and punched the bag six or eight times in quick succession, my strikes hard, fast and tight. I was tiring quickly.

"I heard about his leg. That's a tough break." Vic stood in close to me, leaning past the heavy bag, holding it steady with her body weight and a deep stance that normally made her immovable.

I slammed a side kick into the bag, knocking her back a few feet. The hundred pound black leather bag shook on the chain as she let go and followed me to the water cooler. I filled a paper cup and guzzled down the cold water, hoping I wasn't replenishing my body for another round of tears that bubbled just below the surface. "He won't talk to me. He won't let me help him. And he can't tell me what happened to Levi." I filled another cup and sucked it down, wiping the spilled water off my chin with my tee shirt. My hands shook.

"Will knowing what happened change anything?"

"Now you sound like Brig." I sat on a bench, wiping the sweat off my brow and wondering if this was a typical military approach to the death of a soldier. It doesn't matter what happened as long as the official line is that my brother died a hero.

Vic had been one of the first women to be an Army helicopter pilot and had met Brig while running missions in South America in the early nineties. I didn't think it was a coincidence she had chosen Somerville, Connecticut to settle down and open a gym after my grandmother passed. I wondered if her friendship with Brig went beyond their military training and fascination with covert operations, but I would never ask, and the two of them spent very little time together, so whatever relationship they had, it wasn't a steady thing.

Vic nudged me in the ribs. "Brig's usually right on target. But judging by the look on your face, you aren't about to let this go." She nodded to a couple of young guys stepping into the boxing ring. "Look, I get the truth matters--especially when the facts are sketchy. What story did the military give you?"

I ripped the Velcro straps open with my teeth, sliding my gloves off one at a time. "Supposedly, Levi and Alex were on a mission to enter the safe house of some Iraqi official. They were just there to hack into a computer and get information. The house was supposed to be empty, but at the last minute intelligence came through that there were people inside and they were told to stand down. Details get foggy after that, but the gist is, Alex went in anyway and Levi followed. Apparently they took out one guy but another got off some rounds before backup arrived. Levi was dead and Alex severely injured. They still don't know why Alex went in. Like I said, he has no memory of the incident and there are no eye witnesses.

"And why don't you think it's the truth?"

The two young guys in the ring pummeled each other, grunting and swearing as they went at it and then retreated. "I can't put my finger on it exactly, but it just doesn't feel right to me. Don't get me wrong. I don't want to believe that my brother…it's just that…when it came to Levi and Alex, Levi was always the leader. He had to be up front all the time—taking the risk." My voice shook as I thought about Levi, the times he cut himself--or jumped off bridges-- the hundred things he did that challenged his mortality over and over again. "He would never have let Alex go into a dangerous situation ahead of him, and Lee was the rule breaker. If Alex was told to stand down, he would have listened. I don't know why, but the truth matters here. It just does." I let my tears fall and I looked her right in the eye. "Can you help me find out what happened?"

Vic turned her attention to the kids in the ring who were in a clutch beating the tar out of each other against the ropes. "Knock it off, you knuckleheads, or I'll come up there and tear you apart." Her voice boomed in a loud, monotone way that said she might be joking or serious and you didn't want to find out which one. The kids responded by breaking hold and heading for their respective corners.

Vic looked back at me and then wrapped an arm around my shoulders. "I'll look into it." I straightened up, wiping my eyes and hugging her back. "But don't get your hopes up," she added.

"You know the first place I need to go for answers is Brig. And if he isn't behind us opening this can of worms, it's not likely either of us will change his mind."

I gave her the most encouraging smile I could muster, suddenly feeling a little fragile and desperate for a spark of hope. "I have confidence in you," I said. "If anyone can soften him up, it's you."

Vic gave up a grin, something she didn't do easily or often, and shrugged. "The average man always underestimates a woman's powers of persuasion--" then her face went into mock seriousness mode, "though your grandfather is anything but an average man."

Chapter 5

Mom was dressed in her scrubs and clogs, fixing coffee in a travel mug when I came down to the kitchen the next morning. Her face still looked pale and lifeless, a mask ready to crack with the least provocation. After nearly two weeks of hiding in her room and sleeping, returning to work had to be a step in the right direction. She was lucky Dr. Stevens was willing to give her 'all the time she needed.'

"Do you want coffee?" she asked as I rubbed sleep from my eyes and slumped into a kitchen chair, the sleeves of an extra-large flannel shirt hanging way past my hands and the tails covering my knees. I pulled my feet up onto the chair, my legs disappearing under the shirt entirely, only the toes of my socks poking out.

"Yeah, I guess." I watched her move around the kitchen in slow motion as if she was on autopilot, completely absent from her body and floating somewhere in the periphery.

"Are you planning on opening the antique shop today?" She poured me a mug of steaming coffee and set the milk and sugar on the table for me.

I stirred in a heaping spoonful of sugar and added a quarter cup of milk, stirring and gazing down into my mug so I wouldn't have to meet her eyes and the penetrating sadness that lay beneath the vacant stare. "I thought I'd go see Alex again. I think he'll be coming home soon, but they won't let him out of the hospital until he's ready to deal with taking care of his leg." I couldn't even say the word amputation out loud. The thought of it and the way it looked, all red and raw, made me queasy. I closed my eyes and sipped my coffee trying to banish the image.

Mom remained silent as she finished packing her usual turkey, avocado, and cheese on rye for lunch. She worked as a Medical Assistant at Doctor Steven's office, the family practitioner who had been our doctor since I could remember and who had given Mom a job when we first came to live on Thompson Lake.

"I'll be home around five-thirty," she said, her back turned to me, obviously working hard to control her emotions. I heard the screen door slam and wondered how we would ever get past this. Past the sorrow, the grief, the anger—the loss—the sense that our family was shattered and broken and would never be the same again. My only hope was that down deep, she loved Alex and would find a way to forgive him for being alive while Levi was…

I wrapped my hands around the hot mug, letting the sensation seep into my skin. Warm tears stung my cheeks, reminding me that I was still here and had to go on. I'd learned in martial arts classes that when all hell is breaking loose around me, I needed to stay in the moment, notice all of my senses, be in my body, and breathe in and out. Then my direction would be clear.

I took in another deep breath, the sweet, nutty aroma of hazelnut coffee opening my airways. As I blew on the hot liquid and sipped carefully, I thought about how fractured our family had always been and wondered if Levi's death would be the final straw in breaking us completely.

"It's good that your mother went back to work this morning. I wondered how long she was going to stay locked in her room." Brig stood in the doorway, his broad width nearly filling the opening. He headed straight for the coffee pot and poured himself a huge mug, leaving it black and sitting down across from me. "How are you holding up, Sunshine?"

"I'm okay, I guess. Mom still seems really mad at Alex. I don't understand how she can blame him." My feet fell to the floor and I leaned over my coffee, letting the steam and sweet aroma fill my nostrils. I had found that it was in noticing the simple sensations that kept me grounded and sane, minute by minute. I clung to my cup.

"She's just hurt and angry and sad, and looking for someplace to put it all. She'll get beyond it eventually. Did I hear you say you were going back to the hospital to see him?"

"I think he really needs me right now. He wasn't doing very well with his therapy, and I'm afraid...I can't let him give up." I sighed low and long, suddenly feeling tired and angry again. Emotions ran through me from a million directions, flooding me in a tsunami that I was powerless to control. I held my tears tight in my chest, the injustice of the whole situation making me feel sick.

"If you really want to help him, you'll leave the past alone and help him move forward. He needs to see that he still has a future. He's a smart kid. Just because he can't be a Marine, doesn't mean he can't live a full, productive life." Brig peered over his cup at me as he drank his coffee. "If he was Army or Air force, they'd find a place for him, but the Marines...well...just keep reminding him of who he is. He'll be fine."

I relaxed in spite of myself. Brig always seemed to know just what to say, as if he knew the future and had total confidence that even fate would bend to his will. "I think you're right. He just needs a little encouragement." I intended to deliver just the encouragement he needed, even if it meant kicking his butt.

I parked the Rabbit in the parking garage of the Veterans' hospital and made my way up to

Alex's room only to find it empty. My heart jumped to my throat, the worst case scenario coming to mind. *Alex died from an infection, a complication from his injuries, a guilty conscience, a broken heart.* I made my way to the nurse's station, my hands and feet numb. The nurse directed me to the Physical Therapy department and I followed the yellow stripe down the long hallway, my heart racing in anticipation and apprehension the way it always had whenever I faced Alex head on.

At least it had been that way ever since the first time he kissed me when I was fourteen and he was sixteen—the moment we had become more than friends but not quite knowing what else we would be to each other, especially since Levi was at the center of both our worlds.

My mind spun with questions I promised myself I wouldn't ask him and a year and a half of thoughts I wanted to share with him. All of it disappeared as I pushed through the double doors and saw him standing between the parallel bars holding his weight on one leg, his arms locked at the elbow, his shoulders hunched and head down in concentration. He was wearing the same military issue gym shorts I'd seen him in the day before, but now he was clean shaven and looking determined. His knee was wrapped in a neat criss-cross pattern, the ace bandage conforming to the stump of flesh that was the remainder of his lower leg. The therapist was at the end of the parallel bars holding a wheel chair, cheering him on.

"C'mon, Corporal. You can do this." Her voice was sure and firm, not unlike her stocky frame.

I approached slowly and quietly, afraid to startle him or break his focus. His face was pale, his lips pressed together in a hard line. The muscles of his jaw were clenched as tight as the muscles in his arms, which shook with tension. Just as he looked up and saw me, he collapsed, catching himself before he hit the floor. I ducked under the bars and caught him around the waist lifting him upright as the therapist pushed the wheel chair up behind him. Alex lowered himself into the chair, my assistance no longer required or welcomed.

"Nice save. Thanks." The physical therapist nodded to me, came around and knelt down in front of the chair, checking the wrapping around the stump.

Alex grimaced as he pushed her hands away. "It's fine. Leave it alone. I'm fine." He said again, glancing up at me. "What are you doing back here? Did you come back to interrogate me some more?"

I ignored the jab though the ugly tone in his voice cut deeper than I wanted to admit. "No. Actually, I'm here to see that you co-operate and do exactly as this nice lady says." I smiled from him to the therapist who returned it until she saw the scowl on Alex's face.

"We're done for today." She stood and came back around, dragging the chair out of the bars. "I'll leave you two to visit." She looked down at Alex. "You did great today. Your prosthesis should be ready by Friday, and if all goes well, you should be able to go home the beginning of next week."

Alex didn't respond.

The therapist left us there, her sneakers squeaking across the gym floor as she approached another patient, a young African American man doing straight leg raises on a mat with a ten pound cuff weight strapped to his leg. I noticed a raised red scar from mid-thigh to below his knee. I sympathized, remembering my own knee rehab my first year of high school track when I developed an infra-patellar tendonitis and had my first taste of physical therapy. The profession fascinated me even then.

The gym was wide open with a few other guys working out various parts of their bodies, some with visible injuries, others performing general strengthening programs in an effort to return to their previous level of function after some incident that had derailed their military service. Other than one small curtained area, there appeared to be little privacy in the open space and I felt the tension of silence growing larger between Alex and me.

"Can we go somewhere and talk?" I asked, finally breaking the awkward moment.

Alex adjusted his leg, bending and straightening the wrapped knee, a strange movement that made my stomach lurch. He wheeled away, leaving me standing beside a large fichus plant. Then he stopped and called back over his shoulder. "Are you coming?"

"Yeah." I fell in line beside him and waited until we reached our destination a few minutes later. Neither of us spoke again. He led me out onto a veranda—a lovely view of a perennial garden sporting brightly colored flowers and fragrant roses. I sat on a wooden bench next to where he had stopped and put the brakes on his wheel chair.

"So it sounds like you might be home by next week. That's great, Coop."

He eyed me doubtfully. "Yeah, great."

"The harder you work and the quicker you get better, the sooner you'll be home and…then you can figure out where to go from there." I felt awkward, unable to say what was really on my mind and in my heart. We both knew nothing would ever be the same, but I wanted to believe that he had a future. More importantly, I knew *he* needed to believe it. "So what made you decide to do the therapy?" I asked.

"After you left yesterday, I realized I couldn't sit around feeling sorry for myself anymore." He looked out over the garden avoiding eye contact with me, his hand running along his thigh as if trying to work out the ache in the muscles. "I know if Lee was here, he'd have told me to 'suck it up' on day one." A small smile edged his lips and my heart swelled at the sight.

"No doubt," I said. "My brother wasn't much for putting up with whining of any kind." I pushed my hair back over my ear and stared at his profile wishing he would look at me. He had grown even more handsome over the last year or so, a manly squareness to his jaw and strong features that all but erased the boy I'd known. "Hey, do you remember the time I fell out of Mr. Hollenbeck's maple tree and broke my wrist?"

His smile widened and he glanced at me. "Yeah, how could I forget? You screamed your head off for like an hour. What were you, like six then?"

"Yeah, I think so. I remember Lee carried me all the way home telling me the whole time that if I didn't stop crying he was going to leave me on the side of the road at the nearest bus stop."

Alex laughed. "Which, of course, only made you cry louder."

My face felt on fire. "You guys always teased me about being a total baby."

"It was mostly Lee that did that. I always thought you were tough. Even through your tears, you were still brave. The bone was sticking right through the skin. I bet Lee or I would have cried too."

"Now you're just trying to make me feel better," I said, rubbing my old wrist injury where I still had a scar. What I remembered most about that moment was that Alex had kissed my forehead and told me everything would be all right, and it made me stop crying. He had always had that effect on me—calming, soothing, reassuring maybe. Now, I wished I could do the same for him.

He was finally looking at me, his green eyes sparkling in the morning sun. His face seemed more relaxed, his brows no longer furrowed and creasing his forehead. I felt a warm glow rise to my cheeks as he studied my face. Had I just been wishing he would look at me? I looked away first.

"You've always been the strong one, Jordie. Out of the three of us, you were the one that always knew what was right. You'd follow us only so far and then you'd put your little foot down and say 'NO', like you were the final authority."

"Not that either of you ever listened to me," I chided, nudging his shoulder with my fist.

Reflexively, he grabbed my hand before I could pull it away and he held on, staring at my hand wrapped in his for what felt like a long time.

He looked up at me and slid his fingers through mine, closing them firmly in his grasp. He looked out at the garden, a distant look on his face, as if he were trying to hold on to the present moment and losing the battle. The warmth and strength of his hand wrapped around mine felt good and frightening at the same time, and I held it there, as still as the roses soaking in the sun beside us.

"I'm listening now," he said, his voice coming back to him. He looked from our joined hands to my face, his eyes sad and lost. "Tell me, what am I supposed to do, Jordie?"

My heart ached for him. Everything he thought he was had been blown out from under him. His best friend was dead--maybe because of him-- maybe not. All of the questions I wanted to ask him fell away at that moment. The only question that mattered now was the one *he* had asked. He needed me to be strong and he needed me to have an answer.

"You are going to fight like a Marine--like you've been trained to. You're going to get a new leg, stand up and walk, and get on with your life." My voice sounded strong, determined, positive-- everything that I didn't feel on the inside but wanted to be for him.

"You make it sound so simple." He released my hand and rubbed his thigh again, staring past his knee to where his foot no longer resided.

"It is simple. You just do it. One step at a time." I rested my hand over his, reaching down inside myself for courage, and then I laid my hand on his knee just above the stump. He flinched but didn't pull away. I looked into his eyes, swallowing my urge to cry. "I didn't say it would be easy. But you aren't going to have to do this alone. I'm right here."

He gently removed my hand from his leg and seemed to focus somewhere far away again, his voice falling into that detached monotone of a Marine holding his feelings in check. "You shouldn't be wasting your time hanging out with a cripple."

His words stung, the truth of his condition hitting me harder. "I don't see it that way," I said softly.

"I can't ask you to help me." He stared down at his leg, bitterness and frustration seeping into his words.

"You didn't. I offered."

"I don't want your pity," he snapped.

I moved around to the front of his chair and knelt down so I was looking up at his face. I wanted him to see that I meant what I said. "Listen to me, Coop. You've been my friend since I was six years old. This isn't about pity. I…I care about you." My face felt hot and I knew it wasn't the sun shining down on us that had my cheeks burning. "I think I can help. And I bet if the tables were turned, you'd be there for me."

He studied me for a long time and I forced myself to meet his gaze, ignoring the butterflies that fluttered against the walls of my stomach as if trying to escape. I took a deep breath and waited for him to say something…anything. Finally, he looked away and scrubbed his hands over his face in defeat. He groaned loudly. "I'm probably going to regret this. So, what did you have in mind?"

A smile spread across my face, a weight lifted from my shoulders. "I thought you'd never ask."

Chapter 6

I made a note on the inventory sheet, detailing a small flaw in the neck of an old wine decanter dating back to colonial days, a rare find in such good condition. I set it back on the shelf and finished writing in a ledger. Cursing under my breath about Brig's outdated system, I let out an exasperated sigh. Every Friday I took inventory. Today I counted the antique bottle collection lining the shelves on one wall of the antique shop. The sun shone through the curtains and cast a bright glow on the blue, green and red glass. I dusted off an old ruby red whisky bottle from the 1800's and placed it back on the shelf, adjusting the price according to the collectors book on the desk to my left. I was thinking about Alex when Brig walked in.

"How's it going?"

"It's been quiet. But it's early yet." The summer tourists usually filed in after lunch, looking for old book cases or little antique tables that would go just perfectly with their shabby chic décor.

"I'll have you close up shop around six tonight. Do you have plans with your friends or do you want to eat pizza?" He pushed an old Victorian dresser further back against the wall, making the aisle a few inches wider.

"No plans; pizza sounds good." I tabulated the value of the bottles, my head buried in the musty old ledger book. Brig resisted change and the computer age had not caught up with him. He refused my suggestion to transfer all of the records to Quick books software and spread sheets. You would have thought I'd used foul language. I could not convince him that a computer was a good idea. I'd been shocked when he bought me a cell phone for my sixteenth birthday.

"You haven't gone out much lately." He startled me from my thoughts as he unfolded a squeaky little step stool that looked as much like an antique as anything else in the place. "I figured you'd be enjoying your time away from school with your...what do you kids call it...your BFF's?" He grinned down at me trying to sound hip, but couldn't quite pull it off.

I shrugged and placed the last of the bottles back on the shelf. He was right. I should be doing normal teenage girl stuff, but none of that appealed to me. I preferred being alone, especially now. I realized that I didn't really have a best friend— someone to share everything with. Spending so much time at the gym and on the track, I never felt like I fit in with my high school crowd, and as far back as I could remember, Levi and Alex had occupied much of my time. Now, our threesome felt like a lonely and broken twosome. I sighed as I set the ledger down and reached for a dust cloth. It occurred to me that being with Alex made me feel closer to Levi somehow; probably because each of us had tried so hard to save him from himself. I shook off the memories that rode in on that thought.

Senior year would be here before I knew it and I would have no choice but to see my classmates and friends. For now I needed time alone to process my brother's death. The few girls I considered to be friends understood and would be there when I was ready, but I couldn't explain that to Brig. Nor could I explain my feelings for Alex. I didn't understand them myself. I grabbed the furniture polish and changed the subject. "Are the guys coming over tonight for poker?" I asked.

"Yup. The usual." He climbed onto the foot stool and set about hanging some old lanterns on nails he had lined up in a row on the exposed beams overhead. He met with the same five guys the last Friday of every month ever since I could remember. I wouldn't think much of it, but it seemed strange that I'd never met any of them face to face and didn't know their names. They showed up after dark and left at all hours, no traces of them having ever been there. It was like this private club that Brig kept secret. The only woman allowed was Vic and she only showed up occasionally. I'd learned a long time ago not to ask questions. Lately, it seemed questions were all I had.

"I'm going to pick up Alex at the hospital on Monday. His doctor said he should be ready for discharge by then."

"That's good news." He climbed down off the ladder, his back still to me as he fiddled with some ancient, rusty tools laid out on a table. "I hope you aren't planning to pester him about what happened."

"I won't," I said indignantly. I'd been holding my questions back all week, not wanting to ruin the tentative bond that I'd created with Alex. There would be plenty of time to work up to that conversation once he was back on his feet and doing better.

My grandfather turned to me, his expression doubtful. "I know you, Young Lady. I also know that you talked to Victoria about your suspicions. I told you to let it go, and I meant it." His tone of voice was harsh, meant to intimidate and command, a tone that probably worked well on soldiers in battle and un-cooperative prisoners, but it had little effect on me.

"Why can't you just admit that the story we were given by the military doesn't add up? You knew Lee as well as I did, and it's just possible that things didn't go down the way they said."

He let out a slow breath and scratched his head, letting the stern expression fade. He knew by now that he didn't scare or intimidate me. He also knew I never walked away from a situation once I made up my mind to learn the truth. "I understand you wanting answers," he said. "But at what cost? Do you really want to know that your brother committed suicide? Do you want your mother to have to live with that knowledge? You know what she believes about suicide keeping a soul out of heaven."

My heart thudded against my ribs. I hadn't even said the words out loud or even really let myself think about it, yet I realized that it was all I had been thinking since I read the letter from the military about what happened. Mom's beliefs notwithstanding, I knew I couldn't rest without knowing. I looked down at my feet, unable to meet the cool gray of his eyes. "If that's the truth, yeah, I want to know."

"There's no point in it, Jordan." His voice was angry again, or maybe just frustrated. He had to be as curious as I was. He wasn't a man who liked lies or cover-ups unless he felt it was for the greater good. That got me thinking.

I chose my words carefully. "Right now, I think Alex feels responsible for Lee's death. I don't know what he knows or remembers about what happened, but I don't think it was his fault. I'd like to prove that, and give him some peace of mind. If I find out that Lee…went into a dangerous situation knowing he wouldn't come out alive and that he did it on purpose, I promise I will never tell Mom." I was good at keeping secrets. I folded my arms across my chest and tilted my head, meeting his eyes with the same look I'd given him when I promised to never do drugs or have unprotected sex, (conversations we both agreed to have only once).

He spoke softly, "Do you think your mother hasn't wondered the same thing? She is suffering enough without having you dig up dirt on your brother. She needs to believe he died with honor."

Our gazes locked. "I'm not trying to hurt Mom. I know she couldn't handle something like that, but *I* need to know the truth—whatever it is. And so does Alex. It's not fair for her to blame him."

He shook his head and rubbed a meaty hand along the back of his thick neck. "Don't you have any friends? You should be going to the mall, buying shoes, getting manicures—whatever it is seventeen year old girls do in their free time."

I smiled and wrapped my arms around his neck, resting my head on his barrel-like chest. "I have lots of friends, but you know all that girly stuff has never been my thing." I looked up into his face and blinked my baby blues, giving him the look I knew would melt the last of his resolve. "It's your fault I'd rather be sticking my nose where it doesn't belong. I learned from the best."

A smirk twitched in the corners of his mouth and he wrapped his arms around me, pulling me into a snug embrace. "All right, I'll look into it. But don't say anything about this to your mother and you leave Alex alone about it. He has got enough to deal with."

I squeezed him tight. "Thanks Brig. I knew I could count on you."

Chapter 7

"Who taught you to drive?" Alex gripped the dashboard of the Rabbit.

"Who do you think?" I asked, checking my speed and slowing down a little.

He relaxed and sat back, his face growing solemn as he stared out the window at the passing high school. "Lee, probably; he was a crazy driver."

"Actually, it was Brig. He thought I should learn offensive driving techniques. He says a girl should be prepared for anything," I said in my best growling Brig voice.

I glanced over to catch his grin widen. My heart did another little dance and I wondered just how far I would go to see that smile every day. I couldn't even let myself go there. Alex was in no way ready for my emotional neediness. *Stick to business.*

"It must run in the family, then," he said. "I just hope you're a better driver than your brother."

I ignored the comment, wanting to avoid discussion of my brother's obvious character flaws. Aside from nearly burning down the high school, Levi had wrecked every vehicle he'd ever owned, from his mini-wheels, to BMX bikes, to motorcycles and cars. The Rabbit had actually been lucky to survive. It had a ton of dings and dents, scars from Levi taking a baseball bat to it in one of his fits of rage. We'd gotten most of the big dents out, but the Rabbit wasn't pretty. I braked at the corner and turned left onto Main Street, passing the skating rink and the old town hall.

"This isn't the way to the lake." I felt his eyes on me, another chill raising the hairs on my arms. I clenched my jaw and prepared myself for an argument.

"I know. Trust me. You are going to love what I have planned. Well…maybe not love it…but you'll know it's the best thing for you."

"This does not sound good. Do you mind cluing me in on the plan?"

"Do you always have to know what's going to happen next?

"No, but I like to be prepared." I glanced over, noticing his face had gone pale.

It dawned on me that he was scared. It wouldn't be easy facing everyone and dealing with the stares and questions. I sympathized with him but if he was going to get better, he might as well climb the hard hill first. "You know you can handle whatever comes your way, don't you?" I asked, turning into the parking lot of Vic's Gym and sliding into a space.

Alex let out a groan when he saw the sign on the building. "You're kidding, right? I already have

PT scheduled for tomorrow at the hospital. I thought you were supposed to be giving me a ride home. If I'd known you were going to play a dirty trick like this, I'd have waited for a ride from my mom."

I let him rant for a minute before I interrupted. "I figured the physical therapist could cover the basics. You know, getting used to the prosthesis, doing the whole straight leg raise routine, gait training and stair climbing. But just think about how much faster you'll get better if you add a few times a week at the gym where you can work on your whole body." Before he could argue, I added the challenge, "You do want to get better, don't you?"

"That's not the point…"

"I think it is. Either you want to get better, and are willing to do whatever it takes, or you don't."

"I feel like crap and this thing is already uncomfortable as hell." He motioned toward his new leg which was covered by his jeans and sneakers. If I didn't know his lower right leg was missing, I wouldn't be able to tell with him sitting here in the car. He stared out the window at the front door as if willing someone to pull down the blinds and hang the closed sign out. "I just don't think I'm ready…"

I cut him off again. "What I have in mind for today has nothing to do with your leg. Stop making excuses…"

"I'm not…."

We argued for another ten minutes, until finally he gave up. "Enough already! Obviously, since you're holding me hostage here in the car and you have the keys, I'm not going home until you get your way." He opened the door and climbed out, reaching for his crutches in the back seat. "Going *in* can't possibly be as much torture as sitting out here arguing with you," he muttered.

I inwardly gloated at my triumph and collected the gym bag out of the back seat that I'd arranged ahead of time with his mom. She was totally behind my plan to whip Alex into shape and I'd cleared it with his PT, getting special instructions about the limits of the temporary prosthesis and what to look for if there were problems. She didn't want him damaging the new skin, so we needed to check occasionally that there were no pressure sores developing on the stump. There was no room for squeamishness on my part. I took a deep breath and dug in my heels, ready to face whatever happened next. Getting Alex's co-operation would likely be my biggest challenge.

I had said the word 'stump' aloud to myself a hundred times over the last several days while I researched and read everything I could find on prosthetics, below the knee amputees, and rehabilitation. With the right attitude and proper care, Alex could live a fully functional life. If I had to pin him to the ground, he was going to learn to deal with this new situation. No matter what it took, I wouldn't let him settle for anything less than a full recovery. He had no idea what he was in for and I wasn't about to tell him up front. I hated to be so sneaky about it, but I knew he'd never cooperate otherwise. Stubborn and Marine were words I knew to be synonymous.

Alex followed a few steps behind me, still mumbling under his breath. The squeak of his sneaker over the end of the prosthetic foot came down on the pavement in an uneven cadence signifying his limp. I took another deep breath and promised myself that when I was done with him, that limp would be a distant memory. The more permanent and high tech prosthetic limb that would return him to near full function was still being designed for him, and awaiting necessary adjustments based on how well he adapted to the one he had on, but the casted lower leg, titanium post, and rigid ankle joint would have to do for now.

Vic met us at the check-in counter. She acknowledged Alex with a firm handshake and handed him a key on a small chain. "This'll open up locker number twenty-four. You're welcome to use it whenever you want. As far as I'm concerned you have free run of the facility."

Alex took the key and looked from me to Vic, obviously aware this had all been pre-arranged. "Thank you, Ma'am. But I'd be happy to pay for membership."

Vic waved him off. "I have special rates for military. No charge considering all you've done for your country, Corporal." There was an awkward silence and then Vic turned her attention to me. "I reserved the meditation room for the next two hours. It's all yours."

I thanked her and led Alex to the locker room, handing him the bag his mom had packed with a towel and workout clothes.

"You thought of everything," he said, a sarcastic grimace reminding me of the boy I'd once tripped and pushed face first into a mud puddle.

I turned my back, hiding the grin that crept across my lips. "I'll meet you back here in five."

Fifteen minutes later we sat on meditation pillows facing each other. "Why don't you take off the prosthesis so you can sit comfortably," I said, noticing him squirm and stretch his right leg out straight as if it didn't quite belong to the rest of his body.

He eyed me without humor. "What are you up to, Jordie? I really don't feel like…"

I cut him off again, a technique I'd learned from my mother, no doubt. I had to hand it to her. She was an expert at cutting down on a lot of unnecessary arguing and complaining. She either interrupted or walked away, the latter skill not being my strong suit. "I told you, this has nothing to do with your leg. Take it off and get comfortable. We're going to be here for a while." He didn't move. I reached over and grabbed his artificial foot and pulled.

"Hey! What are you doing?" He wrapped a tight fist around my wrist, stopping me.

"Are you going to take it off, or do you want me to?" I met his gaze with the coolest expression I could drag to the surface. He glared back. His hand felt like a vise around my wrist, on the verge of too much pressure. I held my ground. "I've already seen it, Coop."

After a tense moment, he let out a harsh breath and let go of my wrist, "You're impossible," he grumbled. He yanked up his pant leg and removed the leg with exaggerated movements to express his obvious unhappiness with the current plan of action. He let the sweat pant leg dangle below the knee, the vacancy looming between us like an echo, vibrating as if his foot were still there and invisible at the same time.

"Why are you doing this?" he asked. His voice sounded low and tired.

I waited for him to put the prosthetic leg off to one side and assume a modified version of a cross legged pose. "Because you need me," I said. "Now close your eyes and breathe." I closed my eyes and focused on my breath, still sensing him watching me. My heart fluttered and skipped in response.

"I can't," he said, frustration seeping into his tone.

"Yes. You can. I find meditation very helpful. Vic says meditation is the path to all wisdom."

"You are so weird." He cracked a smile and my heart skipped.

"Maybe I am," I said, my lips twitching in an effort to sound serious. "You're not the first one of my friends to think I'm weird, but meditation does help. Trust me. The only thing holding you back is what's going on in your head. If you can clear and focus your mind, you really can overcome whatever physical, mental or emotional limitations you might be faced with. Meditation is the best way I know of to clear the mind…accept for beating the crap out of the heavy bag, but I figured we should try this first, considering you're still recovering." I crossed my legs into lotus pose, rested my hands palms up on my knees, and sat up tall. "C'mon, it can't hurt to try it." I took a few cleansing breaths, closing my eyes once more.

A moment of silence filled the room before his voice, hollow and empty, broke through. "How is it, that you don't blame me for Lee's death?"

I opened my eyes to see Alex staring at me, a tortured look on his face. My heart pounded louder and steadier while I tried to control my emotions. I wanted to cry. But I knew Alex would take it as confirmation that down deep, I did blame him. When the truth was, I didn't. I needed him to know that truth.

"It wasn't your fault. I know it, and you know it. And if you don't know it for certain, you and I are going to find out together. Now, close your eyes and breathe." I closed my eyes and sucked a deep breath in through my nose, waiting for the pulse in my ears to subside.

"Jordie…I'm sorry…about Lee."

I kept my eyes closed, willing the air to continue to move through me, my calm in the storm. I felt hot tears behind my eyes but I kept them locked away. "I know," I said. The calm I reached for deep inside came out in my voice, and I felt Alex relax—sensed his heart open just a crack.

"Jordie."

I opened one eye. "What now?"

"Thanks for believing in me."

I smiled and closed my eye. "Just breathe, okay?"

Chapter 8

"Don't you think you should stick around today and help Brig at the antique shop?" Mom poured her second cup of coffee, her fuzzy slippers, bathrobe, and the newspaper tucked under her arm, signs she would head back up to her room for another few hours before starting her Saturday. I had already been for a six mile run and was scarfing down a bowl of cereal before picking up Alex for the gym.

"I told Alex I'd be there by nine." I slurped the last sip of milk from my bowl.

"You've been spending too much time with him, Jordan. This is your summer vacation. What about your friends?"

"Alex *is* my friend. Besides, nobody's knocking down my door to hang out. Penny has a lot going on taking care of her mom right now and she's at skating camp practically every day. All my other friends have summer jobs, are on vacation with their families, or are otherwise as busy as I am, so for now I want to focus on helping Alex."

I put my dish in the sink, towering over my mother. Standing as close to her as I had the day of the funeral, our shoulders touching, I realized we hadn't spent more than a few minutes in a room together since that day, let alone had any physical contact. I heard her crying at night and I suspected she heard me too, but it just felt like we were worlds apart in our way of dealing with this horrible loss— and neither of us knew how to bridge the distance.

"Don't forget your obligation to your grandfather. You are supposed to be helping *him*." She stared down into her coffee cup.

"Brig can get along without me for a few hours every day. Why don't you say what you really mean, Mom? That you don't want me hanging around with the person you think is responsible for Lee's death." I stared out the kitchen window, trying to keep the anger out of my voice.

She sucked air through her nose--never a good sign. "Since you mention it, yes," she snapped. "I don't understand how you can stand to be around him after what…"

"It wasn't his fault!" I shouted, at the end of my rope with her bad attitude about Alex.

"The military report said…"

"It was wrong! I don't believe…"

"It's in black and white, Jordan…"

"You can't be serious! How can you be so…so…judgmental…and so…naïve. Like everything the military says is gospel. You are just looking for someone to blame so you don't have to look at the truth… " My blood was boiling and I faced off with my mother, the two of us working up to a full blown explosion of words we couldn't take back.

"And you can't see the truth when it's staring you in the face. Talk about naïve…" She had slammed her cup onto the counter, coffee spilling over onto the folded newspaper.

"What's that supposed to mean?" I asked. My voice sounded extra chilly.

"It means you are only attaching yourself to Alex so you don't have to deal with your own loss. You act like it doesn't matter that your brother is gone…" she was crying now, her words coming out in sharp gasps.

"How can you say that?" I screamed. I'd been trying to hold it together for her, and now she was accusing me of not caring.

"What's going on in here?" Brig burst in through the kitchen door, undoubtedly hearing our raised voices all the way out into the garden.

"Mom doesn't want me to see Alex. She thinks it's all his fault--what happened to Lee. And she doesn't think I even care that Lee is dead." By now my anger was dissolving to tears and I heard my voice pitch into that whiny teenage girl sound that I hated so much when I heard my friends do it. But I couldn't help it. She wasn't being fair.

"I didn't say any of that," she sniffled and lowered her voice, gaining control in front of Brig. "I didn't tell you that you couldn't see him. I just said I thought you were spending too much time with him. You are only seventeen years old, Jordan. You should be out having fun with your friends, not babysitting a Marine Vet recovering from trauma." Her voice shook. "And I didn't say you didn't care…oh what difference does it make?" She turned her back, heading out of the room. "Do whatever you want. You always do."

With that, she disappeared up the stairs, leaving me crying in the kitchen and feeling worse than if she had stayed and fought. "Why does she start with me and then walk away? It's like she wants me to hate her." I sobbed, turning my back to my grandfather and staring out the window at the neat rows of vegetable mounds and prize winning tomatoes, still green on the vines. Tears spilled down my cheeks faster and faster. "I can't stand it. She always runs away from a fight. It seems like she spends most of her life hiding from the truth, existing in her own protective bubble and leaving the rest of us out here to deal with reality."

"Your mom…she isn't strong like you are. She's afraid of all the hurt the world can bring. She's had her fair share of troubles and… well…she thinks she needs to protect herself. It's just her way."

"I wish she were different," I said, wiping my tears away and sniffling hard, stuffing my emotions back into their cramped compartment down deep inside of me, somewhere out of the way where they wouldn't take over my every thought.

"Wishing won't make it so, Sunshine. When it's about family, we have to love people for who they are, no matter what." He wrapped an arm around my shoulder and stared with me out at the garden and to the property beyond. Three wooded acres, two barns and the antique shop, all, three generations old. Family had to be about more than blood and roots. Maybe it worked the opposite way too. I thought about Alex. If you loved somebody for who they were, no matter what, maybe *that's* what *made* them family.

I picked up Alex as planned, the ride to the gym growing conspicuously silent. I didn't want to talk for fear of ranting about my mother's personality disorder, so I turned up the tunes, opened my window and let the car fill with noise the whole way there. The silence seemed to suit Alex just fine.

We had already been to the gym three times during the week and I thought he was beginning to look forward to it. The physical therapist had him walking and stair climbing without his crutches but

Alex's limp was still pronounced and his balance needed work. We had gotten into a routine of meditating for about thirty minutes, a practice that was torturous with him interjecting thoughts every few minutes about how stupid it was. After meditation, we rode stationary bikes for a half hour, stretched, (another exercise in patience since he didn't see the need), and then I ran him through the weight training circuit, pushing him until he grunted and groaned. I couldn't tell if he was grunting in pain, annoyance, or approval, but at least he'd stopped arguing.

I introduced him to the speed bag and he disappeared into the rhythm for a while before I dragged him onto the next thing, one day Pilates floor work (which he said made him feel "sooo girly".) Another day I worked him through a private yoga class, instructing him on modifications for poses that would be impossible without an articulating ankle joint. I couldn't wait for him to get his new leg, which would arrive in another week. He would have so much more freedom once the ankle joint moved. The new vacuum style socket would give him much better balance, stability and control.

With his incision all healed up, I figured today, we would get into the pool. I was as nervous about him seeing me in a swim suit as I was about seeing whether he could still swim or not. It would be a big test for both of us.

There were only a few people in the pool, lap swimmers lined up in three narrow lanes separated by blue buoys. Vic reserved the two open lanes for me to work with Alex. I stepped under the communal shower to rinse off before entering the pool. If I was out of the locker room before Alex, I knew he was stalling. It would be hard to come out in the open in front of people, his leg on display for the first time. I couldn't imagine how vulnerable and scared he must be.

I set the water to cold and shivered for a few seconds before turning it off. It was best to acclimate to the pool's temperature before hopping in. Vic didn't believe in heated pools. When I turned around, Alex was there, leaning on his crutches in his swim trunks and his stump covered with a black neoprene sleeve.

"Ready for a swim?" I asked smiling. It took effort not to look at his leg. I forced myself to lock onto his eyes, something I'd been avoiding for several reasons—not the least of which was the effect it had on my ability to think straight. The jolt that went through me when I stared into the blue-green depths made me shiver again.

Alex stared back at me, and then I watched his eyes trail down my body—all 5'10" and 140 pounds of me. I felt suddenly and completely exposed. He had seen me in swim suits a thousand times when we were kids, but standing here half naked in front of him— I was instantly aware that he had noticed my chill. I turned my back and headed for the pool, anxious to take cover under water.

"That's what I like about you, Jordie; you don't believe in wasting time." He leaned his crutches on a chair and hopped on one foot across the cement, grabbed for the railing, and then launched himself into the pool. He executed a neat shallow dive past my head, then torpedoed through the water and came up half way down the length of the Olympic sized pool. "Whew! That's cold!" He shook out his hair, the spikes standing on end in every direction. His hair had grown out the last few weeks. It looked darker in the water and I liked it a little longer. But nothing made him more handsome than the wide grin he beamed at me. "Pretty good, huh?"

I dunked under and swam out to him, popping up a foot away. "That was fantastic. How does it feel?"

We were shoulder deep in the water and he had to wave his arms back and forth to keep his balance, but he looked happier than I'd seen him

since he'd gotten back. I sensed the freedom and
lightness of his spirit, as if he had found a part of
himself that he thought had been lost. He floated
onto his back, floundering a little then righting
himself again. "It'll take some work, but so far it
feels awesome." He swam to the wall, an awkward
modified flutter kick trailing behind, and his
muscular arms dragging him through the water.

I swam up to meet him, hanging onto the
edge next to him. "You always were a great
swimmer. I hoped this would help."

He stretched his arms out onto the deck, his
back to the wall. His lower body floated upward and
he kicked his legs trying to find a rhythm to balance
the absence of his right foot. "Really, Jordie, this is
great. I appreciate how hard you're working with
me. I don't think I would be this far along if you
hadn't pushed me the way you did. I owe you big
time." He kept his gaze focused on his legs as if
willing them to cooperate. He pumped them in
synchronicity, the left foot churning up the water so
you could hardly tell the other was missing.

I joined him on my back and kicked hard to
match him, both of us causing a roiling eruption of
splashing water. "The only thing I want is to see
you happy and healthy again," I yelled over the
noise.

He stopped kicking and pushed off the wall.
"Race you to the other end." In two strokes he was

already ten feet away. "Hey! Not fair. You had a head start." I shoved off the wall with both feet, closing the distance by a margin, but I knew he would beat me to the other side. I didn't care. I felt like I'd already won in a big way.

Chapter 9

"Hurry up. I don't want to be late for church." My mother had apparently decided that a month away from Sunday morning Mass was more than sufficient grieving time, and she picked this morning to drag me out of bed to make her triumphant return.

"I'm exhausted. I want to sleep in." I stuck my head under my pillow.

"Let's go. No arguments. You have exactly thirty minutes to get up and get ready." She stood in my bedroom doorway, feet wide, hands fisted on her hips like a prison guard.

I eyed her from beneath the pillow and groaned. "All right already, leave me alone. I'll be down in a minute." I heard her footsteps squeak along the old wood floors, each plank carrying a distinct sound so I could follow her down the hall and knew what stair she was on at any given moment. I rolled over and begrudgingly sat up.

I wasn't into church like Mom was. I had a larger view of God. Studying Eastern practices had opened my mind to seeing the bigger picture. I believed in a God that lived inside of me, not in some building where you went once a week to recite your prayers and take communion, making sure you left your dollar in the basket before you escaped your hour of boredom. Somehow, it felt kind of insulting to God. But that was just my opinion and my mother had little tolerance for what I thought about anything. She didn't force much on me. I guess I was lucky that way. But church, she insisted upon.

Brig drove the Land Rover, Mom sitting in the front seat and me staring out the back window watching a cow pasture go by, the black and white heifers chewing the grass and digesting it over and over in their seven stomachs. My own stomach felt queasy just thinking about facing the same cross my brother's casket had rested in front of—the last place I had asked God to watch over him. Since my previous prayers for divine intervention for my brother had obviously been overlooked, I wasn't on speaking terms with God just yet. And it wasn't like sitting in church for an hour was likely to change my mind. I felt like such a hypocrite, not believing in half of what the priest said and yet following like a sheep up to the altar and saying *"Amen"* after communion. But that was a fight for another day. Mom didn't look like she was in any kind of mood to be discussing our different perspectives on religion.

I slid back into the pew beside my mother, Brig inching in alongside me as we all knelt on the pad in front of us and bowed our heads in prayer. I whispered to Brig. "Do you need me this afternoon?"

He glanced at me over his knuckles, "Another hot date?" He raised a bushy brow at me and I saw the teasing spark in his eye.

"Alex thought we could use a little reward for all our hard work the last couple of weeks," I whispered back, not responding to his dig.

"Shhh!" My mother lifted her head and glared at me.

"I'm just saying..." I rolled my eyes at her, irritated by her impatience.

My mother sat back and pulled me along with her. "Do you need to discuss this right now?" Her voice was low, but her eyes looked about to spill over into tears.

"Sorry." I cast my eyes down, a little ashamed that I hadn't thought about how hard it must have been for her to return to church. This had always been her place of refuge. I wondered if it still was, or if she was mad at God, too.

The service continued on like white noise in the background. My head filled with cotton as my mind wandered and my emotions bubbled to the surface. Flashes of memories crashed through the wall I had so carefully placed around my heart-- Levi sitting next to me on this very same bench, pinching me and tickling me to get me in trouble when I would laugh or cry and cause a scene. My mother would come between us and give us that same evil eye that she had just given me, our family as complete as it could be without a father. I hadn't thought of my dad as a part of our family in a long time. Now another piece was missing. All the sadness I'd saved up for the years since he'd died came back in a flood.

"I have to go..." I stepped in front of Brig and escaped up the aisle, making a bee-line for the rear exit. I burst out the doors into the sunlight and could barely see where I was going. Tears cascaded over and I sobbed on the front steps of the church. No one followed me. Why should I be surprised that everyone was oblivious to the breaking of my heart? I had been trying so hard to keep my feelings under control. Now that they were loose, I was afraid I wouldn't be able to stuff them back down. What was I thinking coming here? Anger at Levi, at God, at the war...it all bubbled up and came out in unrelenting tears that I didn't want to cry. I felt so alone. "Damn it! Why?" I cried up to the puffy clouds, not sure who I was yelling at, really.

My mother's voice stopped me. "Jordan." She sat down beside me, reaching an arm around my shoulder. "I know it's hard being here. It's hard for me too." I rested my head against her, happier for her presence than I wanted to admit.

"You know that I miss him too, don't you?" I asked, sniffling to catch my breath.

"I know, Sweetheart. I didn't mean what I said yesterday. You have every right to choose to help Alex. And I know you loved your brother."

I lifted my eyes to her face, seeing for the first time, in a long time, the mother that combed my hair before bed when I was a little girl, the woman who sprayed Bactine on my cuts and bandaged me up when I fell. She was still the same mother who had worried about Levi and lost sleep whenever he was out of her sight, wondering if he would come home unharmed and alive.

"Mom, have you wondered if Lee…did it on purpose?" As soon as the words passed my lips, I wanted to take them back.

My mother's body stiffened. She took in a long breath and let it out slowly before she answered. "All I know is what the report said. Your brother died a hero—saving his best friend."

"Do you think it's possible though? That somehow, Lee found a way to end his life and make it look like an accident so that…"

"Jordan. Stop it." She gripped my shoulders and pinned me with a cold glare. "You have to let this go. Alex…made a mistake. I get that. I don't really care what happened any more. I just want to move on and begin… letting go of your brother." Her voice cracked and she looked away.

Before I could respond or tell her I didn't think Alex had made a mistake, she was already headed for the truck. I let her go. Brig was right. She needed to believe that Levi had earned his place in heaven. It was the only way her heart could stand him being gone. I wasn't so lucky. To me, only the truth mattered.

Chapter 10

"Kayaking was a good idea." I paddled alongside Alex, noting that he took one easy stroke for every two of mine.

"I figured we deserved a day off," he called over his shoulder. The morning light glinted off his hair, the color of a pale moon on a clear night. His tanned muscles flexed and bunched as he eased the paddle through the water. A wash of happiness settled over me—a true happiness I hadn't felt in over a month. Not since...No, I wasn't going there. Not today. I wanted to enjoy this time with Alex-- just the two of us. Not that it was like a date or anything. Alex had given me no real indication that he thought of me as anything more than a friend-- more than Levi's little sister-- other than occasional glances when he thought I wasn't looking. Mostly, he treated me like he always had--friendly, but hands-off.

Except for one, long ago kiss...

I leaned back and soaked in my surroundings, my chin raised to the sky. The sun warmed my face and the serene call of the loons on the lake vibrated in the air, the sound bouncing off the Berkshire Hills. I drew a deep breath and let the life around me fill my soul, and I thought about his

lips on mine, warm and moist. I thought about a
sunny day behind the barn when he had kissed me
long and slow. When I opened my eyes, Alex was
staring and smiling--the kind of smile that said he
definitely wasn't thinking about me like a sister.
Maybe there was hope for us after all. Or maybe I
was reading way too much into it.

"What were you just thinking about?" He
wore a curious grin as he peered over his shoulder,
eyeing me as if he had been reading my thoughts
and knew the answer already. I felt my cheeks get
warmer and I picked up my pace, my Kayak pulling
up beside his.

"I was just thinking what a perfect day this
is."

Alex took two more hard strokes. Then he
lifted his paddle out of the water and laid it across
the edge as the boat drifted silently along the
surface of Thompson Lake. What was he up to? The
south end of the lake ran along the nature preserve,
its coastline devoid of houses and docks. Up ahead
was a small beach surrounded by thick pines,
maples and oaks, a few birches dotting the forest
like white knights guarding the woodland
inhabitants.

"What are we doing here?"

"I made us lunch." He added, "Don't worry,
I didn't try to use a stove or anything. It's just
sandwiches." His boat slowed down and I steered

past, pulling around him and gliding the kayak up
onto the sand.

"It's still nice of you," I said. A flush of
warmth ran through me, thoughts racing to
determine his intent. I was surprised when he asked
me to go out on the lake, but I thought it would be
good therapy. I hadn't expected a lunch date. I
climbed out of the boat and dragged it up onto the
beach, removing my life vest and chucking it into
the cockpit. I adjusted my shorts, tugging on the
hems to make them an inch longer. My legs were
seriously growing too long for my body. I lifted the
tee-shirt over my head and tossed it in the boat, a
little self- conscious of wearing a skimpy flowered
bikini top underneath, my boobs filling it out nicely
if I did say so. Sammy had picked it out saying,
*"The orange and yellow totally catches those red
and gold highlights in your hair. Stop hiding that
killer body, Dude."* Right about now, I wondered
why we couldn't go back to those 1930's style
swim suits that came down to your knees and up to
your chin. I held my breath and waited to see if he
noticed me.

Alex pulled the twelve foot Pungo 120
alongside mine, dropped his vest on top, and
reached in the dry well to extract a plastic container
with lunch for two. He was becoming adept at
negotiating uneven surfaces with his prosthesis, but
the sand had to be an extra challenge. He glanced

up at me, stumbled slightly and recovered, a flash of frustration passing over his face. He shook it off and beamed that easy smile at me that made my heart leap. He stopped and stared, his expression faltering just enough for me to see that he *did* notice. Okay, so maybe he was interested. My goose bumps did a cool dance on the surface of my skin.

Alex cleared his throat and turned his back, tossing his tee-shirt onto the hull of the yellow boat. "It's the least I can do to repay you for all the hard work you've been doing to help me out." He plucked out a blanket he had rolled in a waterproof bag and laid it out on the sand, settling down and taking a spot while situating his leg. "I hope this thing doesn't rust up or get sand in it and start sounding like I'm grinding my gears." He rapped on the hollow plastic below his knee and shot me a sarcastic grin.

It was my turn to stare and clear my throat. Even if my eyes were traitorously disobeying my commands to look away from his shirtless and very muscular chest, I managed to find my voice. "It's going to be awesome when you get your new leg. You'll be a lot steadier on your feet and you'll be able to go running with me and…well, if you want to that is."

It suddenly occurred to me that I had more or less taken over his life and even more weird was that he had let me. Part of me was smugly satisfied about it and the other part of me felt a wary knot forming in my gut. Being supportive of his recovery was a given , but my heart was far more invested in our time together than was practically safe. A shot of fear ran through me for the first time. What if I was wrong about him? About us? About everything?

He spread out the food and handed me a bottled water, twisting the cap off first. "Why wouldn't I want to?"

"It's just that…I know I've been kind of…"

"Bossy?" He took half the sandwich in a bite and chewed, eyeing me over the water bottle as he slugged it down.

"I wouldn't have used that word, but…well…yeah," I said, smiling and looking down at my peanut butter and jelly sandwich. He handed me a bag of potato chips. I stared at him in awe. "You remembered."

"How could I forget? I don't know anyone else who likes potato chips on PBJ's." His ears turned a shade of pink and he looked away.

I swallowed the urge to cry. My heart swelled to near bursting—over a stupid sandwich. What was happening to me? I had loved Alex since I could remember. A silly crush on the boy down the street, but this felt different. I was suddenly scared…terrified. We'd grown closer these past weeks of training and therapy, but we had both been so focused on his recovery, I hadn't paid attention to how different it felt to be with him. What used to be a warm, shy, longing now burned a hot white hole in my heart that sent an ache down into my bones--an ache that nothing could ease except his smile or the thought of his touch. In that moment, I knew I was falling in love, but I had no idea how he felt, and the thought had me petrified. What if he didn't feel the same way? I sipped my water, pondering my options, and then took a deep breath. The direct approach, I decided. "Alex, what's happening between us?" My cheeks felt on fire, but I had to know.

He shifted uncomfortably. "I...I don't know. We're just...being friends, aren't we?"

My stomach sank. "Friends...of course. We've always been friends, right?" I took a bite of my sandwich and crunched on the chips, the taste no longer as appealing as when we were little. Another reminder that we weren't kids anymore. The passage of time, and war and death had changed us. Our one kiss had been a mistake, right? We were just playing at being grown up. It didn't mean anything. Besides, what Alex needed right now was a friend. I could do that. I could just be his friend. I clenched my jaw and forced my emotions down. My heart hammered in my chest as we both looked out over the lake, the tension growing between us.

"Hey, I remembered something about what happened," he announced, drawing me out of the funk that had my head spinning. He sat up straighter and caught my full attention.

"What did you remember?" My heart sped up another beat. This moment was what I had been waiting for—for Alex to recover his memory, to tell me the truth about Levi.

"It's not much, really." He slouched and stared out at a row of ducks paddling along the shoreline. "I keep hearing this kid crying. Not a baby…a kid about seven or eight…crying. I see flashes of the house…a window…people inside…I don't know." He shook his head, his voice sounding lost and confused.

"Do you know what it means?" I didn't want to get my hopes up, but it was the first time he had volunteered information or was even willing to talk about the incident. I knew he'd been seeing a counselor and I let that be private for him, resisting the urge to ask him how it was going. I let my other questions drop to the background in my busy head, my emotions so close to the surface I wanted to crawl under the blanket and hide like a sand crab.

"I'm not sure, but I think it has something to do with why we went into the house in Fallujah." He shrugged his shoulder. "I hope I'll remember more." His face took on a hard, faraway look that made my chest ache. I had no idea what he'd gone through over in Iraq, but I could only imagine he had seen more than any nineteen year old should ever see.

"Why would the military be so sure that you entered the house first?" I asked.

"Our squad leader gave us our assignments. I was supposed to go in and hack into the computer and Lee was my backup. Two Marines covered us from a nearby rooftop and another two had the street and the alley. It was supposed to be a simple in and out." His voice had taken on a monotone and now wavered. "I remember getting the call to stand down, and then I can't remember what happened next until I woke up in the hospital...." He looked down at the prosthetic limb and then looked away again. The lake seemed to offer him a grounding point to the present.

I didn't press him for more, despite the thousand questions that battered my brain. I touched his arm, warm and solid, and he smiled over at me, coming back fully to the moment.

"We'll work on it in meditation. Maybe you should try acupuncture—to clear your meridians," I said.

I took the last bite of my sandwich as he rolled his eyes and shook his head. "You are so weird." I tossed my empty water bottle at him and he caught it in mid-air.

"Your cat-like reflexes are going to come in handy when I get you in the sparring ring." I lay back on the blanket and closed my eyes, soaking up the sunshine and trying not to think about the house in Fallujah or the memory of Alex's kiss. It was pointless to dwell on the past. He couldn't force himself to remember and I couldn't force myself to forget. I ignored the ache deep inside and listened to the sounds of the lake--the birds singing, the water lapping gently on the shore. I reminded myself of a lesson I'd learned in yoga classes. To gain what you desire, you must learn to let it go--a strange paradox that I'd never quite understood.

"Jordie." Alex's voice cut through all the other sounds and made goose bumps rise on my skin.

"Yeah?" I opened my eyes and shielded the sun with my hand so I could see his face. A serious expression confronted me and my muscles tensed.

"You know I care about you, right?" His eyes held an intensity that ran another jolt through me.

"Yeah, I know."

"I mean…I really care about you. It's just…I have a lot of stuff to work through. You understand, don't you?"

I wanted to say *"No, not really,"* but I did understand. The time for us to talk about our feelings would have to wait. His recovery came first. "Of course I do, Coop. You've been through a lot."

"So have you." Without warning, he reached over and brushed the hair back from my face, tucking a stray curl behind my ear. The sensation of that one simple touch reached all the way to my belly and made my toes tingle. My pulse jumped and my skin felt hot from the inside out.

He leaned over me, blocking the sun. We looked at each other for a long minute. I thought he might kiss me—willed him to do it-- but then the tortured look in his eyes faded and he let out a breath as he backed away and stared blankly out over the lake. Sadness and disappointment settled over my soul. I could see the guilt on his face. He felt responsible for my brother's death. How could I expect him to see beyond the weight that rested so heavily on his shoulders?

"You have to stop blaming yourself, Alex. Whatever happened, you need to forgive yourself and look to the future. You know that Lee would never have blamed you." I sat up and peered out over the lake with him, only half seeing the beauty beyond the dark cloud that hung over us both. "It's probably what he wanted, anyway." My voice sounded small and more fragile than I'd intended. "And if he wanted to die, there would have been nothing you could do to stop him."

Alex laid a hand on my arm, the warm contact touching a part of me that felt much deeper than skin. "I understand why you would think Lee wanted to die, but he had changed. The Marines gave him a purpose…a reason to live. He wouldn't have tried to kill himself, Jordie, especially not while putting me at risk. You're wrong if you think otherwise." He let his hand fall away and I instantly missed his touch. My head ached with confusion.

"Then why did he go into the house when you were ordered not to and he knew it wasn't safe? I know you, Alex. The only reason you would have to go against an order was if you were following my brother." The anger I'd been containing crept out in my words.

His jaw ticked. "I don't know. I wish I did." His voice sounded so far away and detached, I wanted to reach out and pull him back, but he added in a hoarse whisper, "All I know is the military record shows that I got my best friend killed."

Chapter 11

I'd been thinking about what Alex said all morning, seeing the tormented look of guilt and shame that shadowed his handsome face. Mom and I had gone to church and Brig had stayed behind to open up the antique shop. Business had picked up over the last week and he wanted me to work the rest of the day, but all I wanted to do was find out if he had any new information that might help clear Alex's name.

"I thought you were going to look into it?" I rubbed the wood polish into the old maple nightstand, the scent of lemon oil permeating the air.

"I called in a few favors and read over the squad leader's report. It seems pretty clear that Alex jumped the gun. He made a mistake, Sunshine. It happens to the best soldiers. I blame his squad leader for putting two wet-behind-the-ears Marines into a bad situation. They never should have been on a special-ops mission in the first place. I don't care how easy a job it was supposed to be. It was just poor judgment all the way around."

"I just think…"

"Listen to me, Jordan. You have to let this go now. You aren't helping Alex by dwelling on the past."

"I'm the only one who *is* helping him," I snapped. Furniture polish sloshed in the container as I slammed it down on a seventeenth century sideboard next to me.

"Settle down there, Young Lady." Brig eyed me severely. "I know you're angry. You have every right to be, but it won't help anything to chase after some crusade that you can't win. Sometimes, life is unfair and you just have to deal with it. Do you understand?" His tone softened a bit but still held that air of authority that meant the question was rhetorical. He took the rag from my hand before I could polish a hole right through the wood.

Tears burned behind my eyes. My pulse grew in my throat like the blood would spurt out my jugular or the top of my head might pop off if I didn't hit something or scream very soon. "No I don't understand! I know things didn't happen the way they said it did and I'm going to find a way to prove it!" I turned to storm out of the antique shop, and Brig caught my arm.

"This will not end well, Jordan." His steely blue eyes penetrated through me and might have terrified someone else—someone who didn't know the depths to which my grandfather could love. I could see the pain in his eyes behind the glare and I knew he was wondering, too. Did Levi commit suicide, or did Alex really make some horrible mistake that ended in tragedy for all of us? And was Brig willing to let Alex take the blame if he didn't deserve it? I couldn't believe he could live without knowing the truth.

I pulled my arm free. "I'm going to look for answers with, or without your help."

Alex was the only one who could tell me. I had to help him remember—but how?

I stomped out of the shop just as two very prickly gray haired old ladies walked in. With a satisfied smirk, I left my grandfather to fend them off. It served him right.

"Alex doesn't want to see you." Mrs. Cooper glanced over her shoulder and stepped out onto the porch, locking and closing the door behind her. She adjusted her briefcase strap on her shoulder. Her slim brows furrowed in concern and fatigue shadowed in her pretty features.

"What do you mean--why not?" I had a sinking feeling in my stomach and my palms started to sweat. The July heat wasn't helping. Perspiration rolled down my temple and I pulled my ponytail tighter, shifting a Red Sox cap down over my eyes to block the sun. I'd taken it from Levi's old room.

It helped to keep a piece of him close to me—a
reminder of good times.

"Alex got his discharge papers yesterday.
He hasn't come out of his room since." Mrs.
Cooper's blonde hair was perfectly held in place
with what probably took an entire container of
hairspray in this humidity. She was in a light cotton
suit and her face was made up as if she was heading
out to a business meeting. At 3:00 on a Saturday?
Didn't she ever take a day off? I couldn't leave
Alex alone. He must be feeling like crap. He
definitely didn't need any reminders of all he'd lost.
His discharge papers couldn't have come at a worst
time.

Mrs. Cooper stood in my way. I could see
she wasn't planning to invite me to stay, and rather
than argue, I smiled sweetly and said, "I understand.
I'll give him a few days and call him to see how
he's doing." *Like hell I would.*

Her face relaxed. "I'm sure he'll get past
this in a day or two. Thank you for understanding."

She followed me off the porch and waved as
I walked down the driveway toward the street. My
house was less than a quarter of a mile away and I
had walked, so it was easy to act as if I was headed
home. I waited for the sound of her BMW to fade
away, and doubled back. If Alex was avoiding
company, he probably wouldn't answer if I rang the
bell or knocked. I checked the front door. Yup, she

locked it. Probably the back door, too. She struck me as someone thorough and security conscious. I paced the length of the porch a few times until an idea formed.

I remembered Alex sneaking out on occasion when he and Levi would skulk off to some midnight keg party. Bonfires and summer parties were a common occurrence on Thompson Lake, although the local cops had come down hard on under-age drinking the last few years. I made my way to the back yard and craned my neck trying to detect any signs of movement. If I remembered correctly, Alex's room was the one on the right, a small balcony leading to a double wide set of French doors covered with sheer curtains.

Fragrant yellow roses on a thick vine twined their way up the old trellis attached to the house right below the balcony. I studied the lattice, doubtful it could hold me but unwilling to be deterred. There were enough open spaces where the roses hadn't filled in that I could climb up and hop over the balcony, but the wood itself looked pretty old and worn. It had been a few years since Alex had used this escape route, but it must be sturdy enough for me if he could climb up and down.

I took a deep breath and started to climb. About half way up, I heard a creak and my foot dropped through the broken wood into mid-air. I held tight with both hands, thorns from an underlying stem and splinters biting into my fingers as I searched for another foothold. My hat fell off and I reached for it, nearly losing my grip. If I fell it would be a ten foot drop onto a stone patio. My heart lurched and I grabbed onto the trellis with both hands, stopping to catch my breath and recover.

The rest of the climb turned out to be relatively easy other than the fact that the roses seemed to have a mind of their own and lashed out at every opportunity to leave scratches everywhere my skin was exposed. In shorts and a tank top, it left little of me that wasn't stinging or bleeding by the time I reached the top and pulled myself over the railing. Not my brightest idea.

I peered in the glass doors and saw the room was empty. The sheer curtains were drawn, but I could make out the space clearly. At least I'd gotten the right balcony. There was a shelf with stereo speakers and a rack of CD's, a television, a desk with a state of the art computer system and an entire book case loaded with sci-fi books and technical manuals along with a dozen plaques and awards from science fairs. Alex was such a geek. I loved that about him. He was so different from other guys I knew from school--guys who were afraid to look too smart and hid behind their football uniforms or pothead status to keep from landing on the geek squad. Alex had always been--just Alex.

Now that I was here, I should probably go in. I slowly turned the handle on the door and opened it just a crack. A burst of cool air hit me. I listened carefully, a chill crawling up my spine at how silent the house was. I pushed the door open and walked in, about to call out to Alex. A blur hit me from behind and the air rushed from my lungs. Two strong arms wrapped around me as I sailed through the air and came down hard on the bed. Instinct kicked in and I twisted, my elbow snapping out and catching Alex on the side of the face as I rolled onto my back.

We both screamed--me from shock, him from pain. "Alex! I'm so sorry. Did I hurt..."

"Are you crazy! What the hell are you doing sneaking into my house? I could have killed you!" I stared into his face suddenly aware he was on top of me, pinning me to his bed, a savage look in his eyes.

My heart raced and the air-conditioned room did nothing to relieve the heat that coursed through my body. I wanted to respond, but my words caught in my throat and all I could do was lay there motionless beneath him trying to recover my breath and figure out how to get him to stay exactly where he was. Nose to nose and eye to eye, we were as close as we'd ever been to each other. The weight of his body and the warmth of his breath on my skin sent shivers of tension through me that settled into a

blissful swirl in my belly. I curled my fingers
through his and felt the tension shift between us.
His expression changed from one of anger
to…before I could define it, he rolled off me and sat
up, swinging his legs over the edge of the bed, his
back to me. I gulped in a few deep breaths, willing
my heart rate to come back to normal.

I lay still, the sensation of him on top of me
lingering like a kiss. I blinked a few times to
recover my focus and found my voice. "I'm sorry.
Your mom said you didn't want to see me so I…"

"So you broke in," he snapped. "Jesus,
Jordie. You nearly gave me a heart attack." He
dropped his head into his hands. "I really could
have hurt you."

I sat up and slid over next to him. "Well,
you didn't. If anything, I nailed you. Let me see
your face." When he looked up at me, I saw his eye
lid already swelling. "You'd better put some ice on
that."

"I don't need any ice." Then he grabbed my
hand. "You're bleeding," he said, a note of panic
rising in his voice. "Are you all right?"

Raised pink scratches marked my arms and
legs; a particularly nasty one on my left forearm
was oozing little droplets of blood. A few splinters
and scrapes marred my palm, but overall I was no
worse off than after a good sparring match. "The
roses got me." I flashed a grin at him, embarrassed.

"We'd better get you cleaned up." He stood, slightly unsteady as if he'd forgotten about his prosthetic leg, and returned from the bathroom a minute later with a bottle of hydrogen peroxide, tweezers, and a bag of cotton balls.

"Hey, you got your new leg." I noticed his limp was almost gone and his gait looked steadier. The titanium post now had a spring-loaded articulating ankle joint that flexed when he walked. If he had shoes on and long pants, I would never know the difference. Hoping we could change the subject away from him not wanting to see me, I focused on the state-of-the- art prosthesis. "It looks amazing—totally functional."

"Yeah. It's working out pretty well-- although it makes me feel like a cyborg." He sat beside me again, his weight dipping the mattress and making me slide closer. His temper had cooled and his lip twitched into a small smile which, as usual, made my heart sing. He pulled the splinters out of my palm, eyeing me as I sucked in a sharp breath. "Sorry," he said, making quick work of a few more splinters and cleaning the scrapes on my palm. He silently tended my wounds, his complete focus drawn to the task at hand. I hated to admit it, but it felt good to have someone looking after me for a change. It occurred to me that I had spent most of my life taking care of everyone else. He dabbed at the cuts on my arm, his touch gentle and sure. A feeling of deep contentment grew inside me. I liked this new feeling—probably way more than I should. I avoided eye contact with him, certain he sensed my hesitation.

"Your mom told me about the discharge papers. I'm really sorry, Alex." I didn't know what else to say. The silence grew awkward between us as I focused on the cool sting of the antiseptic and the gentleness of his touch. My belly fluttered and I tried to ignore the warmth that radiated between us. He smelled like soap and some manly scented deodorant that made my nose twitch and my mouth water. I stared at his green eyes, a little more blue today with the turquoise tee shirt he had on. I thought about what it might feel like to nuzzle my lips into the soft spot at the base of his throat just above his collar.

"It doesn't matter," he sighed, "I couldn't perform my duties anyway. It's not like the Marines could use a guy with only one leg." He screwed the cap onto the bottle and set aside the cotton balls.

"That's not true and you know it. With or without a leg, the Marines would be lucky to have you. You're brilliant." I looked around the room at all of his science awards. "Look at this place. You are amazing. If they can't appreciate what you have to offer, than that's their loss and they are idiots."

He looked at the shelf and shook his head, his gaze dropping to the floor as if he was searching for something he had lost. "Please go home and leave me alone."

"I'm not leaving you like this. You can't give up on yourself. There is so much you have to offer the world. You just need a little time to figure it out."

He stood and stalked across the room, opening the bedroom door and standing aside. "I need you to leave, Jordie." He hesitated. I saw him swallow and my heart leapt to my throat. Confusion and fear buzzed in my head like angry bees. He straightened his shoulders and cleared his throat. "Don't come back. I don't want to see you anymore."

The pounding in my chest moved to my ears. Uncertain if I'd heard him right, I didn't want to believe him. "You can't mean it. What about training? What about…"

"You've helped me more than you know, but I don't need you to…I can do the rest myself. I need to do this alone. Please. Leave."

My legs shook as I stood and a lump formed in my throat. I wanted to argue, but I knew the next words out of my mouth would be something embarrassing and would be followed by a flood of tears that would make this harder for both of us. I made it to the door and turned to face him, holding back my hurt and frustration with every ounce of strength I had. "I'm sorry you feel that way. I thought…we…"

"You thought wrong." His voice was hard, his expression cold and empty. He stared me down until I couldn't stand to look at him another second. The tears fell from my eyes and I swiped them away, my heart shattering like hot glass under cold water.

I turned back one more time, ready to beg, ready to do whatever it took to stay close to him. He looked like he could care less. My blood boiled, driving my temper to surface. "Fine, but maybe I won't be around when you change your mind."

"Maybe." He stood military straight and stared past me to the stairs. He couldn't have hurt me worse if he'd called me a fool.

I strode past him. "Good-bye, Coop."

Chapter 12

A sharp pain shot through my wrist. I
ignored it and hit the heavy bag again, an unladylike
grunt escaping my lips. I followed with a
roundhouse kick, a wheel kick and a back fist,
releasing what amounted to a loud growl aimed at
the defenseless bag.

"Anything I can do?" Vic grabbed the
swinging black leather as the chains rattled
overhead.

I turned away, my breath coming in ragged
gasps, a cramp forming under my ribs. I bent over,
hands on knees. A bottle of water appeared under
my nose. "Thanks." I twisted the cap and chugged.

"I suppose this has something to do with
Corporal Cooper's absence here in the past week."
Vic sat on the bench and patted the spot next to her.
Reluctantly, I plunked down on the bench.

"He doesn't want to see me. He says we're
done." The words tasted bitter and the lump that had
been in my throat all week felt like I'd swallowed a
peach pit. I had tried to put him out of my mind. I
went to the movies with Pen and Katie, hung out at
the mall, spending my meager income on stupid
shoes and makeup I would never wear, and ran past
Alex's house twelve times hoping he would see me

and come out to grovel. No such luck. I leaned back against the wall, the cool concrete easing the itch of sweat trickling down my spine.

"You've got to give him some time. I know it's hard, but you need to be patient." She let out a sympathetic sigh. "What set him off?"

"He got his discharge papers."

"I see. That would piss off any Marine who didn't leave by choice. It's programmed in. You know how it is. Duty, honor, loyalty...*Semper Fi*, and all that. He feels betrayed. He's angry. He feels terrible about Levi. The boy's got a heap of dung on his plate and not two slices of bread to go with it. You can't take it personally."

"It's just that he is so smart. He has so much potential and he just can't see it." I realized the ache that had taken up residence in my heart was as much for him as it was for me. "It would be such a waste for him to give up on himself." Even if he didn't want anything to do with me, I wanted the best for him.

"Has he seen the military's investigative report?"

"I don't know. I don't think so. If they gave him a copy, he hasn't shared it with me." Another wave of emptiness and hurt washed over me. I hated that he shut me out. What I hated even more was how much I wanted him back! I missed the shy, '*I'm-thinking-I-might-kiss-you*' sparkle in his green eyes and the '*don't-even-think-about-resisting*' smile that went with it. I'd only caught glimpses, but I was clearly sucked into the romantic notion that maybe, just maybe, Alex loved me back. I refused to believe I'd read the signals wrong.

"Typically, you need a security clearance to see special ops reports, but if he could get his hands on that, it might put this thing to rest once and for all. He would know for sure what happened and he could move on." She patted my leg and nudged me with her shoulder. "And so could you."

I let out a rush of air, my shoulders relaxing a fraction. "So how does one go about acquiring these reports?"

"Well, as I said, you would need a security clearance. Maybe Brig knows somebody."

My shoulders tensed up again. "He won't help me. He's made it pretty clear he wants me to leave this alone." My brain started spinning, the seed of an idea sprouting like a bean. "You've been a big help, though. Thanks, Vic." I gave her a quick squeeze and stood.

Her dark brows arched, a noticeable contrast to her almost white hair. "I don't want to know what you're planning, but whatever it is, I had nothing to do with it and don't get in over your head."

"I'll be careful. Don't worry." I headed for the shower with the thought rolling around in my head--*I'm already in way past turning back.*

I dressed quickly, slipping into a pair of shorts, a tee shirt and sneakers. I pulled my hair back into a ponytail and jumped into the car. I needed to see Alex and tell him about my idea. He might not go for it right away, but I was sure I could convince him. The hardest part would be getting past the small issue of him not wanting to see me. Vic said it wasn't personal, but I had my doubts. It felt very personal to me. But given all he'd been through, maybe I had pushed him too hard. Maybe he just wasn't ready to let himself get too close to anyone, especially the sister of his best friend. Not when he was feeling so responsible. How could I be so dense?

I stopped at his house first but Mrs. Cooper said he'd left a couple of hours ago and taken her car. He hadn't said where he was headed and I could see she was worried. Where the heck could he be? I drove to Somerville, my heart pounding with the rhythm of the music on the radio. I checked the pool hall, circled the parking lot at the mall, tried his cell phone a bunch of times and finally decided it was futile. He could be anywhere.

I turned around and headed back toward the lake, a nervous twitchy feeling taking over. Something was wrong. I could feel it. He wouldn't do anything stupid, would he? No. I comforted myself in knowing that he of all people was unlike my brother. Alex was not self-destructive by nature. He had fought for Levi's life dozens of times— probably kept him alive much longer than he would have ever made it without such a steady and level-headed friend.

Then I zipped past the Old Thompson Lake Tavern and spotted the blue BMW. I hit the brakes and backed up, pulling into the parking lot and kicking up dust. Yup, it was Mrs. Cooper's car alright. Crap. What was he doing at a bar? Beside the fact he wasn't legal, this particular bar attracted a pretty rough crowd. Mostly bikers passing through or low life regulars who stayed and drank until they could barely walk, let alone drive. The local cops patrolled the parking lot every hour or so trying to keep the idiots from getting behind the wheel.

The bar, an old barn-style building, had a run-down, country boy feel to it. Antlered heads of deer and mounted fish on wooden plaques hung on the exposed beams overhead. The stench of stale beer and fried food hit me as I entered through the front door. The place was busy for a Saturday afternoon. Several leather-clad, bearded men sat stationed around a pool table, while the bar stools were filled with middle aged men and a couple of guys in their twenties, knocking back shots and beers enough to have them swaying in their seats. I saw Alex right away, sitting at the bar staring at the flat screen TV, a Red Sox vs. Yankees game keeping his attention. The big game explained the crowd.

I approached cautiously, uncertain about the reception I was about to get. Heads turned and I felt my face heat up as several pairs of eyes stayed glued on my boobs. What was I thinking? I had no business being here. But then again, neither did Alex.

Alex had on a USMC tee-shirt stretched tight over his muscular chest and shoulders. His blond hair was combed back, longer than I'd seen it since he was in high school. With a couple days' stubble, he looked much older than nineteen and the bartender must have decided not to card a Marine with a prosthetic leg, figuring he'd earned at least the right to have a few beers. Alex wore shorts, either trying to make a statement about his leg, or beyond caring what anyone thought. I slid onto the bar stool next to him and the bartender, a pinched-face man with a huge gut, smirked at me. His expression said, *"Don't even try it."*

"Could I get a ginger-ale please?" I asked sweetly. He looked from me to Alex and back again as Alex nodded to acknowledge me.

"What's a nice girl like you doing in a place like this?" Alex said. He seemed to think this was funny because he laughed and slapped a twenty onto the counter and downed the rest of his beer. "Keep 'em comin', Tommy." He slid the bottle across the mahogany and the bartender sent a full one back.

"Drinking is not going to help." I eyed him as he drew a long swig off the fresh beer.

He set the bottle down hard and glared at me, turning his attention back to the game. "What are you doing here, Jordie?"

"I came to get you out of here. We need to talk." The bartender set my drink onto a coaster and shook his head as if I was creating some kind of drama he wanted no part of. I took a long sip through the straw, a fizzy tickle hitting my nose and making me blink.

"I already said what I needed to say to you. You need to leave me alone. I'll be fine." His words slurred a bit and it was clear he was anything but fine.

"At least let me drive you home. You are in no condition to…"

"What are you, my mother now? Just go home and stop bugging me. Man, you are such a pain. Just like when we were kids. Always tagging along, getting in the way, ruining our fun."

His words stung even though I knew he didn't mean them. Or maybe he did. I was always a third wheel when it came to him and my brother, but there were times he had made me feel like we were the three musketeers and that I was more than just Levi's kid sister. I wouldn't let him push me away. "Whether you like it or not, Marine, you need me. Now get your ass out of that chair and let me give you a ride home. I think you've had enough."

He slugged the rest of the beer and slammed the bottle down, "In case you haven't heard, I'm no longer a Marine. But, you're right. I have had enough! Enough of you trying to run my life." He ran his hands through his hair, his jaw tightening. "Let me make this clear. I don't want you in my life right now." His voice escalated and the bartender gave us both a dirty look. The two guys that were seated a couple of stools down busted out laughing at some comment one of them had made and then had the stupidity to repeat it out loud.

"If he won't go with you, sweetheart, you can take me." The comment came from the skinny guy with bad skin and greasy hair.

His buddy who was no less of a derelict, and no more appealing, piped in, "You can have us both. Two of us has gotta be better than a one legged ex-Marine." He belched and laughed again at his own hilarity.

My blood surged and my mouth took over. "I'd rather a one legged Marine than a two headed ass," I sniped. My nerves crackled with the anger that rose from somewhere deep inside me. I stood and faced the two jerks, my fingers flexing instinctively. "How dare you insult a man who has fought for your right to be a jack-ass. Fought to keep you safe in your own country so you don't have to live in fear every day that someone is going to drop a bomb in your back yard..." I was just heating up when Alex grabbed my arm.

"It's not worth it, Jordie. These guys are idiots." A smug smirk crossed his face and I immediately had a bad feeling. He added, "Ugly-ass idiots too."

Both men stood and I felt the energy in the room shift. Beyond the ball game, conversation came to a halt. Tension hummed in the air as Alex stepped in front of me and faced off with the two men. He stood taller than both of them, but they were either too drunk or too stupid to stand down. Before I had the chance to enjoy seeing Alex mop the floor with them, a third guy rounded the corner from the men's room. He stood six foot-four and had to weigh at least two hundred and sixty pounds. He sidled up to the two men who were smirking like they had just pulled out a grenade launcher.

"Is there a problem here?" he asked, stepping in front of the other two men.

"Great, the three stooges." Alex apparently couldn't resist poking the porcupine, a move I would have expected from Levi—not the mild mannered Alex Cooper I had grown up with.

Considering the odds, I suddenly missed my big brother more than ever.

At this point the bartender was reaching for the phone and I knew things were about to get uglier. My heart hammered in my chest and I willed Alex to back down. I grabbed his arm and stepped up beside him, trying to capture his gaze, which was piercing darts into the big man's face.

"Let's just leave, okay, Coop?"

The skinny guy laughed and mimicked me, *"Let's go Coop, okay?"* He snickered and bumped elbows with the other guy, pointing at Alex. "Is she your mama, or just your whore?"

I felt Alex go rigid. Crap. Before I could say another word, he shot a punch out at the big guy, no doubt realizing to get to the skinny one, he had to go through the brick wall first. The brick wall staggered backward but recovered quickly. His eyes grew wide and then narrowed to slits. He came at Alex with both hands. Alex side-stepped awkwardly but managed to shoot his new foot out, evade the man's grasp and send the guy flying past him. The barstools scattered like bowling pins. Alex had his back turned waiting for the man to get up when the skinny kid jumped him.

The chaos that ensued happened so fast, I didn't have time to think before I reacted. When I saw the third guy make a move to gang up on Alex, I let a round house kick fly and nailed the guy in the gut. He doubled over and I dropped an elbow hard on his upper back, a precise blow I knew should send a paralyzing jolt down his spine. He crumbled to the floor.

I turned to see Alex struggling to keep his balance with the skinny guy hanging on his back. The big man climbed to his feet and charged, swinging a meaty fist at Alex's head. Alex ducked and the fist collided with the skinny guy's face, sending him reeling backward. I stuck out my foot and watched him sail through the air, landing on his back with a thud and a loud grunt.

Alex took on the big guy, blocking several blows and taking a hard shot to the jaw before he struck back. His hands moved lightning fast and within a few skillfully executed moves, he dropped the guy on the floor so hard the glasses behind the bar rattled. A wave of relief swept through me. I'd had my doubts for a brief moment. Alex shot me a huge grin, sending my heart into overdrive. I resisted the urge to jump up and down clapping, but I had the desire to kiss him in the worst way.

Before we had a chance to gloat, sirens blared in the distance, and grew louder by the second.

Chapter 13

"You kids better get out of here. I don't want the cops finding anyone in here without legit ID." The bartender stood behind the bar, a baseball bat in hand, looking prepared in case the brawl threatened to escalate further.

I grabbed Alex's arm and pulled him towards the door. The tension in the bar had fizzled, the other patrons returning to their drinks, the three guys on the floor groaning and beginning to stir. "Let's go!"

Alex followed me out and I dragged him to the Rabbit. He resisted. "I have to get Mom's car."

I pulled harder. "No you don't. You are coming with me." The sirens wailed close by. "We don't have time to argue. Get in!" The last thing he needed was to get arrested, and calling my mother to pick me up at the police station would not be the highlight of my day.

Alex grumbled and climbed in the passenger side. I tore out of the parking lot and headed in the opposite direction of the sirens, leaving a cloud of dust in my wake. My heart pounded and sweat beaded on my forehead. Every nerve in my body was strung tight with the adrenaline rush that coursed through my veins. I had been sparring and practicing for nearly five years, but I'd never been in a real fight.

"That was…awesome! I can't believe we did it."

Alex laughed. "Your first bar-fight, huh?" I glanced over at him, grinning. He smiled and then pulled it back, rubbing his jaw, and wiggling a tooth with his tongue. "The big guy had a mean hook."

"You were amazing. He must have outweighed you by fifty pounds and you clobbered him."

"You weren't so bad yourself. Remind me never to make you mad."

I laughed, the adrenalin finally wearing down and my heart rate settling. "Where should we go? I don't want to take you back home yet. You don't want your mom to see you like this, do you?"

"No, I guess not." He looked out the window, a somber expression taking over his face.

"Don't worry; I'll take you back to get her car later--after you've had a chance to sober up." He didn't respond and the car grew silent. The rumbling sound of the little diesel engine and the hum of the tires rolling on pavement filled the space between us.

"I suppose I need to say thank you…again," he said. "Why is it every time I turn around, you're there saving me from myself?" Sarcasm couldn't cover the sincerity behind his words—or the frustration.

"That's what friends are for, right?" I kept my eyes on the road, my face heating up. I really wished I had AC in my car. I rolled the window down letting in a rush of warm air.

"After what I said to you, I didn't think I'd see you for a while."

"You can't get rid of me that easy." I smiled over at him, trying to lighten the mood.

"I appreciate all you've done for me, Jordie. But…I don't deserve your friendship. How can you even look at me, knowing that I'm the one who caused Lee's death?" His voice was soft and low as he stared out the window, cow pastures and rolling hills speeding past as we headed out of town.

"Let's get a few things straight, Coop. Even if…and I mean *if* you made a mistake or an error in judgment or something…and I still don't think you did…Lee was killed by an Iraqi bullet. He was fighting in a war, and that means every minute of every day, he was taking his life in his hands. We knew this could happen when he went over there. I know…"

He cut me off. "It should have been me," he said softly, his throat tight, his voice cracking.

"You're wrong. Lee would have wanted you to be the one to live." My own voice shook with the effort to hold back tears.

"I keep trying to remember why we went in the house. If I was team leader and I got the word to stand down…if I knew it wasn't safe…I wouldn't have…" he shook his head, his hands covering his face to hide his tears.

I laid a hand on his shoulder. "I know, Coop."

He pulled away and leaned his head on the window, his shoulders shaking as he cried. Tears streamed down my own cheeks and I brushed them away, not willing to give in to my own grief while his seemed so raw. He needed me to be strong. A few minutes later, I pulled into a dirt parking lot and turned off the car. We sat quietly for a long time, both of us unable to find any more words, his tears finally drying up.

"Let's take a walk," I said. I felt like we both needed to be close to Levi. I hadn't known I was even headed here, but now I knew we had landed right where we needed to be. This had been one of his favorite spots. A wooden sign at the edge of a trail read, Wolf Den Falls, one of his favorite places.

Alex looked up and a sad smile curved his lips. "We used to come here all the time. I haven't been here since…" he swallowed the rest of the sentence. "Let's do it," he said, clearing his throat.

We hiked down the trail in silence, the sense that we weren't alone buzzing in the air between us.

I could hear Levi's laugh, his dark sense of humor a source of constant strain between us. He used to say I was the angel and he was the devil in our family. He believed I was the one who kept the balance between good and evil, and I had the strength to keep the scales tipped in the right direction or it would be the end of civilization as we knew it. A part of me had always felt like the fate of the universe rested on my shoulders, thanks to him. Now I knew it was true—maybe not the universe, but something very important hung in the balance and the weight of it rested on me. I didn't want to let my brother down.

Dappled sunlight spread through the trees as we made our way up and down the rolling trail. I felt Alex watching my back and listened for signs that he was having difficulty with the terrain. Even with his prosthetic limb and a few too many beers, he kept pace with me. We walked about a half mile when the sound of rushing water reached my ears. A few minutes later the tree line broke and we stood below the falls, the forty foot cascade tumbling over rocks and ledge on its way to the deep pool below. The sun sparkled on the water and created a rainbow effect through the fine mist before us.

"Wow. I forgot how beautiful this place was." Alex settled himself down on a boulder and I sat beside him. I took in the view and enjoyed the cool air rising off the water as it rushed past us over mossy rocks.

"I don't think we ever appreciated real beauty when we were younger. It was all about the fun and seeing what we could get away with." I smiled, remembering scaling the cliff up to the falls, Levi taunting me the whole time. He was the first to jump and then Alex would follow, leaving me standing at the top with my heart in my throat, terrified and exhilarated at the very idea of dropping into unknown depths. Levi would call up from below, *'Just jump!'*

Some part of me knew I could trust them—if not Levi, then Alex. So I jumped, my arms and legs flailing to keep me upright. I copied them and crossed my arms at my chest and kept my feet together so I would hit the water in a streamlined position and then push off from the twelve foot deep bottom and torpedo to the top, gasping for breath—amazed I was still alive. I knew Levi and Alex wouldn't have let anything bad happen to me. My heart ached for missing my brother and I felt my eyes watering again. As if he'd read my mind, Alex wrapped his arm around my shoulder and pulled me closer.

I rested my head on his chest and let the tears fall. "What are we going to do without him?"

"I ask myself the same question every day," he whispered.

After a minute, I sat up straight, remembering why I had gone looking for Alex in the first place. "I have an idea." I wiped my cheeks with the backs of my hands and sniffled.

Alex looked serious. "This is going to be bad, isn't it?"

I ignored his teasing. "If we could get a hold of the military's investigative file, it might help you to remember or give you a clue as to what really happened that night."

"I tried. They said it was classified." He pulled back, his gaze studying the falls.

"There has to be a way you can get a look at the file."

He eyed me dubiously. "What do you suggest I do, hack into the Pentagon?"

"Wasn't it you who hacked into the high school computer and changed Lee's grades from failing to passing so he could pass junior year?"

"Right. And I got caught--and expelled, I might add." He climbed to his feet, pulling himself up by the limb of a small tree growing out of the rocks. "Besides, the pentagon is a little more complicated than high school."

I waved off a bee. "But you are so much better at it now with all of your military training. Wasn't it your specialty or something? You can do this. C'mon, what have you got to lose?"

"Um…my freedom." He frowned and raised a brow. "This is the Pentagon we're talking about. I could go to prison."

My idea suddenly sounded stupid. What was I thinking? I sighed and climbed to my feet beside him. "You're right. It would be crazy to try something so stupid. Besides, you probably couldn't do it, anyway."

"I didn't say I couldn't do it. I just said it would be taking a huge risk."

We both looked up at the falls and then down at the deep pool of water beneath. I heard the mischief in his voice, "Are you thinking what I'm thinking?"

Chapter 14

"You cannot be a part of this, Jordie," Alex argued as he closed the door to his room. We had been arguing for the better part of an hour, standing on the porch until the mosquitoes found us and we were driven inside.

"I'm already in this whether you like it or not. Besides, it was my idea." I plunked down on his bed, crossed my legs and folded my arms, ready for whatever came next. I could do this all night.

"It doesn't matter. These are classified files. Do you understand what that means? If I get caught..."

"If *we* get caught."

"Fine," he sniped, "if *we* get caught, we could both go to Federal Prison."

"Brig would never let that happen." I was probably being naïve, but I was not letting Alex shut me out again.

"That's not the point...look..." he huffed out a breath, exasperated. I was clearly wearing him down. "If I get caught..."

"*We.*"

He rolled his eyes. "*You* need to be as far away as possible. The law calls it plausible deniability. If you are questioned, you can honestly

say you had nothing to do with it." Alex sat down at
his computer.

"I would already be lying. I'm staying. Now
stop wasting time." I got up and stood over his
shoulder. The computer screen kicked to life.

"Man, you are as stubborn and thick headed
as a…"

"As every other Dunn you've ever met?" I
smiled down at him, reveling in the smidgeon of a
grin that crossed his lips.

"At least sit across the room with your back
to me while I'm subverting national security." He
glared at me and pecked away at the keyboard. He
stopped, green eyes glancing up at me sternly. "Go.
Sit. And be quiet."

Instead, I wandered around the room picking
things up and putting them down. The ugly green
ceramic box he'd made in eighth grade, the old
brown insulator we found along the train tracks,
now filled with screws, washers and loose change.
A hundred memories of our years growing up
together—all of them connected to Levi. I picked
up a picture of Alex and his dad on a fishing trip
when Alex was about eight. I recognized the Four
County Fair tee shirt he wore from that year,
thinking back to my first summer on Thompson
Lake when we'd first met, him picking me up off
the ground after I'd fallen off my bike—my first
excursion without training wheels.

"Have you ever heard from him?" I asked, examining the picture, trying to remember a time when I hadn't seen the hurt and haunted look behind his young eyes. I'm sure it didn't help that he had grown to look very much like his father.

Alex peered over his shoulder. "No. Why don't you leave my stuff alone and chill?" His annoyance should have been expected. He hadn't heard from his dad since the day the guy walked out when Alex was twelve. He didn't like to talk about it, but I knew it still bothered him that his father lived out there somewhere but never cared enough to make a phone call. My stomach turned at the hurt his father's neglect must have caused Alex over the years. How could a father abandon his only child? My heart ached for him, knowing how the absence of my own father left a gaping empty space behind.

"How's it coming?" I asked, setting the picture down and running a finger along the titles in his bookshelf. There was a row of sci-fi paper backs, gothic novels, and manga, along with a tall stack of collectible old Marvel comics Brig would have killed to get his hands on.

"This is going to take some time. Why don't you run down to the kitchen and fix us some sandwiches or something?" We'd made it past his mother who was steamed about him disappearing with the car, but looked immensely relieved when we came in. Until Alex announced we were going to his room, at which her mouth dropped open and nothing came out. I didn't really want to face her again.

"I'm not going anywhere," I said stubbornly. "I'll be quiet, I promise." I proceeded to pace and fidget for another twenty minutes before cracking. "Tell me what you're doing." I leaned over his shoulder, our heads side by side looking at the screen.

He let out a deflated sigh, his fingers dancing over the keyboard. "You are such a pain."

"I consider that my best quality, thank you." We glanced at each other, smiling, a moment passing between us, warm and comfortable like fuzzy slippers and hot chocolate.

"I've made it through the firewall. I had to re-rout my connection through several bogus servers so they won't be able to identify my IP address. But I won't have long once I'm in. It'll take me a couple of minutes to run my decryption software, but I should be able to download the file to the flash drive before they catch on." The screen blinked, new pages popping up one after another as he tapped the keys furiously.

"May I ask where you got a hold of decryption software?"

"I could tell you, but then I'd have to…well, you know." His lips curved into a small smile.

"Seriously, Coop? I think we're past the 'I'd have to kill you' stage. I already know way too much. Spill."

"I helped write it," he said absently. "As long as the government hasn't changed it in the last six months...hey, I'm in!"

I leaned over to read the pages that zipped past, lists of files flashing and winking, all marked CLASSIFIED.

"I've got it. I found the file. Be quiet and let me concentrate." Taptaptaptaptap. The whir of files downloading and then Alex hammering away again until the screen went blank and he pushed away from the desk in triumph. "The boys at Langley will be scratching their heads after that ride." His grin widened as he pulled the flash drive and stuck it in his pocket.

"What! You're not going to let me see it?" I popped up straight, arms crossed and ready to pester him until I got my way.

He stood and faced me, a good four inches taller than my 5'10" and looking down at me with a smirk and a stubborn set to his bruised jaw. The green in his eyes sparkled and I felt myself caving already. As soon as he put his hands on my shoulders I knew I was doomed. "I need you to go home and give me a day. Just a day," he added before I could cut him off with an argument. "I need to do this alone. Let me look over the file and see if it clears up any questions. I promise I'll call you tomorrow and tell you what I find."

The unexpected power of his proximity and strength of his hands on my arms made me weak kneed and unable to stand my ground. And if I wasn't dissuaded already, I all but swooned when he leaned in and laid a gentle kiss on my forehead. He was fighting dirty and I didn't care. I soaked in the sensation of his soft lips and the tingle that shimmied all the way to my toes. When he looked down into my eyes, the expression on his face rendered me speechless. All those sharp angles disappeared in a softness that reminded me of warm summer days when he was just a boy, of climbing trees, swimming in the lake and racing to the dock. I could drown in those eyes and never come up for air.

My heart fluttered and my cheeks grew warm, the silence between us filled with a hundred memories and one long moment that could change us both forever. I studied the curve of his lips, imagining how they would taste and feel against mine, willing him to kiss me. I laid my hands tentatively on his chest, struck by the firmness under my fingertips. His heart hammered and mine skipped a beat faster to match his. *Breathe*, I reminded myself.

He was inches away, his voice barely above a whisper. "No matter what I find in that file, I want you to know...you have given me...well... you helped me find *me* again, and I'll never forget it."

Tears stung behind my eyes and I blinked them back. The intensity built to a thunderous wave crashing in my head, his words touching me deeply. I had to tell him how much he meant to me. I knew it was a terrible risk (a flash coming to mind of the last time I had said the words), but he had to know. "Coop...you know I..."

Before I could say it, he kissed me. Those lips I'd been imagining were suddenly pressed against mine, moist and warm and soft. A groan escaped as my whole body surrendered to the moment, reveled in the contact between us, wanting more than I knew I should. I kissed him back, pressing my body against him and wrapping my arms around his neck to pull him closer. His hands went to the small of my back to hold me there as if I might pull away—an unlikely possibility from where I stood. I had dreamed of this moment since I was old enough to know Alex was the only boy I wanted to kiss. Now I was in his arms, wrapped in the strength, tenderness, and passion I'd always known was Alex.

A knock on the door interrupted the moment. Alex pulled away and I let go, gasping for breath. My fingers went to my mouth as if to hold onto the lingering sensation of his lips on mine.

Mrs. Cooper spoke through the door. "Do you two want to come down for supper? You're welcome to stay, Jordan." Did parents have some kind of radar that told them when to interrupt at exactly the worst time?

"We'll be right down," Alex answered, his face flushed. He eyed me cautiously for a moment. "I'm sorry about that."

I wasn't sure if he meant the kiss or the interruption, but either way, the spell was broken and I needed to put some distance between us. The humming in my body needed release and I didn't think staring across a dinner table at Alex was going to help. What I needed was a good long run. I took a deep breath which cleared my head enough to find my voice. "Call me tomorrow?"

"You can count on it." Alex quirked a little smile at me and my heart melted. I followed him to the door. He faced me, his hand on the doorknob. "Whatever happens next, I promise I'll do the right thing. No more screw ups." Eyes the color of sea glass, stared down at me with a look so serious, a shiver ran down my arms.

"It wasn't you, Alex." My voice sounded so sure. "It was never about you."

I knew it had to be Levi. As much as it hurt to think my brother was so desperate that he would risk his best friend's life to do something stupid, I knew both of these guys better than anyone. Alex and Levi had occupied most of my life and I had no regrets. In my heart, I knew Levi had lived his life on borrowed time. It hadn't come as a shock when we'd gotten the call about his death. Somewhere inside, I'd half expected it. What I hadn't expected was the impact. Mom still slept at weird times and wandered the house at night, crying. Brig acted like his same old solid self, but I caught the sad, faraway look in his eyes when he thought no one noticed. Me—I sat up late at night re-reading every letter, e-mail and postcard he'd sent, trying to find the answer to the stupid, unanswerable question of '*why*'.

But worse than all of that was the look in Alex's eyes--the haunted emptiness that took over his face every time he thought about Levi. Crushing guilt screamed behind his blank expression. I could always tell, and I saw his guilt now. I reached up and touched his cheek, "Whatever you find, it is not going to change how I feel." I looked at him hard so he'd know I meant it.

He pressed my palm against his cheek and closed his eyes, drawing a deep breath as if committing the sensation, or maybe my words, to memory. When he opened his eyes, he kissed my palm, sending a quiver to my belly. "We'll talk tomorrow."

The quiver dissipated as soon as he let go of my hand—replaced by a hollow sensation in the pit of my stomach. The absence of his touch hit me immediately and I had a terrible feeling about what was to come.

Chapter 15

Mom gave me an earful when I got home. *"...irresponsible of you to leave Brig to work alone for the afternoon, no phone call, didn't know where you were..."* blah, blah, blah. I heard about half of her rant, my mind still whirling about the days' events. If she only knew--I'd been in a bar room brawl, come close to jumping off a cliff with Alex (our better judgment had prevailed on that one), and committed a Federal Offense all in the span of a few hours. But none of it compared to the excitement that had every cell of my body buzzing over our kiss.

I lay on my bed staring at the ceiling. I replayed the moment over and over, hearing Alex's apology, *"Sorry about that."* Was he sorry he kissed me? Sorry we were interrupted? My stomach twisted, uncertainty making my nerves twitch, as I tapped my fingers on the mattress.

I sat up. I paced my tiny room. Pink walls and flowery purple curtains--a decorating choice I'd made when I was fourteen and now hated--closed in on me. I could have done something about it, but I had planned on leaving for college next year and it didn't seem worth the effort. Taking over Levi's room was out of the question, although the room had more space and a better view of the lake. Another twinge of sadness gripped my heart. Why did life have to change so fast—so completely? What was the use in planning on anything?

Up until a couple of months ago, I thought my life was planned out. Moving far away from Thompson Lake had seemed like a good idea. I wanted to get away from my mother's depression, her self-absorbed silence, and the inevitable drudgery of taking over the antique shop when Brig decided to throw in the towel and really retire. Not that I didn't love the shop, but I had bigger plans. I had hopes of being accepted for early admission to the pre-med program at either Harvard in Boston or Stanford in California. I had also applied to John's Hopkins and Columbia. My grades and a track scholarship should get me several scholarships to the college of my choice. Being at school far from home had been very appealing when I thought Alex didn't want me. But after today, all of my plans left me feeling lost.

I pulled out the box from under the bed. A shoe box from the Merrill hikers I'd bought a year ago. I lifted the lid and sifted through the letters, reaching for the one I wanted to read again. Unfolding the wrinkled and well-worn page had become a secret addiction. I couldn't go to sleep without reading it every night. I pressed the paper flat on the bed and smoothed it out.

Hey Sis,

I would love to tell you everything is great, but I know I can tell you the truth. It's hot and dry and sandy. Wearing a flack -jacket and full gear in this heat sucks big time. My equipment belt weighs a ton and my rifle is part of me at all times when I'm out in the field. I don't know why I keep volunteering for maneuvers, but it beats sitting around waiting for something to happen.

Life here is full of fear. The people are afraid. I can see it in their faces. Worse, I know I am just as afraid as they are. Anyone could be the enemy, so you have to always be on guard.

I'm tired all the time. I miss home every day. I miss you. You understand me better than anyone. Accept maybe for Coop. I know he misses you too. He won't tell me why he hasn't answered any of your letters. But I think he's afraid too. We don't talk about it here, but we're all afraid for our lives. I think Brig understood, and that's why he kept Coop and me together I used to think I wasn't afraid to die, but it's not true anymore. I think about it every day. Dying that is. I can't get it out of my head. It isn't like it used to be. Now it's more like I am surrounded by death and I'm trying to conquer it somehow. I hope that makes sense and doesn't make you worry. I'm really holding up all right.

Coop's staying tough, too. No matter what, we have each other's back.

That brings me to what I really wanted to tell you. I've told Coop that it's OK with me if he loves you. I've known for a long time that you might end up together and I've come to the conclusion that life is short and you shouldn't waste time with regrets. I want you both to be happy. I don't want you to worry about me. I'll be okay no matter what happens. You have enough on your shoulders with Mom and Brig. Tell them I love them. I'll send Brig an e-mail. Remind him to check. I know he doesn't open his e-mail very often. LOL. I love you little sister, and I'm sorry I'm not there with you. So is Coop.

> *Love,*
> *Lee*

I shook my head through my tears, more confused than ever. I lay down and fell asleep, the letter curled in my hand.

Chapter 16

The next morning I went to church—
willingly. Resistance seemed pointless, so I sang the
hymns, half-heartedly recited the profession of
faith, and asked for forgiveness for my sins. I
wondered if impatience was a sin as I went up to
receive communion. I tried not to think about Levi.
Instead I focused on Alex, who had taken over
pretty much every thought in my head since he
kissed me. Even my dreams were filled with flashes
of what came beyond his kiss. I blushed, noticing
the mosaic form of the Virgin Mary etched into the
stained glass window beside me. The light and
warmth of the sun glowed down on me bringing an
unexpected wash of serenity. For the first time in a
long time, I felt glad to be in church, even if I didn't
believe everything they taught.

No one spoke on the way home. Mom drove
the CU-V and Brig stared straight ahead, his eyes
far away. I sat in the back seat, catching up on all
my texts. I had a twinge of guilt that I hadn't seen
my friends much at all over summer break, and here
it was, almost September. Where had the summer
gone?

I had completely engrossed myself in Alex and I didn't feel sorry about it. I could be myself with him, and I know he would always be my friend. The attraction part turned out to be the most amazing surprise. Not that I wanted him, but how *much* I wanted him. A constant dull ache had settled into my lower belly, a slow burn that sparked to flames whenever he was near. His scent, the sound of his voice, the intensity in his eyes—all made me wonder how I could possibly ever feel this way about anyone else. I wanted him to be my first, maybe even my only. The thought brought a rush of warmth to my center, the spot just below my belly button we called our lower dan tien in martial arts, or the second chakra in yoga--the place where all life comes from and our creative energy lies. I definitely wanted to create some energy with Alex. My face went hotter. I started contemplating birth control. Not a topic I wanted to bring up to my mother. Maybe I would talk to Vic. If I could hold off another few months, I'd be eighteen and not have to worry about talking to my mother.

Eighteen, finally. I had waited forever for the happy occasion when I could be on my own, go to college, travel, and see something—anything beyond Thompson Lake. The lake felt sad with Dad gone, grandma, and now Levi. Winters were too long, and summers zipped by like dreams.

The short few months I'd spent with Alex
were filled with a mixture of emotions I would have
to list to name. Sadness was the one emotion we
both shared. We'd lost so much. But mostly, I felt a
deep sense of contentment around me every time he
was near. I wanted this feeling to go on forever. His
smile lit my day—and my body—on fire. Whether
he felt the same was anybody's guess. I needed to
find out before I did something stupid like throwing
myself at him.

We pulled into the driveway and my heart
jumped. The blue BMW sat in the parking lot of the
antique shop. Alex leaned up against it, looking like
a model for the Gap. Nobody should look that good
in a pair of jeans. His hair brushed the collar of a
sage green shirt, which his shoulders filled out
nicely. His arms unfolded and he stood to meet us
as we parked.

"Hey, Coop. What's up?" I asked, hopping
out of the truck, my heart slamming against my ribs.
I realized Alex was facing my mother and Brig for
the first time since the funeral.

"I came to see you." He glanced from me to
my mother. "All of you."

I thought Mom might have a melt down and
go all psycho on him, but her reaction surprised me.
"Of course. Why don't we go inside and I'll make
us a snack."

Alex, Brig and I all stared at her. Brig spoke first. "That's a good idea. Come on in." He wrapped a bulky arm around Alex's shoulder and pulled him toward the house. Alex looked back at me, his eyes filled with some unreadable emotion. My stomach tightened. A bad feeling ran through me.

Once we sat around the kitchen table, my mother had crackers and cheese set out and iced tea poured before Brig had finished the small talk of "How is your mother?" and "Hasn't it been a hot summer?"

Alex cleared his throat and took a slow breath as Mom sat down across from him. His tanned face was a little pale, his eyes wide and empty, and his voice came out in a monotone. "I came to tell you how sorry I am about what happened to Lee. I take full responsibility. I've recently come into some information which leads me to believe I gave the order to move in and Lee followed me. I wish I could tell you why…" he faltered, "but…Lee's death…it was my call."

For a long moment, silence and the ticking of the wall clock filled the air. Blood pounded in my ears. No. Something wasn't right. My mind screamed. If it were true, what now? My whole assumption was wrong? Levi didn't kill himself? No. I would never believe it was Alex's fault.

"No!" the word jumped out of my head and into the air. "That's not true. It can't be."

A brief desperate look peered out behind Alex's eyes, and then he stared straight ahead, unfocused and distant again. "I can't apologize enough for what happened and I hope someday you can all forgive me. But I understand if you prefer that I keep my distance from your family." He stood, squared his shoulders and saluted Brig, who was already on his feet. "Sir, my deepest condolences." He turned and walked out the front door, the screen slamming behind him.

I gaped at the door, paralyzed. I looked to my mother, who sat staring wide-eyed, her eyes glassy from unshed tears and shock. I looked to Brig, who just looked back at me, sympathy and understanding in his eyes. I raced to the door and blasted through the screen.

"Alex Cooper! You stop right there!"

He froze in place, half way to his car. "I'm sorry, Jordie. I know it wasn't what you wanted to hear." He kept his back turned to me.

"What I wanted was the truth. If this…if this is really the truth, then I…just have to accept it…get past it and move on." I swallowed hard, a flash of doubt creeping into my head. "It doesn't matter. I forgive you, Coop." Tears streamed down my cheeks. Desperation welled inside me when he didn't respond. "I can't lose you too. Not like this. Not now." He took another step. My voice dropped to a whisper. "I love you…please…don't go."

He stood absolutely still without even a hint of a breath. I waited. I'd said and done all I could. Now it was up to him. My fingers curled into a ball. Time stood still. Alex didn't turn around. In fact, he strode toward his car. My heart sank, my breath caught in my throat. I would not dignify his actions by sobbing openly. I wouldn't. I held back the tears, swiping at my face with the heels of my hands. My hurt, humiliation, and anger all screeched in my ear demanding I do something. I stood rooted to the ground. Alex pulled open the car door. I couldn't believe he was leaving.

Then he pulled out my Red Sox hat and turned to me. Our eyes met and we started towards each other before my feet knew what they were doing. He stopped just short of me and I wanted to throw my arms around him...or punch him in the nose. I couldn't make up my mind. But then I saw the look in his eyes--his blank, haunted look had returned.

"I found this in the rose garden," he said.

"Yeah, I must have dropped it."

"It had Lee's name. I wondered..."

"Don't you remember when Brig took us all to that game at Fenway? We each got a hat and stuffed our faces with hot dogs and soda." I half smiled, trying to dispel the crackling tension between us.

Alex face softened for an instant. "Yeah, right. Brig made us write our names in them so we wouldn't mix them up. I guess I lost mine." He looked down at the inside of the hat; LEE in faded black ink lined the rim.

I reached out and took the hat, examined the letters and handed it back. "You keep it.

His eyes flashed. "You sure?"

"Yeah."

He nodded. "Thanks."

"Why didn't you write to me?" I asked, my throat tight and dry.

I could see I'd caught him off guard. He opened his mouth and then closed it. Seconds ticked past. Finally he sucked in a breath and exhaled slowly, apparently coming to a definite conclusion. "I thought if anything happened to me over there, it would be easier for you if I didn't…encourage you." His shoulders had straightened again and I saw the Marine appear before me, cool, controlled and maddeningly distant.

"Encourage me? So it would have been better for me to have you die, forever wondering how you really felt about me. Not having one memory to hold onto to let me know if you loved me or…" I couldn't utter the "not." The word caught in my throat. I hadn't meant to say anything about love, but there was the word, hovering in the air between us.

A flash of hurt crossed his face, and then he composed himself and stared past me. "I didn't want to make promises I couldn't keep." His tone shifted and sadness seeped in between the words. "You say you forgive me for what happened to Lee. But I don't know how you can, and I don't know if I can forgive myself." He looked down at me and let the mask fall away. The grief and guilt I saw there squeezed my heart. "Don't you understand? I can't look at you without seeing him. I wake up every night, screaming over something hiding under the surface in my head--something I can't quite reach. I look down at my leg and I relive the moment I woke up without it, and realized I would never again be the same person . I had an AK47 blast my leg off and I don't remember it. I ordered my best friend to walk into an ambush...and I don't remember why." He turned his back on me again, this time to hide the emotion that rode to the surface. "I am no good for you, Jordie. I am way too messed up right now and you have to leave me alone to figure it out." He headed for the car again.

"C'mon Coop. Please talk to me. I can help you." The desperate part of me, the little girl who couldn't take another abandonment, called after him. "Coop, wait!"

He stopped. "Let me go, Jordie."

My throat burned with tears. "Why did you kiss me yesterday?"

After a long silence, he looked over his shoulder, his expression achingly cool, "It was the only way I could think of to keep you from saying something that would make this so much harder for both of us." He turned away again. "I have to go. Please don't follow me. And don't call me."

I stood glued to the spot, shocked, hurt, and angry. A deep sense of loss paralyzed me as I watched him get in the car and drive away. He didn't look back. Numbness overtook my limbs. I wanted to run after him. I wanted to scream and cry at the injustice of life—how unfair he was being. My insides felt like they'd been torn out and left on the ground. I hurt for him, for me, for Levi, for my mother, for Brig. Grief washed over me and I fell to my knees sobbing in the driveway, the dust from his tires settling into a cloud around me.

Chapter 17

I don't know how I made it through the next few days. I felt like I had lost Levi all over again. Maybe my mother was right. Maybe I needed to be close to Alex so I wouldn't have to deal with my grief over the loss of my brother. But I knew there was much more to it. I loved Alex so much; my whole body ached at the thought of not being with him--ever. I felt like I had swallowed broken glass. I went through the motions of my life, realizing on the third day I should eat and shower and come back to the world. I couldn't sulk over Alex forever. I had a life to live—as desolate and pointless as it seemed now.

I ran, avoided Mom and Brig as much as possible, and kept to myself, or hooked up with friends. I tried to stay busy. Work at the antique shop occupied my afternoons and each night I sat quietly through dinner, Mom and Brig eyeing me with concern and watching me pick at my food. The days turned into a week and gradually two, but every day seemed endless and horribly lonely. I'd stopped texting and e-mailing Alex after the first week when I got no response. Maybe he had never

really cared about me. My heart broke apart in
increments, day by day, hour by torturous hour.
Sometimes my stomach churned, burning with
anger, and then I was swamped with an acute
sadness from missing him.

Life continued on and I was dead, I
decided. This is what a ghost must feel like,
wandering through a life that's no longer theirs. I
wondered if Levi was close by, watching me
struggle to just keep breathing every day. Is this
how he felt--desperate to escape the pain of living?
But I suppose if I were dead, I wouldn't hurt like I
did now. I wanted my life to make sense, but
nothing made any sense without Alex.

I excused myself after dinner and dishes and
hid away in my room again. I stuffed my ear buds in
and sprawled on my bed, letting the music take me
away. Tears spilled from my eyes and ran down my
temple as a *Lady Antebellum* song came over my I-
Pod. '*I need you nowww…*' I was in the throes of a
really great cry when I heard pounding on my door.
I rolled over and yanked the ear buds out. "What?"

"Can I come in? I'd like to talk to you."
Mom's voice echoed on the other side of the door.

Crap. "Come in," I grabbed a tissue and
sighed. I really did not want to hear anything she
had to say. She had gotten what she wanted. Alex
was guilty and out of my life. It must have killed
her not to gloat.

166

She opened the door slowly and inched her way in. I realized she hadn't been in my room for a very long time. Months, years maybe? I couldn't remember the last time. The room was a mess. I hadn't had any energy or desire to clean up after myself when I could barely walk in a forward direction. She gazed around the room, taking in the pictures of me sprinting over the finish line at last year's state championships, the medals and trophies, the stuffed animals hanging in a net in the corner. My laundry covered most of the floor, causing a brief crinkle of my mother's nose.

"I need to say something to you." She moved the stack of books and sat in the chair in front of my computer.

"What is it?" I asked, preparing myself for an "*I told you so.*"

"I'm sorry about Alex...about your friendship. I know how much he means to you." She reached out with a shaky hand and touched mine..

Part of me wanted to pull away, but another part—the part that craved some connection, some bridge back to my mother, kept still. I glimpsed the mother she had been when my father was alive. I realized I had lost them both the day my father died. I held her hand, wondering why she had suddenly changed her mind. "Are you sure?" I asked. "I know you wanted us apart."

"I thought I did." She glanced down, her eyes brimming with tears. "I thought if I knew for sure Alex was responsible, I could find peace in Levi's death...but that didn't happen. I feel terrible for Alex--and for you." She let out a sigh and pulled away from me.

"I don't understand." I kept my own tears in check, not quite trusting this unfamiliar version of my mother. Maybe her counseling was finally helping her.

She kept her gaze focused on my feet and caught some tears on her knuckles. "You loved and accepted your brother for exactly who he was, something I could never do. He changed from a sweet little boy into a young man I had no control over. He refused help. I couldn't undo the damage that was done." She broke into full tears and sobbed openly, her hands covering her mouth. "It was my fault."

I grabbed the box of tissues and handed one to her. She took it gratefully.

"You blame yourself?" I tried to make it a question and not an accusation.

"Do you remember when we lived with Auntie Theresa?" she sniffled, blowing her nose hard into the tissue.

"I remember a little. I was pretty young," I said. I had the feeling I was about to learn a new piece of the puzzle that was my brother.

My mother swallowed and gulped in a breath, and then let it escape with a shudder. "I caught Uncle Ted touching Levi...inappropriately." She put her hands over her face, breaking down again. "I confronted him...he denied it. He threatened me...he threatened to have you taken away from me...he was a police officer. I didn't know what to do. I called Brig and he came to get us." She sobbed and wiped her eyes with a handful of tissues. "Theresa divorced him and Ted disappeared."

I stared blankly for a long time, both stunned and saddened about how Levi must have felt, what he had been through. "Do you know if he..." I couldn't say the words. I couldn't even let myself think the thought. But I already knew the answer. "Did it happen more than once?" I asked, my throat so tight I could barely breathe.

"Yes," she whispered, her shoulders shaking as she sobbed.

I couldn't cry. Tears seemed beyond me, like I'd known this ugly truth all along and had buried it deep inside with all of the emotion and confusion that went with it. All that was left was to fill in the blanks so I could see the whole picture. "Did he...what about me?" Bile rose in my throat. I was so young, what if I didn't remember...

"No." My mother's hand tightened around mine, an urgency in her voice that gave me a moment of relief. "No, it was only Lee." Her face flushed with anger and disgust. "He only wanted boys, from what I understand." She couldn't meet my eyes and I watched her struggle to gain control.

I needed to understand how this could happen. "Didn't you try to get Lee into counseling? Didn't you talk to him about it?"

"I just wanted to put it behind us. I wanted him to forget. I thought he would get over it...I couldn't deal with it...after your father died...I just couldn't face what a failure I had been. When I finally tried to get him help, it was too late. He refused to go, and I couldn't force him. You know how he was." She broke into another round of tears and sobbed uncontrollably, uttering whispered regrets. "I should have protected him...he was my little boy..."

The look on her face as she moaned the words ate a hole through the hardened shell around my heart. Tears found their way to the surface and spilled silently down my cheeks. My mother shook and rocked back and forth, holding her arms across her chest as if hugging an invisible child against her. "I'm sorry...so sorry..."

I let the tears fall, a crushing sadness moving through me like a boulder rolling down hill, gaining speed and momentum and heading straight for my very foundation. Everything shifted when the truth hit me. I let out a sob and my mother fell into my arms, sitting next to me on my bed and holding me as we both cried and cried. The rush of emotion lasted so long; I thought we might both collapse from exhaustion. Eventually we let go of one another.

My mother looked at me hard, taking my chin in her hands to force eye contact. She looked tired, worn out by carrying this secret for so long. But something in her eyes seemed different—a resignation maybe—like telling me was the last piece of some puzzle that promised to put her back together. There was a new strength in her voice. "I know Alex would never have done anything to intentionally harm Levi. I know how devastated he is. I'm so sorry I didn't understand sooner." Mom wiped the tears on my face with a fresh tissue and tossed the handful into my over-flowing trash bucket. They landed in the corner. She looked around the room again. "We really need to redecorate this room."

I smiled weakly and hugged her. "I'll be leaving for school next year. I don't see the point."

"Don't remind me. It's going to be hard to have you gone." A sad expression flashed across her face. She shook it off, swiping at another tear. "I love you, Jordan. I only want what's best for you."

"I wish I knew what was best. I used to think medical school was what I wanted. I thought I would specialize in psychiatry. I guess I thought I

would understand Lee better." My limbs felt so
heavy. "I'm not sure. I don't know what I'll do.
Besides, I don't even know if I'll get into the
schools I applied to. It all seems so unimportant
now." I sighed, surprisingly warmed when my
mother rubbed circles on my back.

"You'll figure this out. You still have your
senior year ahead of you to think about it. School
starts next week. Why don't you and I take a little
trip? We haven't been anywhere in ages." Her face
grew somber. "If we don't do it now…I'm afraid
I'll have missed my chance to make things right
between us." She took a long, tired breath, her
regret palpable. "Besides, I think a change of
scenery will be good for both of us."

The thought of spending time alone with my
mother for several days made my stomach spasm. I
hadn't had time to make sense of all she'd said. She
had known my brother had been molested. She had
run away from it. My brother buried the pain and
she let him live with it all alone. It hurt that he'd
never told me, but I understood. He couldn't have
told anyone if his own mother wouldn't
acknowledge the truth. Now that she confessed her
sins to me, I'm just supposed to forgive and forget?
She was willing to let Alex pay for Levi's death.
Her offenses loomed before me, and a fresh seed of
resentment took hold. "Only if you do something

for me," I said, my voice going colder than I'd intended.

"Why do I think I'm not going to like this?" Her brow furrowed.

A smirk of satisfaction crossed my lips before I could stop it. I'd heard those words before and it usually meant I had the upper hand. "I want you to talk to Alex. Explain what you just explained to me and apologize to him. And apologize and make up with Mrs. Cooper. Then I'll go on vacation with you."

"That is blackmail, Young Lady," she said sternly.

"Maybe, but those are my terms. If you want a one on one girl's week—maybe our last chance *ever*—you'll do it." I resisted the urge to fold my arms, knowing it would not help my case, and might, in fact, cause her to dig in her heels.

"You are way too much like your grandfather."

"Not an insult, Mom. So, is it yes, or no?"

Chapter 18

Of all places we could go for a
vacation, Mom wanted to take me camping and to
the beach. "We could both use the fresh air," she'd
said. She promised me she had been to see both
Mrs. Cooper and Alex and had delivered on my
demands, calling me "an emotional terrorist" as we
packed up the truck. Knowing that she had forgiven
Alex and told him about Levi's past somehow made
my angst a little lighter. It had to have made a
difference for him to know the truth and know that
Mom wasn't going to hold a grudge. I'd insisted
Brig go and check on Alex to make sure he was
okay and that he knew Brig didn't hold him
responsible either. Brig hadn't come back this
morning and I hated to leave not knowing how
things went. I packed my sleeping bag, pillow, and
Levi's old duffle bag. It said 'DUNN' in large block
letters across one side, the USMC eagle and anchor
emblem on the other. Mom eyed me crossly when
she saw me stuff it into the back.

"Why didn't you use the luggage I gave you
last Christmas?" She loaded the cooler into the back
seat. I could see this trip wasn't going to be a time
of reminiscing about my brother. Mom cringed as
she placed her bag on top of the army green duffle. I

guess she had a right to try not to think about Levi.
Everything seemed to be a reminder. I hoped this
weekend wouldn't be too hard on either of us.

We hadn't been camping together in years.
Brig brought us several times the first few years
we'd come here, but once I hit my teens, I'd resisted
camping like the plague. Bugs, dirt, and sleeping on
rocks--not my idea of a good time.

"I'm saving it for school next year. I didn't
want to ruin it by bringing it camping," I snapped.
The thought of leaving home had kept me going at
one time, now the idea terrified me. I couldn't
imagine moving away from Alex, not seeing him
again. My stomach felt sick when I thought of the
expression on his face when I'd seen him last. He
had seemed so beaten, so far gone. *He'll be all
right*, I reminded myself. *He just needs some time.* I
chucked my pillow on top and climbed in,
wondering if I could wait for him if it took months
or even years for that time to be up. Whether I went
away to school or not, I needed to let him go. I
forced the thought to the back of my mind.

Mom wanted to drive, which gave me a
chance to text Penny and ask how her mom was.
Last I had heard, she was nearing the end of a long
battle with cancer. Penny must be freaking out. I'd
call her when I got back. I looked over at my own
mom, struck by a sharp pang of gratitude that she
was still here and still healthy—other than some

scary bouts of clinical depression. Not lost on me was the possibility I might have one more chance to get to know her without the heaviness that clung to her like a demon. Maybe unburdening her conscience had helped her in some small way because she seemed more centered and grounded the last few days. It was the last long weekend of the summer and I would spend it trying to relax on the beach and attempting to find something to talk about with my mother.

Before I knew it, we were on Route 2, heading for the Rhode Island Beaches. We would set up our three man dome tent at a nearby campground that had a lake with trails and clean bathrooms from what I remembered. Mom and I talked intermittently on the two hour drive. She asked me mundane questions about my friends, what classes I would take this year, and which college I preferred, Columbia or Harvard. She picked the two closest schools to home—shocker. I answered with what I knew she wanted to hear and wished I could have gotten out of this torture before it even started. It would be a long four days, but it was worth it to know she had forgiven Alex and moved from hating him to speaking of him with sympathy.

"I know you miss him, Jordan, but try not to sulk. There's nothing you can do except be patient and let him work this all out on his own. He has a lot of healing to do. We all do," she added as if I didn't know already. "He'll come around. Maybe by the time you're through with college, he'll be in a better place and you two can reconnect."

Did she really think she was helping me? "I *don't* want to talk about Alex." I stuffed my ear buds in and disappeared into my music, *Pink's* latest tunes bumping in my head until we pulled into the campsite.

Setting up was a disaster. Neither of us had put up the tent in three years. It smelled musty and we fought over which poles went where. We argued over where to put the tent, whether to put the tarp under or string it up over the picnic table in case of rain (my idea), tying it into the trees, or staking it to the ground (her idea). What should have taken an hour ended up taking three, and by the time all was said and done, I was sweaty, tired and starving and the mosquitoes were ferocious. What had I gotten myself into? I smacked another bug and scratched my shoulder blade.

"I think we should go out to dinner. It's too hot out to start a fire and I can't find the propane tank for the gas grill." Mom picked through the kitchen box, pulling out matches, candles, and bug spray and putting them back in, letting out a frustrated sigh.

"We came a hundred and thirty miles to go out to dinner?" I grabbed the bug spray and applied

it generously to my legs and arms, giving one last
blast to my head and holding my breath. So much
for enjoying the fresh air. I clenched my teeth and
wiped the sweat from my brow with my tee shirt. I
was clearly in no shape to be seen in public. "I'll
stay here and make a peanut butter sandwich. I need
to eat now." I dug through the bags and slapped a
sandwich together while Mom stared at me, her
eyes showing the strain of trying to keep it together
and sound positive.

"I guess I'll be back in a while then," she
said. "Do you want me to pick you up anything?"

She grabbed the keys and I grumbled a "Not
unless you can fit a five star hotel into the C-UV,"
as she climbed into the truck. She glared at me,
backing out of our site and onto the dirt road
leading out of the campground. I watched her go
and breathed a sigh of relief, muttering about how
long the next four days would feel. I wolfed down
the rest of my sandwich, inhaled a carton of
chocolate milk, and changed into my bathing suit. I
needed to cool off and it was still light enough that
a swim in the lake made more sense than fighting
the returning beach crowd for the showers. The
camp ground appeared to be sparsely inhabited at
the moment, but I expected campers to be pulling in
next to us any time now. Then I'd have to put up
with noisy little kids or middle aged honeymooners

grunting and groaning all night long. The thought
made me irritable on several levels.

I took in the empty sites all around me. It
was only Thursday. People wouldn't be arriving
until tomorrow. Good. I didn't want to see anyone
anyway. People sucked.

Then I noticed the quiet. Nothing but birds
tweeting—first one—then another far off, replying
in the same sing-song tone. Then only one bird
called. No reply. He sounded so singular and sad
and lonely. I brushed off the thought of Alex and
pulled my hair back into a ponytail, tightening it
against my head hard enough to give myself a little
snap of pain—*smarten up idiot. It's over with Alex.
Get on with it already!*

The lake was a fifteen minute walk down the
main road, but I checked the camp map and saw a
short cut through the woods to a smaller pond.
Maybe if I played my cards right, I could avoid
talking to anyone at all for the rest of the week. I
wasn't afraid to be alone, and I was in no mood to
be polite. I slipped shorts up over my bottoms, tied
my hiking boots on, and wrapped a towel around
my neck.

I consulted the map one more time and made
my way through the woods toward the pond. The
path was well worn but growing steeper by the
minute and I had a moment of doubt as to the
wisdom of my choice. Forging on, thinking it

couldn't be much further, the woods closed in around me, an eerie silence sending a chill across my skin. My boots slipped on the small stones, forcing me to sit on my butt to get down the next sharp drop. The trail narrowed and I caught my breath, nearly sliding off a shear edge and tumbling down the hill. I clung to a tree branch and eased myself down a rocky precipice wondering what lengths I would go to, to be alone.

Twenty minutes later, I came to a crystal clear glacier pond, a few scrapes on my hands but no worse for wear. In spite of the rough hike, I decided it was worth it. The place had a magical feel to it like I'd stepped into a fairy tale. I half expected a wood sprite to greet me or a water nymph to break the reflective surface of the peaceful water. The pond looked more like a lake, much bigger than it had appeared on the map. There wasn't a soul around. I tried to push away the dark shadow that hung over my soul. I wanted to enjoy this moment of connecting with nature, but self-reflection was a dangerous luxury I couldn't afford. It would inevitably lead to more tears and frankly, I was tired of crying.

The sun sat low in the sky, an orange ball that promised another long, steamy day ahead. I threw my towel onto a rock and kicked off my boots, the warm sand, inviting under my toes. I shimmied out of my shorts and waded into the pond up to my thighs. A cold chill trickled up my spine. I thought of Alex for the millionth time in the last week, my heart taking another plunge into the depths of despair. I let out a frustrated growl. I hated being this out of control of my emotions. Maybe he had found closure in telling me to take a hike, but I didn't get to say what I wanted to say…should have said…needed to say.

"You stubborn, pig-headed, pain-in-the-ass…jerk!" I yelled to the leaves on the maple tree nearby. I felt stupid, but it was good to vent. A smidgeon of tension dropped from my shoulders. I did it again. "How could you be so selfish?" I shouted. "How could you walk away from the one person who knows you best…and still LOVES you…even though you are maddeningly stubborn and…and emotionally…immature!" I screamed. A flock of geese took flight off the surface of the still water.

I had to laugh at myself. Not because I was wrong, really, but because it was a terribly one-sided argument and I was acting a bit like an irrational shrew. It felt good not to have to hold back--to be what Mom and Brig and…Alex…needed me to be.

I sank under the water up to my chin and felt the chill all the way to my bones, all of the heat I'd built up cooling instantly. I couldn't be mad at him. He was an honorable guy who thought he was doing

the right thing by taking responsibility for a
mistake. A part of me still couldn't believe it was
Alex's fault. Where Levi was concerned, anything
could have happened. But the other part of me—the
part that had worried about my brother and lied to
protect him--knew that if Levi walked willingly to
his death, my silence was the lie that made it
possible. Maybe that was the truth I was trying to
get to. I dunked under and came up slowly, dipping
my head back and letting the water pour over me as
if seeking some kind of baptism or forgiveness.

I still wondered if things would have been
different if I'd said something about his cutting, but
I had the feeling it was one more thing my mother
couldn't have handled. On some level, I knew she
had always known and that it had been her job, not
mine, to do something about it. Maybe someday, we
would be able to talk about it, but not now. My own
grief was too raw to face my part in protecting the
lies. Another sharp pang of anger and regret twisted
inside me. We had all failed him miserably and I
couldn't lay all the blame on her.

At least now we had the knowledge that he
died with honor, a fact that would no doubt give my
mother a sense of peace. She couldn't have lived
with it if he had killed himself. She would say it
meant he couldn't go to heaven, but I didn't believe
her. God always seemed bigger than that to me. I
didn't think God would hold it against a kid who

had been so hurt in life he couldn't bear to live with the pain. My heart ached for Levi. I wish he had told me. Tears ran down my cheeks again. Frustration with my grief, my weakness, the unrelenting sadness that filled me to overflowing, sent me into a rage. "WHY?" I screamed to the heavens, knowing not even God himself would be able to make me understand.

I splashed the cold water in my face, and dove under, coming up only when my lungs were close to bursting. I swam hard for the center of the large pond, the water growing icy cold around me. The bottom, which a minute before had appeared as a soft sandy beach ten feet below me, disappeared into darkness. I swam in long strokes taking me further from shore until my arms got tired and I rolled onto my back to float. I peered up at the dimming sky, its afternoon blue turning to an evening violet and crimson. The sun still shone through the trees, but it wouldn't be light much longer. I should probably head back in. I righted myself and began to tread water, realizing I'd swum out farther than I thought.

The pond was silent and growing dark with shadows. A looking glass reflection of trees and the splash of the sun's last rays glittered across the surface. An owl hooted in the distance and frogs croaked out a symphony along the edges of the ancient glacier pond. It dawned on me I was in water that could be a hundred feet deep, and my heart beat quickened.

I took a stroke and then two more before I felt the first cramp. A small stitch in my side. I tried to keep swimming, but the cramp spread to my calf, then lower. Crap! I grabbed for my toes which followed the spasm in the arch of my right foot. My mother's voice came to my head—something about not swimming until at least an hour after eating—a lesson I thought stupid at the time. A peanut butter sandwich and chocolate milk? Really? My toe cramp started to dissipate and then my calf tightened painfully again as soon as I kicked towards shore—too far away. I'd never make it. The pulse in my throat pounded. I struggled to relax, float, and breathe. I was quickly tiring and the edge of panic rose within me. No one knows I'm here. Crap! Crap!!

Water splashed into my mouth. I spit it out, choking. I clutched my side. Another cramp—harder—took my breath away. I went under…kicked my way up. My leg seized. I went down again. I pulled my way to the surface and gulped for air. My body felt like a cinder block, heavy, solid, and sinking fast. I went under a third time. Fear gripped my mind. I couldn't think. I clawed my way up, my legs numb and useless. I gulped for air, but hadn't quite hit the surface. My lungs filled with water—panic—choking—

I heard my mother, crying, *"Don't leave me."* Then I saw Levi reaching out to me beneath the murky water and felt myself drifting towards him. This must be how it was for him. Dying wasn't so bad after you got past the fear.

I reached out and brushed his fingertips. He smiled.

So dark—so quiet—I slipped away.

Chapter 19

I felt myself drifting--up or down—I
couldn't tell. Floating—being pulled—carried. I
blinked and saw the sky above, stars twinkling
against a deep purple canvas. I saw Alex's face
silhouetted against the night shadows. He hovered
above me, his face close, calling my name but
distant. Was this what it felt like to die and go to
heaven?

"Jordie, can you hear me?" His voice was
muffled. He sounded panicked, desperate, gasping
for breath.

I choked up pond water, coughed, gagged.
He helped me turn on my side, and held my hair
back, the elastic long gone. I gasped for breath as he
laid me back down. "What…happened?" My ears
felt full of cotton, my head pounded.

Alex grabbed me and pulled me onto his lap,
holding me tight and rocking back and forth. "Oh,
God. I thought I lost you!" His warm lips felt nice
on my forehead, the heat of his body bringing me
closer to life. I began to shake, my limbs trembling
painfully as the numbness wore off.

"How did you f-f-f-find me?" I asked, the
fog clearing slightly as he sat me up. My throat
burned and it was hard to swallow.

"I saw you head down the trail alone and I...followed you."

I held my head in both hands trying to make sense of everything. "Why are you here?"

"Brig asked me to go on a camping trip with him. I had no idea you were going to be here." Seeing me shiver uncontrollably, he wrapped a towel around my shoulders and pulled me close beside him. The sand felt warm, but the sun had all but disappeared and a chill closed in around us. "I'm just glad I made it to you in time." He crushed me against his chest and I let myself snuggle into his neck. Oh, yes. Heat infused me. I snuggled deeper, wrapping my arms around his warm, hard torso. If this was what heaven was like, I had surely died. "Can you stand up?" he asked. The gentleness in his voice started a warm fire in my chest.

"Not yet," I whispered, my teeth chattering violently. He settled his arm tighter around me. I lifted my eyes to look up at him, catching a glimpse of the vulnerable, insecure guy I'd known--and fallen in love with--when I was in the ninth grade. I remembered the day he went from being Levi's friend to possibly the love of my life.

I was fast becoming a tall, gangly, jock and he was...Alex...soft spoken, cute, in a Great Dane sort of way--not quite sure of his own size and strength, awkward but graceful at the same time-- and hiding behind glasses and a computer screen.

Then one day we were joking around. While showing him one of my martial arts moves, I knocked him onto the ground and landed on top of him. His glasses had flown off and we were nose to nose, seeing each other as if for the first time, those beautiful eyes piercing straight through to my soul. I know he felt it too. A moment of recognition so true and pure, you know you will never be the same again.

He was so sweet, his crooked smile hurt and vulnerable. I knew what he'd gone through with his dad and I felt bad that Levi kept getting him into trouble. He was a nice guy who had hooked up with the wrong friend. From that day forward, I never saw him or us the same way. I became secretly fascinated with Alex Cooper.

My shivers brought me back to the moment. His chin rested on my head and his arms seemed to be everywhere. He rubbed my back, my shoulders, and stroked my hair. I felt the blood coming back into my extremities. My mind cleared and I remembered the last time we saw each other and how he'd walked away from me. All the hurt I'd been steeped in for the past two weeks rose to the surface, giving me a mental slap back to reality. I sat up, immediately regretting the loss of his warmth. "I have some questions for you."

"Look, you're freezing, and we have a long hike back in the dark. We should get going." He pulled away and slowly climbed to his feet. It was then I noticed his leg.

"You got another new leg." This one strapped on the same suction cup kind of way, but the titanium rod was replaced by a flat curved lower leg and foot which looked a bit like a ski.

He looked down. "It's my running leg. I just got it this week. I guess it works pretty well for swimming too." He flashed me a grin in the dark that fell around us. A half-moon rose up over the pond and the sky was bright with stars. He extended a hand out to me.

I let him lift me to my feet. I wobbled, my legs still not quite ready for land. His hands came around my waist to steady me. I held onto his arms and looked him in the eye, one side of his face in complete shadow. "I don't think I can make it back up the hill in the dark. It's a long hike and it gets pretty steep in spots. Can't we just make camp here?"

He tensed and hesitated. "I don't think that's a very good idea," he said.

We stood toe to toe, bodies touching in so many places, my nerves felt instantly hotwired. I placed my hands on his bare chest and he shivered. "I think you should start a fire," I said. I bit my lower lip, feeling heat rise in my cheeks, my breath shallow. "Let's make camp here." In response, he went to that still place inside himself, fighting some internal demon that had him paralyzed in the moment. I pushed away and punched him in the arm, hard. "Are you afraid you can't control yourself around me?"

"Ouch." He mock flinched and rubbed his arm. "I nearly drowned saving you and now you're punching me? Maybe it's *your* self-control we should worry about." He waggled his brows at me.

"Don't worry. Your virtue is safe with me." I rolled my eyes at him. "Look, I don't have my cell phone and I can't see you and me stumbling through the dark and falling off a cliff or something just because you don't trust yourself to be alone with me. We are definitely safer here." Challenging his resolve seemed like a good way to force his hand. Besides, I was going to get answers to my questions—one way or another.

I had barley finished my thought when he pulled me against him, "You think so?" he asked, his eyes lit with fire, and then he kissed me. I didn't fight him. In fact I think I grabbed his hair in both hands. Questions could wait. His hands tightened on my waist and we stayed pressed together for a blissfully long time, his lips locked hard against mine, his tongue thrusting again and again, leaving me dizzy and confused. Then he pulled away, his face close to mine so his words came out breathy and warm. "Still feel safer here?"

My fingers and toes tingled, my breath came
in waves. I managed to steady myself. "I always
feel safe with you, Coop." My voice was a whisper,
a sensual sound I didn't know I could make. Afraid
the moment would disappear too soon, I draped my
arms around his neck and smiled. "I haven't
thanked you for saving me."

Exasperated, he relaxed and held me close
again. "You are impossible." Then he laughed, a
quiet chuckle in the dark, "Consider me thanked."
He kissed my forehead, a gesture that would never
lose meaning to me. There was tenderness behind it
I craved more than even I wanted to admit.
Somehow it felt like a promise. I hoped I wasn't
wrong.

"I still have questions," I said, caught in this
tempting embrace neither of us could seem to pull
away from.

His voice came out deeper and softer than
usual. "You are relentless. Not to mention too
trusting for your own good. If I was any other guy,
you could be in real trouble."

"If you were any other guy, I'd have
knocked your butt on the ground and out-run you by
now." He laughed and then his expression grew
serious.

"I can't spend a night alone with you. It
wouldn't be fair to either of us." He pushed my hair

out of my face and stroked my cheek, sending a tingle all the way to my toes.

"Haven't you figured out life isn't fair?" I said quietly, the darkness filling in around us. "If anyone knows that, it's you and I."

He groaned in frustration, his fingers tightening around my arms. "What do you want from me, Jordie?"

I used the calmest, most self-assured tone I could muster under the circumstances—what with our bodies vibrating with tension against each other. "For now, I want you to start a fire and keep me warm. Then, talk to me and tell me what's going on with you. In the morning we'll walk up the hill and work it all out, okay?" I waited for his response. The truth was I didn't know if I could be next to him all night without my hormones cutting loose, but all I could think about was lying in his arms and feeling his warmth around me. Getting some answers would be an added bonus. I fluttered my lashes in the dark, wondering if he could see me. "I need you to do this for me, Coop."

He let out a long sigh and released his hold on me. "Brig is going to kill me." He scratched his head in defeat. "I'll go get some wood."

Chapter 20

Alex was remarkably resourceful. He brought back wood and plenty of tinder to start the fire. He'd been much more prepared than I, and had a backpack with supplies, including a lighter, a folded up rain poncho, and some power bars. Oh, and then there was a flashlight with dead batteries, and a cell phone with no reception—signs we were meant to stay right here together, in my opinion. He threw me a USMC sweatshirt and before long, we were sitting on the poncho next to a roaring blaze sharing a vanilla almond super packed protein bar. I finished the last bite and chewed forever, my jaw tiring before I swallowed. My stomach felt slightly less hollow. I took a slug off his water bottle and handed it to him.

Alex sat close beside me, his body warmth shielding me from the cool air at my back. He tossed the wrapper into the flame and capped the water bottle, setting it aside. The crackling fire radiated heat to my legs, the numbness finally leaving my toes. His shirt, my shorts and a towel hung on sticks drying out. My hair had dried into a tangled mess I kept tucking behind my ears. I thought about what a close call today had been and I shivered again, leaning into the solid warmth at my side.

"Thanks, Coop. I owe you." I glanced up at him.

He smiled down at me, spiky blonde hair looking like a halo in the firelight. He had gotten it cut short again since I'd seen him last. "Let's call it even, okay?"

My heart lurched, catching the tender look in his eyes. Why did he have to be so cute? And smell so good? My mind spun with possible scenarios of how the night would go, but at least I was certain that by morning, I would know how Alex felt about me once and for all. I couldn't take all of this cat and mouse game with him. I also needed him to level with me about everything he knew. I hated to ruin the mood, but the questions in my head wouldn't stop churning. "Coop, if you really want to call us even, I need to know what the report said."

His smile faded and he stared into the fire for a long time before speaking. I waited patiently, my heart in my throat. When he started, his voice was cool, controlled. How did he so easily shut down as a person—become a Marine—in the space of a breath.

Alex stared into the fire, focusing intently on the flames. His voice seemed detached from his words. "If the report is accurate, Lee and I were told to stand down when it was discovered the house we were set to enter was occupied. Thirty seconds later, my voice came over the com saying '*We're going in.*' Twenty seconds after that, gun fire broke out. Two dead Iraqi men and your brother and I were the only ones found inside. Since I was supposed to be lead man, and no one actually saw which of us went in first, the squad leader assumes I made the judgment to go in against orders, and…it resulted in casualties."

"If there weren't any eye witnesses, you don't know if all that's even true. Nobody does… unless you can remember." I touched his arm and waited for him to look me in the eyes—to come back to me from wherever he had disappeared to.

His brows drew together, his jaw clenched. "Don't you think I know that?"

"I'm sorry, Coop. I wish I could help. Have you been doing your meditation?"

He rolled his eyes at me and shook his head. "It doesn't work for me. I can't get out of my head." His voice dropped in volume, sounding strained. "I close my eyes and all I see is Levi, bleeding out."

The image twisted something inside me and I closed my eyes. I saw Levi reaching out to me under the water, our fingers barely touching. I opened my eyes. "You remember Lee…dying?"

"Yeah. That's *all* I remember."

"Did he…did he say anything?"

Alex went very still, his voice lowering to barely above a whisper. "No…I don't think so. I remember that he looked at me from across the floor…I couldn't reach him…I couldn't…help him."

I swallowed back tears that scorched behind my eyes. I imagined how painful it must be for Alex to live with such a terrible memory. I cleared my throat and stared at the flames willing the tears back down, trying not to see the picture in my head of my brother's life draining away and Alex lying helpless with his leg shattered. My stomach clenched and I squeezed my eyes shut tight trying to stay focused on my questions. I needed to know everything. I shook off the horrible image. "Why were you going into the house? What was on the computer you were supposed to hack?"

Alex resumed his unaffected Marine voice. "I can't tell you that. It's classified. I don't see why it matters."

Frustrated, I flexed my fingers, balling them into fists to keep my impatience from surfacing in an argument. "You aren't in the Marines anymore, right? So it wouldn't be like breaking the rules to tell me."

"I suppose you're right," he let out a breath and pulled away from me, awkwardly shifting to stand on his new prosthesis which probably wasn't really made for the sand. He tossed another log on the fire and grabbed the warm towel off the stick. Then he sat back down beside me, covered my bare legs, and curled his body around me again. I shivered against him, the anticipation killing me. Everything inside of me wanted to tackle him to the ground and make him talk, but I felt the fragility of the moment. He was about to open up and let me in. I held my breath a second longer.

His body relaxed beside me as he took up the conversation, the moment of hesitation past. "The report said that the two men in the house ran a human trafficking operation. Kids mostly--selling them as servants or sex slaves to perverts. They use the money to fund terrorist activity. I didn't know until I read the file."

"Do you think Lee knew?" I sat up onto my heels, pulling the towel tighter around my shoulders.

He cocked his head. "I don't know." His green eyes sparkled with the reflection of the flames and my pulse jumped a beat faster. "What are you thinking?"

I hesitated. This was no time to be delicate. "My mom told you about what happened to Lee when he was little, didn't she?"

"Yeah." He looked down, avoiding eye contact. "I always wondered. Lee acted funny about stuff sometimes."

I could see his cheeks flush and I moved on, not ready to deal with my brother's abuse on any deeper level. Then I thought of something Alex had told me when we were kayaking on Thompson Lake. "Wait. Maybe there was a witness." I sat facing him, the fire warm at my back. "Remember you said you heard the sound of a kid crying? Is it possible there was a boy there--a kid in trouble?"

"There was nothing in the report about a kid, but there may have been a child in the house. I can think of crazier scenarios." He glanced from me to the fire a few times before settling his gaze on the flame.

"Remember how Lee used to go mental with bullies in school who picked on littler kids? If Lee saw or heard a kid being abused, I can't imagine him standing by and watching. Maybe he rushed in to save a kid and you just went in after him. The call to your squad leader wasn't specific about who went in first. It could mean anything." I was on a roll and I thought he would stop me and tell me I was way off, but a flash of recognition came over his face.

Now I could see the wheels in *his* head turning. A smug grin curved his lips and I saw the old Alex emerge.

"What are you thinking?" I asked. I pushed my hair back over my ear, turned to face the fire again settling in next to him, and tossed another stick into the flames.

"I think you're brilliant." He flashed a heart melting look of pride my way and a warm puddle pooled in my chest. His expression shifted to serious. "In hind sight, knowing what I know now, I can't see any other reason Lee would have broken protocol."

"Unless he was trying to commit suicide," I added softly, staring into the flickering light as if I could burn the image of Lee slicing a blade across his wrist out of my mind.

Alex wrapped an arm around my shoulders and pulled me close. "I told you. I don't think he did. Lee was different over in Iraq. He felt like he belonged there. Like it was his chance to do something right. He was a good soldier. He never would have let me down." Alex's voice had grown quiet, and I saw him looking down at his leg.

"I'm so sorry, Coop--about your leg. You're right. Lee would never have wanted this to happen to you." I felt tears behind my eyes again and blinked away the burning sensation.

"I think we should try to get some sleep. Your mom and Brig are going to have half the state looking for us when we don't show up tonight. Brig knew I was going after you, so at least they know we're together." He looked down at me awkwardly, a flash of guilt on his face. "We need to leave and get back by dawn. We don't want the Rangers out combing the park."

I thought of my family and how worried they would be about me. My mother must be freaking out right about now. A twinge of guilt crept over me. She had lost so much—suffered so much. Worrying that she had lost me too must be killing her. Brig would keep it together—keep her together—until morning. I hated to think about the moment I had to face them both. I would be grounded until I went to college. Another pang of something beyond worry and near panic balled in my stomach. What would happen to me and Alex when I went off to college? Was this my only chance to be with him? When we went back to our lives tomorrow, would he walk away again? Questions sprinted in my mind.

Alex tossed several more logs on to burn and I got up to check on my shorts—still damp and cold. I left them hanging by the fire, excused myself to find a tree and came back shivering again despite the blazing inferno.

"If anyone's searching for us, they'll find us with a signal fire this big," he said. Alex settled onto the poncho, sprawling out on his side facing me and the fire. He patted the space in front of him. "Come on. Let's keep you warm. I'll behave. I promise."

I bit my lip to keep from showing how happy that made me. I crawled down and spread the towel over both of us and backed up against him as close as I could. His body tensed at the contact and then relaxed around me. I snuggled into him, my practically naked backside fitting into the firm curve of his body, his arms pulling me closer still. He covered me with the smoky towel and tucked himself around me like a cocoon. "Get some sleep, okay?" he whispered, his breath tickly and sweet on my cheek.

"Yeah, like that's gonna' happen," I said, every nerve in my body humming with warm fuzzies.

Chapter 21

I resisted the urge to toss and turn, sensing that every small movement I made exacerbated a rather embarrassing condition Alex was doing his best to ignore. "Hold still. Will you?" He groaned after I squirmed, trying to dislodge a stone from my hip.

"Ouch! Your leg is cutting into my ankle." I pulled my leg free from under his prosthesis.

"Sorry. I'm not used to sleeping with this thing on, but I'm at a slight disadvantage without it, so..." he sucked in a breath. "Jordie, you're killing me here."

I had pressed my hips against him to get away from the hard, sharp stick digging into my thigh and felt...oh. I sucked in a breath too. "Sorry. I thought that was a...well...maybe if I turn over..." I flipped around and found myself facing a hot wall of smooth flesh. His chest was bare, his abs rigid and he was watching me with a tortured expression on his face, his cheeks red even in the firelight. "I'll stop moving now," I said, snuggling down close to him and tucking my arms in front of me so we could both be spared my boobs touching him. Even through the sweatshirt, my breasts ached, the tips sensitive. Heat radiated between us and I lay still, my breath shallow.

"Coop," I said softly, "why did you come after me today?"

He sighed. "I guess I wanted to apologize. I know I left things…I know I hurt you. It wasn't my intention."

I lifted my chin so I could meet his gaze, his eyes so sad and serious. I wanted to erase the last two weeks of hating him for walking away that day. I smiled up at him. "Apology accepted."

"Even though I'm a stubborn, pig-headed, pain-in-the-ass, jerk?" His eyes sparkled in the firelight, crinkling at the edges.

"Oh, you heard me, did you?" My face went hot. I stared at his chest. What a beautiful chest it was, too. Muscled, smooth, only a few course hairs down the center. I swallowed.

"I deserved it. Don't worry about it."

"Good night, Coop." I kissed the little hollow at his throat that I knew would feel amazing against my lips and sighed, wanting so much more but knowing the time wasn't right. Not yet. We had a lot to work through. But this…tucked up against him, warm and feeling safe…this was a great start.

He settled his arms around me again and I felt him relax. I dozed in and out after a while, waking occasionally and realizing where I was. My muddled mind processed all that had happened, trying to find answers to the questions that still hung between us. I had no idea what the future held for him…for me…for us. Wrestling with my doubts was getting me nowhere. My body felt hot and achy in places that only seemed to come alive around Alex. I pushed the need down and closed my eyes. For now, I would lie there enjoying the feeling of his arms around me, our bodies close, the whisper in the trees, and the crickets chirping their song into the night.

Sometime later, I felt Alex tense, his alertness waking me instantly. "What is it?" I asked, my eyes trying to focus in the dark. The fire had burned down to a low flame; hot glowing coals radiated a dim circle of light nearby.

"Shhh." We lay still for a few more seconds. "Something was out there. But it's gone now."

My heart kicked against my ribs. "What do you think it was at this hour?" I wondered if there were wolves or bears out in the dark and I shuddered.

Alex was quiet for a few minutes and then he wrapped his arms tight around me again, relaxing as I snuggled in under his chin. "It's nothing. Probably a skunk or a raccoon. Go back to sleep. You're safe."

Those words sent a tiny spear through my heart. Was I really safe with Alex? Physically, I knew I couldn't be in better hands. But I didn't think my heart could take it if he pulled away from me again. If I could only get him to see that we belonged together. That whatever he was going through, I wanted to be a part of it and help him through it--that we were always better together than apart. If I could help him see he was still whole and that he had an amazing future in front of him.

I stroked a finger along his collar bone and felt him tense in response, but he didn't complain. His skin felt smooth and warm and his neck smelled so good I couldn't resist the urge to kiss him there. My lips parted and my tongue found the tender flesh that rose with goose bumps. When I pressed my hands to his chest, his muscles expanded, flexing in response. His heart beat against my hand like a bass drum, strong and rhythmic, racing under my touch. He arched his neck, giving me a better angle, a strangled groan of surrender escaping his lips as my kisses became less gentle and more urgent.

The more I tasted of him, the more I wanted. His breath came in short bursts and his body shuddered, his arms pulling me tighter against him. My lips seemed to have a mind of their own, exploring his neck and working their way along his jaw, a day's beard growth fuzzy against my cheek. In spite of a tiny voice screaming at me from somewhere way in the back of my head to '*stop*', I found my hand gliding down his chest and skimming over the ridges of his abdomen. He sucked in a breath like he'd been stabbed.

He rested his hand over mine and squirmed away from my lips. "Jordie, you have to stop. I can't...we can't...I promised..."

My face burned and I felt his rejection like a slap. "I'm sorry. I thought you wanted...never mind." I turned away from him and stared into the glowing embers of the fire. My chest ached and my body cooled with just the few inches of space between us. I heard him let out another groan, and then he slid in behind me again, the evidence my kisses had been effective pressed against my lower back. My head spun with confused emotions. I wanted him so badly I could scarcely stop myself from attacking him, but he made me so mad...always treating me like a child...like I didn't know my own mind...like I didn't know what I wanted. Like he didn't want me the way I wanted him. The physical attraction was obvious, but he might feel the same with any other half naked girl in the middle of the night. Why couldn't he just tell me how he felt?

"Hey, you okay?" his voice whispered on my hair and sent a chill along my skin. I shivered and he wrapped me snug in his arms again. I lay silently fuming while trying to soak in the feeling of being there with him. Maybe this was enough. It had to be, since he obviously wasn't willing to take advantage of the situation.

"Yeah, I guess," I said softly, my temper cooling. "It's just that...I hoped...maybe you felt the same way about me that I feel about you." I felt my face get hot and was glad he couldn't see me.

Alex tensed. "Things are complicated. You're only seventeen. You have to finish school. You still have college...I don't know where either of us will be or what I'm going to do..." he exhaled, frustrated.

"That's kind of the point, isn't it?" I asked, my voice sounding chilly. "What if all we have is right now? The universe doesn't seem like it cares about our timeline for life or where we're all going along the way." I thought about Levi, my dad, Alex's leg. "I almost died today, Coop. What if tonight is all we have?"

Alex rose up on one elbow and I rolled onto my back, staring up into the face that I'd seen change from a boy to a man, the star filled sky looming above. He swept my hair away from my face and ran a finger gently along my cheek, my jaw, and then my lips, his touch leaving a trail of tingling warmth behind. "Can't we just take things slow? See what happens?" He smiled that Alex smile that made my heart melt and I couldn't be mad. He was trying to be honorable—do the right thing—again. Crap!

I gazed into his eyes, only shadows in the glowing embers of the fire, and smiled. "Okay, you win. I'll be patient and behave. But you have to promise me something."

"What kind of promise?" He smiled warily.

"Promise me we'll always be friends."

His smile faded and his eyes widened, a haunted expression flashing across his features. Then, just as quickly, the smile returned. "That's an easy one," he whispered. Alex touched a finger to my nose and followed it with a kiss, so tender, my heart skipped a beat. "Now, go to sleep." He settled me in his arms once more and we lay there listening to each other breathe, the sounds of the night gathering around us.

I wondered about that look—the one I knew he got when he was thinking of Levi--and I couldn't help but wonder if my brother had asked him to make the same promise.

Chapter 22

The sky turned from black to a deep purple, and then the rosy pink of unripe peaches as morning dawned. A fine mist settled over my skin and in spite of the chill it brought, Alex's arms around me and his furnace of a body next to me made me feel toasty warm.

"You awake?" he asked.

"Yup." I yawned and stretched, feeling his body respond to my movement. "Did you sleep?" I asked, knowing he hadn't slept any more than I had.

Tired eyes glanced down at me. "Not much." He rolled away and I instantly missed his warmth and the closeness we'd shared the night before. He tossed me my shorts and said coolly, "We'd better get back."

So much for his promise to be friends. He acted like it had all been a dream. The look on his face evolved into that Marine face, and I didn't like it one bit. "What's your hurry? Are you anxious to face Brig and my mom?" I asked, sarcasm seeping into my voice.

"I don't want them to worry any longer than necessary—something you might consider." His stern expression sent a nudge of shame through me, pricking my pride.

"No, you're right, of course. Let's go." I got up and slipped my shorts on, tied my boots and grabbed the towel. The fire was long dead, a pile of hot ash left behind on the sand.

After we each hit the trees for a pit stop we made our way up the trail, neither of us saying much. I took the lead and felt his eyes on my back, a tension running between us like a rope. What kind of bee was in his shorts this morning? I wanted to ask if I'd done something wrong, but I wasn't sure I wanted to hear his answer.

Alex mumbled under his breath and grunted a few times, the path growing steeper and winding precariously along a severe drop off reminding me of how dangerous it would have been to attempt it in the dark. The sun broke through the trees and the air lost some of its chill. Mosquitoes began to buzz happily around my head, adding to my annoyance.

I had bigger things to worry about than Alex's brooding. I wasn't looking forward to facing Mom, let alone, dealing with Brig. What had he been thinking bringing Alex camping at the same place Mom and I were staying? Had they planned this together? To get Alex and me to work things out? It seemed unlikely my mother would approve of such a plan. Despite her acceptance of his apology and her letting go of blaming him, I knew she still had reservations about us being more than friends. She reminded me every chance she got, he was 'too old' for me (which was ridiculous since there was only two years difference between us). I guess in terms of experience, we were worlds apart. But the thing that really mattered between us, the undeniable connection we'd shared since we were no more than children, had to count for something.

We climbed silently for almost an hour, slowed by Alex's leg and his being unaccustomed to the new prosthesis. I heard him struggle behind me and by the time we reached the top, he was limping, his breath labored. I'd stopped offering to carry the back pack and asking if he was okay about half way up, since it seemed to annoy him and the only answer I got was 'fine'.

When we reached the camp site, my mother was already up and sitting at the picnic table, her hair a mess from running her hands through it and her face the shade of a parsnip. When she spotted me, a wave of relief rushed across her face and she ran to meet me.

"Oh, God. Thank you God." She grabbed me and hugged the stuffing out of me. *Maybe it would be all right. She didn't seem too mad.* She pulled back and her face went from relief to fury in a millisecond. "Where were you? I have been worried sick about you! Of all the thoughtless, irresponsible..." blah, blah, blah. *Here it comes.* She didn't even give me a chance to breathe, let alone speak and tell her I had almost drowned and

Alex saved me. She grabbed me and hugged me again, her eyes filled with tears. "After Lee...I couldn't lose you too," she choked out.

Maybe I would just leave the near death experience part out. I hugged her back.

"I'm okay, Mom. Alex and I just got talking and then realized it was too dark to walk back. We decided to camp on the beach and head back this morning. Alex's phone wouldn't work...I'm fine." She continued to alternate hugging me and then glaring from me to Alex who had sat down at the picnic table and was stretching his leg out. He winced.

At this point, Brig rolled out of the tent, dressed in fatigues, hiking boots, and a fishing hat loaded with lures. He approached with caution, eyeing Mom as if she was a hand grenade and he was ascertaining whether the pin was still in or not. He glanced at Alex. "Glad to see you two made it back in one piece. I trust you took good care of my granddaughter."

"Yes sir." The two men exchanged a look and then I noticed Alex rubbing his knee, a habit I hadn't seen him do since he was in the hospital before the stump fully healed.

"I think you should take your prosthesis off and let me check for pressure sores. It couldn't have been good for you to wear that all night with it being wet and all—and then walking two miles up hill this morning." It was the first time I considered that his bad mood could have something to do with him being in pain. Maybe it didn't have anything to do with his feelings for me. I felt instantly better...and then infinitely worse for being so stupid and self-centered.

"Its fine, Jordie. Don't make a big deal out of it." He lowered his leg from the picnic table bench and made an effort not to cringe as he bent the knee.

Before I had a chance to argue, my mother piped in. "I'd like to speak with you alone, Jordan. If Lee...I mean Alex," she corrected, her cheeks flushing, "says he's fine, let's leave him alone to get settled in his own campsite."

Brig had set up two small dome tents in the site next to ours. He had a screen room over the picnic table and tarps above (and below) both tents, the upper tarps strung to the trees in such a way as to ensure rainfall would run away from the site. Compared to the pitiful mom-and-me fiasco, it was the Taj Mahal. Brig exchanged a look with me and then my mother.

"Why don't you ladies go get cleaned up and I'll make us a nice breakfast?" He pressed a firm hand onto Alex's shoulder. "Maybe we can still get some fishing in this morning before the bass get filled up on mosquitoes."

It was barely seven o'clock, and we were the first to arrive at the showers-- cement walled cubicles with slatted wooden benches and plastic curtains sporting as much hot water as two quarters could by—approximately four-and-a-half minutes worth. With the characteristic hairball in the drain, I left my flip-flops on.

"What were you thinking?" Mom called from the stall next to me, completing her lengthy lecture while she washed her hair. "And what was Brig thinking coming here with Alex?" Obviously, she was as surprised by Alex's presence as I had been. "Not that I'm not grateful you weren't stuck out there all alone last night, but still…"

"I was thinking, I didn't want to fall off a cliff in the pitch dark," I called back. The water timed out, leaving me to wipe the residual suds off with a towel. I hated camp showers. I dragged an '*I'm an angel*' tank top over my head, donned a sweatshirt, clean shorts and my hikers, and wrapped my head in a towel.

When I came out, Mom was already combing out her hair and pulling it up into a ponytail. Standing side by side staring into a foggy mirror, I hated that we looked so much alike. I mean it was good to know I might still look young and pretty in twenty years, but I couldn't help feeling like I didn't have anything that was truly mine—not even my identity. I was her daughter, Levi's sister, Alex's friend—something—I still wasn't sure what I was to Alex.

I left my hair down, deciding to let it dry naturally. With the humidity heavy in the air, it would take about an hour and my hair would be curling and waving like medusa, and I'd be forced to pull it back.

"I hope you didn't do anything foolish." Mom's voice reached my ear, calling the night before to attention. She had no idea how close I'd come to being foolish. I prick of pain went to my heart that Alex had pushed me away when I offered my virgin-self up to him—the jerk. I gave one last look in the mirror, scowling at my reflection.

Maybe it was time to change my look. If I just pulled the long layers back into a clip and let some strands hang around my face…maybe a little makeup…. Crap. A mosquito landed on my forehead, bit me and then evaded the slap that left a red mark between my eyes. Why would God even create stupid insects that bite? I scratched the welt, making it puff up into a pink raised dot.

"*Blah…blah…*you have your whole future ahead of you. I don't want you making a choice that will put an end to all of it," Mom's voice sounded like another mosquito buzzing in my head. I raked a brush through my hair and grabbed my bag, tired of listening to her reprimanding tone. Did all mothers have the ability to make every question sound like an accusation meant to make you feel stupid?

"Alex was a complete gentleman, Mom. Nothing happened, so stop freaking out. I'm sorry I worried you, okay?"

She didn't let up.

"Couldn't you have planned your time better? Honestly, Jordan. I didn't sleep a wink. Even after Brig said he knew exactly where you were and that you were safe. If I didn't trust him so completely, I would have had the police and the FBI out searching the park."

We walked up the road toward the campsite. "How did Brig know where we were? I know he saw Alex follow me, but how did he know for sure everything was okay?"

"How does Brig know anything?" Mom shrugged and sent me a look that said, '*Don't ask*'. "When it comes to bad situations, he always seems to have a handle on things." As we approached the miniature tent city we'd created, I smelled coffee and bacon and my stomach growled in response. One of these days I would ask Brig all of the questions I'd held back. I tossed my bag in the tent. At least Mom had packed the air mattress. Maybe I'd get a better night's sleep tonight. I shook off the fatigue and headed for the smell of coffee.

"Jordan."

I turned back. "What now?" My patience was wearing thin. I had a lot on my mind and I was in no mood to be grilled all day by my mother.

She dropped the subject and wrapped an arm around my shoulder. "I'm just glad you're back safe." I let her kiss my cheek and then she released me.

I don't think she'd done that since before Levi died. An indescribable ache washed over my heart—the stark awareness that Levi's death had changed us both forever. I felt my mother's grief like a pulsing dark spirit that hung around her, making her eyes perpetually sad. Another wave of guilt surged up inside me. Why did I have to be such a jerk? Mom did not need to be left wondering whether I was dead or alive all night, no matter what the reason I'd let it happen.

I gave her one more tight squeeze. "Mom, I'm okay. Nothing bad happened. Alex was with me. And you know I can take care of myself. Have a little faith in me, okay?" I thought about what it would have done to her if I had died yesterday and wondered if I should tell her just how much she owed Alex. Instead, I kissed her cheek and gave her a teasing smile. "You won't be able to watch over me every minute once I leave for school." My stomach soured at the thought. What was I going to do about Alex? I had no idea. But at that moment, all I could think about was staring at him over a

hearty breakfast and remembering what it felt like
to be wrapped in his arms.

Chapter 23

Brig and Alex had their heads together when Mom and I popped into the screen room. Alex's prosthesis leaned against the picnic table and my heart dropped. Crap. I knew before I saw what they were looking at, what I would see. My mother wasn't so fortunate.

"Ohhh," she gasped, raising her hand to cover the sound. Her eyes went wide and her face drained.

Alex draped a towel over the stump, which was oozing blood from several blisters that had formed and broken open. "I'm sorry, ma'am. This isn't the place…I'll go in the tent…" he glanced from me to my mother, clearly mortified by her response.

"No. It's fine," Brig said. He glared at my mother and shook his head. "You stay right there and fix up your leg, Son. Katherine can work on scrambling some eggs." The Coleman camp stove was set up on a small table in the corner of the screen room. He turned his attention back to Alex. "Jordan and I can help you get patched up."

My mother stared for a second longer, her breath steadying and her color returning. "Don't you think you should see a doctor, Alex?"

"You're probably right, ma'am, but this is the only leg I brought with me and I don't have my crutches. I figured I'd be hanging out fishing all weekend. I hadn't planned for the hiking." Alex pressed the towel harder around the stump to stop the oozing and keep the swelling down, and then glanced up at my mother again. "I'm really sorry about this, ma'am."

"Please, don't apologize." They exchanged a long look, my mother's eyes tearing up. "I'm the one who's sorry…" she looked away. "Let me get started on breakfast." She rounded the table and turned her back to us.

I let out a long breath. The last thing Alex needed was my mother's pity. He had enough guilt already. The look on his face told me he was thinking the same thing. I sat on the edge of the picnic bench and faced him, keeping my expression cool. "You could have told me you were in pain. We could have stopped and taken breaks or something."

"You can't help but take advantage of an opportunity to give me a hard time, can you?" He all but scowled at me.

Brig grinned, his blue eyes shifting between us. "All righty, then. I'll get the first aid kit." He headed for the Rover mumbling, "I knew it…"

"Let me take a look," I said. I raised a stern brow in hopes that the assertive approach would gain Alex's cooperation while simultaneously hiding my nerves.

He huffed back. "Don't make a big deal out of it, okay. It looks worse than it feels." Reluctantly, he removed the towel.

I had prepared myself for the worst so it didn't look that bad. I'd seen his leg enough times, it no longer shocked me to find the smile-like scar a few inches below his knee instead of a calf and a foot. I examined the leg without touching it. I knew Alex didn't like anyone touching his stump. There were four blisters, rubbed raw and still oozing clear liquid mixed with a pink tinge of blood. Alex dabbed at the sites with the wet towel. Sweat beaded along my forehead. At eight in the morning, the sun was hot, the air humid. Today promised to be a blazing inferno. I had to find a way to keep the skin dry and padded. I forced a smile. "No worries. I know just what to do."

Brig returned and laid out the first aid supplies on the picnic table. "You should have everything you need there. If not, there's a store about ten minutes down the road."

I looked through the kit. I could make do with what there was. The physical therapist had explained how to treat pressure sores and I remembered pretty much everything she'd said. I'd also spent a lot of time surfing the internet. You can find out how to do anything on You Tube. "Brig, can you get me a rolled up blanket and another clean towel?" I asked.

He grinned down at me proudly. "I knew I could count on you to take charge." He flashed a knowing look at Alex whose lip curved into a quick smile that appeared to be involuntary. He let it slip away as Brig disappeared toward the tent.

"You sure you got this? I can take care of it myself."

"I got it. No problem. It'll be easier this way." I said reassuringly, arranging and taking note of my supplies.

Once Brig returned, I had Alex lift his leg and rolled up the blanket under his knee to bolster it so he wouldn't have to hold it up. I picked up the anti-septic spray and opened a few gauze pads. "This might sting a little." I sprayed each wound and dabbed them dry, keeping my attention focused on my task. Alex stayed perfectly still, watching me carefully. I glanced up and gave him a quick confident smile. "Here, cut four circles, two inches around, and cut donut holes in the center." I found a small pair of scissors and handed him a quarter inch thick neoprene elbow brace Brig had bought two winters ago when he'd had a tendonitis from too much shoveling. Alex busied himself cutting up the brace as instructed, catching on to my plan immediately.

When I was sure the skin was dry, I opened a foil packet marked antibiotic cream and squeezed a drop onto a sterile cotton swab. Covering each blister with a smear of cream, I plastered a 2x2 square over each of the raw spots, and placed the circles of neoprene on top—essentially creating a spongy buffer so the sores wouldn't make contact with the prosthesis. I wrapped a thin layer of rolled gauze around the stump to hold them in place, making sure I used a figure eight pattern to avoid cutting off circulation. I taped the end and lifted my hands, "Voila!"

"Thanks." Alex rolled the stockinet over the end and nodded approval.

"That should do it," I said, satisfied I'd done a good job and that we had solved the problem for the time being. "We'll want to check on it every few hours and make sure the sores aren't breaking down worse. You should leave the prosthesis off as much as possible for the next day or so. Limit your walking and if it hurts, take some of these and get off it." I handed him a bottle of Advil.

Alex took it and eyed me. "Thanks, Doc."

We exchanged brief grins, my face growing hot under his scrutiny, my mind spinning with thoughts of the future and all of the questions it brought with it.

Brig broke the silence. "Nice job, Sunshine." He patted my shoulder and helped me pack up the first aid supplies. "That's pretty impressive. You have a knack for this kind of thing. You'll be a great doctor."

"We'll see," I said. Alex studied my reaction, probably asking himself the same questions I was asking myself. What would we do if I went away to med school for eight years?

Leave it to Brig to stay focused on what was important. "I'll set the table," he said. He tossed some paper plates and plastic forks at us with some napkins.

"Breakfast is ready." Mom dragged a large pan over to the table, while Brig filled plastic cups with orange juice. Mom grinned, always happiest while feeding people. "You two must be starved. You missed dinner last night." She scooped large heaps of scrambled eggs with cheese, mushrooms, onions and bacon all mixed together onto our plates and sat down across from Alex who had faced forward, his leg now hidden beneath the red checkered table cloth.

From a distance we must have looked like any other family, no apparent pieces missing. A pang of emptiness, leftover grief, welled inside me. Looks could be so deceiving. I stared into my plate.

"You made slop," I said, addressing my mother with a frown, tears welling in my eyes.

Alex elbowed me. "It was nice of your mom to make us breakfast. Don't be such a pain."

"I'm not!" My mother and I smiled at one another, both of us wiping tears off our cheeks. Alex frowned, confused.

"Jordan and Lee used to ask me to make them slop for breakfast on Sunday mornings. It was kind of a ritual when they were little." She smiled sadly. "I haven't made it in a long time."

I took a bite. The creamy, salty, eggy flavor burst in my mouth, the bacon just a tad chewy. Perfect. "Thanks, Mom." I said through a half full mouth, happy memories brought to light in an instant. A warm glow rose to the surface of my heart.

Alex's expression changed too. I saw the sadness there, but I also sensed something inside him healing, breaking free--as if his own memories were knitting together to form a patch over the holes in his soul. I wondered if he felt the same warm glow I did. I could only imagine how he must feel, sharing this moment with us--being part of our family again. He took a bite and chewed slowly, a small grin coming across his face. "Excellent. Thanks, Mrs. D."

A sudden rush of emotion filled my chest. Mom returned the smile, the first real one I'd seen in months. "I'm glad you're here, Alex," she said.

The awkward moment passed, the mood changed to one of happy banter between Brig and Mom. Alex and I chowed down breakfast like we hadn't eaten in a week. After I'd finished my second helping and Alex was polishing off his third, the conversation fell to Brig.

"See, now isn't this nice? I knew it would be good for all of us to get away and spend a little time together before Jordan starts back to school." He wiped his mouth and slugged down his coffee.

Mom eyed him suspiciously. "You mean this wasn't some random coincidence, you and Alex ending up here at the campground?"

"Random and coincidence are not in Brig's vocabulary, Mom." I smiled broadly at my grandfather. "You should know by now Gramps always has a plan, and he doesn't do anything without a good reason." I ignored Brig's expected glare, got up, and poured everyone more coffee, and then settled onto the bench next to Alex who was popping a grape into his mouth from the bowl Mom pushed in front of him.

Brig spoke in his own defense. "I had no ulterior motive than wanting to spend some quality time with family and getting in some fishing." He hid behind his mug, taking a slow sip.

Mom and I exchanged a knowing glance. He was definitely up to something. Mom interjected. "Well, I came here to spend some girl time with my daughter, so you boys can do all the fishing you want, but Jordan and I are going to lie on the beach down by the lake today, and catch some sun. How does that sound, Sweetie?"

"Um—okay." Thank God I'd brought a book to read. Hours of lying in the hot sun talking to Mom might as well be a CIA interrogation. Alex shot me a sympathetic look.

"Maybe after Brig and I finish catching our dinner, you and I can go to a movie—if it's okay with you Mrs. D."

After a prolonged silence, she flashed a lame smile. "I suppose so. I guess Brig and I can entertain ourselves by playing cards or something."

I knew she wasn't as happy about Alex being here as she'd said. She was probably even less happy about us spending time alone together. I wasn't sure if it was because it made her think about Levi and made her sad, or if there was more to it. As far as guys I could be going on a date with, Alex Cooper was far from a bad idea in my book. Then it dawned on me. OMG! He'd asked me on a date. Hadn't he? Our first actual date!

Chapter 24

"I'm just worried about you. I don't want to see you get hurt." Mom handed me two ends of the blanket and we laid it out on the white sandy beach, the expansive lake only ten feet away. The commotion of kids swimming and splashing, parents chit-chattering, and the lifeguard whistle signaling a rebel camper to stay inside the buoys, filled the air around us.

I tossed my copy of *Abraham Lincoln: Vampire Hunter* onto the blanket and kicked off my flip-flops. "Alex is not trying to hurt me. He's just confused. He needs a little time, that's all. Stop worrying."

"It's my job to worry about you." She settled herself onto the blanket and slathered sunblock up and down her arms and legs, handing me the tube of SPF 45.

I sighed and took it, half-heartedly repeating her procedure, knowing she would point it out if I missed a spot. "I hate to keep reminding you, but I'll be eighteen in two months." I watched Alex and Brig rowing a small boat away from shore, rods and tackle boxes packed for a day of bass fishing.

"So you keep saying, but you'll be living at home for at least another year and Alex...he has no direction right now. He doesn't seem to be able to focus on his future. Not that I blame him," she added hastily. "He has a lot of adjusting to do. I just think it would be best for you if you didn't get overly involved and attached." She lay back on the blanket, her one piece bathing suit covering the C-section scar she'd gotten while giving birth to me. I guess it meant I owed her something.

I stared out at the lake. Brig and Alex grew smaller on the sun-splashed water, sparkles dancing around them as if they were merely a mirage in the distance. "Coop just wants to take it slow," I said remembering his words from last night and wondering how slow he meant to go. The knot that formed in my gut told me it would be way slower than I wanted. There was a niggling doubt as to whether we wanted the same thing or not in the long run—which for me, was for us to be together. I wasn't so sure Alex really wanted us to be together. He kept pushing me away, but then he would kiss me and say something sweet and my heart would fall all over itself.

"As much as I hate it that you might be all the way out in California next year, maybe an acceptance to Stanford would be best for your future. It would give you both some time and distance to figure out what you want." Behind her sunglasses with her face lifted to the rays, Mom could have been talking to the five year old making mud pies three feet from our blanket.

"Or I could get accepted at Harvard and be only two hours away." The thought of coming home on weekends and seeing Alex gave my heart a little jump. Weekends wouldn't be enough for me, though. I could tell already. Something about him drew me like a wave to the shore, an inevitability that left me helpless to change the force of it. Maybe it was our shared childhood, a thousand memories of laughing together and the interwoven experiences of growing up side by side. Or maybe it was Levi that strung us together and I didn't want to let go of the tenuous thread for fear of losing the connection to my brother that still lived in my heart. All I knew was that whatever switch had been turned on after that one moment back in ninth grade, I couldn't turn it off, and now all I could see was that without Alex, it felt like I had no future at all.

"Are you even listening to me, Jordan?"

"What?" I'd been daydreaming and she was still talking about colleges.

"Your father insisted you were born for greatness. He dreamed of you going to an Ivy League college, becoming a doctor and doing amazing things with your life. He would be so proud of you, honey." Her glasses were tipped down her nose and she had her full attention on me, her eyes misty.

Talking about my father's great expectations for me made me uncomfortable. It seemed like a lot of pressure coming from someone I barely remembered. "I know we've been planning on Medical School since I was ten, but…I'm just not sure it's exactly right for me now." I knew I was risking a scene with this topic, but I wanted her know about my doubt.

She sat bolt upright. "Of course you are going to medical school. It's what you've wanted forever." She followed my gaze out across the lake, her eyes narrowing. "This is exactly why I don't want you so involved with Alex. I fell for your father my senior year of high school and before I knew what happened, I was an eighteen year-old wife and mother with no opportunity to go to college and get a degree."

"I'm not you, Mom. Besides, you could have gone back to school at any time. You still could. Why don't you stop using Lee and me as an excuse for not living your dreams…"

"That's not fair, Jordan." We faced off on the blanket, our voices rising and drawing attention from a few parents who corralled their children to another spot on the beach away from the two angry ladies. Mom's face had the hurt look of a puppy who'd been scolded. "I sacrificed a career so I could be home to raise you and your brother and support your father in his law practice. I always thought there would be time for me to go back to school once you were older, but then…your father died and I had to work to support the family. I just don't want you to make the same mistakes I made."

"Thanks for pointing out what a mistake I was," I said, more harshness in my tone than I'd meant to use.

"I didn't mean it that way," she huffed, clearly exasperated with me. "I meant that you have the opportunity to have an amazing future—a career. You should see the world and do all of the things you want to do before you settle down with a guy." Her tone softened. "I understand how you feel about Alex, but you have to know…he will never be able…people who have been through wars never get over what they've seen. It changes them, and Alex has had an especially difficult experience. It's going to take him a long time to recover fully. Your going away to college will be the best thing for both of you."

A lump formed in my throat and tears burned behind my eyes. "Do you regret marrying Dad?

"Of course not," she said softly. "I wouldn't trade one minute of my life with your father—or with you and your brother. I loved my family—I love you." We exchanged a long look until she gazed out at the lake. "But I hadn't planned on being a widow at twenty-four. Life would have been…different if I had gone to school…gotten a degree." She lay back down on the blanket, slid the sunglasses over her eyes, and turned her head away, signaling the end of our conversation. "I don't want you to find yourself alone with no options if your relationship with Alex doesn't work out."

I wanted her to be wrong, but what she said struck a chord. Maybe Alex had been trying to tell me about his doubts about his future and I hadn't wanted to hear it. From here on the beach, he and Brig looked like tiny action figures, poised in a row boat, fishing rods in hand. I had to believe that Alex would find his way—that he would see a clear path to his future and that his plans would include me. After all he had been through, I suddenly wondered if I wasn't the person holding him back.

Chapter 25

As promised we ate fish for dinner. Three trout, two large-mouth bass and an old boot made up the day's catch. The old boot was thrown back along with a dozen sun-fish, and both Brig and Alex were a deep shade of red-brown like native warriors. I was a lobster. Red stripes marked all of the areas I'd missed with the sun block and I'd forgotten my face entirely. My cheeks and forehead felt hot and tight, my nose stiff.

"Are you sure you still want to go to the movies?" Alex looked on with sympathy as Mom spread after sun moisture lotion loaded with some kind of numbing agent to cool the burn on my skin.

"Absolutely. I'm fine." I rubbed the lotion on my nose and cheeks, and winced at the sting that felt like I was rubbing my face with sandpaper.

Alex looked doubtful. "We can do it another time."

"No. This is great. I'm fine." I pushed Mom away, giving her the eye that said, *Stop, before I have to resort to a snotty remark.* I was going to the movies if I had to bring a cooler full of ice to stick my face in. The only movie theatre in a thirty mile radius was an old Drive-In that had been open for decades. I couldn't wait to be alone in the CU-V with Alex. Then we'd see if he was interested in me.

Another shudder ran through me. Great, now I had the chills to alternate with the flames of hell. The thought of Alex touching me suddenly didn't sound so appealing. Crap.

"Take it with you," Mom said, a mild look of satisfaction on her face. She handed me the lotion.

Contrary to fearing the movie would be a disaster, I had an amazing time. Throughout the eighties double feature horror fest, I screamed repeatedly and nearly jumped into Alex's lap a couple of times. We ate popcorn and laughed out loud at the stupid hair styles and funky clothes. We lay out on the hood of the CU-V on top of a blanket, leaned against the windshield, and looked up at the stars.

Alex seemed lighter, more the old Alex I remembered. During intermission, we stayed there in the quiet and talked about the stars over Iraq, Alex describing in detail the beauty of a pitch black sky with no light pollution anywhere to be found in the desert. He lowered his voice and inched his hand across the blanket until he found mine, our fingers exploring until they settled as if knowing right where they should be. Our hands found a natural comfort in each other, my pinky resting between his ring and middle fingers, a perfect fit— an undeniable connection.

I listened to the sound of Alex's soft voice, my heart thumping a brisk pace as the warmth of his shoulder touching mine seeped into my skin, setting my sunburn on fire. I didn't care. I could have stayed there forever, the stars bright in the night sky, our heads nearly touching. The sky spun above me until the creepy music at the start of the next horror flick shattered the quiet of the moment. I closed my eyes through half of the movie and laughed hysterically through the other half, Alex making stupid faces trying to distract me from the freaky saw guy.

When the movie was over, Alex apologized. "I'm really sorry about the dumb movies. Next time, you pick."

Next time? "That sounds great." I tucked my hair behind my ear and glanced at him. "But honestly, Coop, tonight was perfect."

We stared for a minute, the two of us smiling and not saying anything. I thought he might kiss me. I could tell he was thinking about it the way he stared at my mouth. Instead, he leaned over and kissed my forehead, the heat of his lips setting fire to my face, reminding me of the sleepless night ahead.

"Let's get you back to the campsite." He leaned back to his side of the vehicle and I jumped as a car beeped at me to slip into line. I shifted into gear, the spell broken.

I followed the traffic as it snailed its way toward the exit, sad the night was over, but truly feeling wiped out from overexposure to the sun. I yawned, realizing I hadn't checked on his bandages. "How's the leg feeling?"

"It's doing okay. But I can't wait to take this thing off."

I knew he was referring to his prosthesis and I realized I hadn't even thought about it all night. The more time I spent with Alex, the less I noticed his leg. I wasn't sure if I should feel good about it being an afterthought, but I realized then, that I didn't think of Alex as a handicapped person or anything less than whole.

We pulled into the campsite at midnight, the lantern still lit in Brig's tent. He was probably up reading the latest James Patterson novel, anticipating the ending by page number one hundred.

Alex walked me to the bath house and waited while I took a cool shower, the relief instantaneous on my skin. "Everything okay in there?" he called in response to my moans and groans.

I let the shower run as long as my quarters lasted. "All good!"

I threw on a loose tee-shirt and some soft sweats, and slipped on my flip-flops, my hair wet and soaking the back of my shirt. When I ran a brush across my head, I squealed. "Ahhh! Ouch!" I left my hair to dry in a tangle and collected my belongings. My face was pink as a Victoria's Secret shopping bag.

"You sure you're okay?" Alex took the bag off my shoulder and handed me the flashlight.

"Yeah, other than my wounded pride." I felt foolish not having taken better care of myself. "I look like a beet."

He laughed. "The prettiest beet I've ever laid eyes on."

"Thanks," I said lamely. I felt less than pretty at the moment and yet his words rendered me speechless. My face grew hotter against the cool night air, quiet crowding in around us. Neither of us spoke again. The campers were all in bed and nothing sounded but the occasional rustling of a tent or a small animal in the woods.

We walked shoulder to shoulder in the dark, sharing the one ray of light from the flashlight on the ground, and guided by a few glowing fires still burning in the night. Everything else was as black as tar around us. Trying to be as quiet as possible became a game between us as we walked stealthily along the gravel path.

Before long, we stood between the two tent cities, the flashlight casting a long beam across the pine needles. The light was out in the tent and the campground was completely still as if we were the only two people on Earth.

"I guess we should go to bed now," I whispered. I blushed in the darkness realizing what I'd said.

"Yeah, I guess…"

He closed the distance between us and leaned silently towards me, his shadow causing my heart to leap and my breath to stop before reaching my lungs. I didn't move a muscle—and then, his lips hovered over mine, our foreheads meeting. His hands cupped my head, gentle and barely touching me. I lifted my lips to his and inhaled the scent of him--buttered popcorn and the scent of woods and soap. Our lips pressed together and our tongues found each other, a few gentle passes and then both of us searching more urgently, an in and out rhythm that felt natural and primal. I fought to stay still, not to let my hands grab onto him and kiss him like he'd never been kissed before—like I'd never kissed anyone before, but I knew this was what we both needed--the chance to know each other in this new way; to explore slowly, and enjoy every step. After a perfect—if all too short—ten seconds, he broke free and inhaled deeply, as if to take the taste and scent of me with him.

"Good-night, Jordie." He let me go and took one military step back like he'd just followed an invisible order to stand down. I laughed and shook my head.

"Good-night, Coop." I crawled into my tent and handed him the flashlight. "Hey Coop. That was the best first date ever."

A broad grin captured his face in the shadows and his shoulders relaxed. "Me, too.

Chapter 26

The next morning came way too soon. I slept better than I thought I would and when I came out of the tent, Brig's Rover was gone. It was barely after sunrise. Thoughts of my brother crowded my mind. A tiny part of me felt guilty about what happened with Alex last night. Somehow, Alex and I being together—being so happy—seemed like a betrayal.

I checked the fire pit in our campsite—cold. I stepped quietly over to the guys' luxury suite and found the coals hot enough that I could stir them and start a flame. I warmed my hands and added a few logs (neatly stacked and covered under a tarp).

"You're up early." Mom appeared behind me.

"I couldn't sleep anymore," I said.

She busied herself setting up coffee to brew, an old hand at starting the Coleman stove. "Did you have a good time last night?"

Crap. I didn't want to start with her. "Yeah, it was nice." I pulled the sleeves of my hoodie down over my hands, shrugging in order to warm up.

Mom eyed me through the screen room. "Just nice?"

"What do you want me to say, Mom? It wasn't like we rented a motel room or anything. We went and watched horror flicks, we ate popcorn, drank soda…the usual, you know. We're friends."

"Oh? Is that all?" she pressed.

"Grrrr…Mom. Stop. Please. I cannot talk to you about Alex. I don't know what's going on, okay? Leave it alone. I have to go pee."

My hasty departure ended the conversation. I couldn't tell her what was going on because I didn't know myself. It was obvious Alex was attracted to me. We'd definitely gone beyond being just friends. But I couldn't help wonder what would come next? Alex seemed like he was coming around, but he still hadn't really talked about how he felt or what his plan for the future was. For that matter, I wasn't sure of my own plans. Why did life have to be so uncertain? So complicated? So confusing?

Since I wasn't up for another day in the sun, we decided to spend the day at the Crystal Mall, school shopping. Shopping, I could wrap my head around. It would be good to have the only complication for my brain be what shoes went with which jeans. I wasn't usually a fashionista, but I liked the idea of starting fresh at the beginning of a school year. I'd been saving a little of my paycheck every week and Mom would pitch in the other half. A new look, a nice outfit or two, knew shoes…maybe a new bag. Not to mention all those wicked cool writing utensils, customizable notebooks and colored sticky pads.

I was a hopeless nerd when it came to school. Yeah, I fit in with small groups of friends in almost every clique, but being the best in my class had been a goal since childhood, so I spent a lot more time in books than I did with a social life. When I wasn't studying, I was at the gym, running, or working. I had a moment to consider what I was running towards, or maybe…what I was running away from.

One more year of high school and then what, med school? Leave home and move far away…from Mom, Alex, Brig, the antique shop, Vic? Everyone and everything that mattered to me was here. It seemed Alex wasn't the only one who needed time to work out a plan.

Mom and I came back from shopping—a successful trip in my opinion. We'd found a ton of bargains and stretched our dollars so I ended up with four new outfits, two pairs of shoes (buy-one-get-one-half-off), and enough school supplies to provide for an entire sixth grade class. I loved taking notes in pencil. I liked knowing I could erase a mistake and start fresh.

It was well after lunch time when we pulled in and parked. The first thing I noticed was that the

Rover was back. Then my eyes honed in on a shirtless and sweaty Alex, chopping firewood like he was stocking up for the winter. He took another swing with the axe, his shoulders bulged, his chest flexed, and I drooled. He had on well-worn jeans that sat low on his hips, the arched bones and contoured muscles of his abdomen drawing my attention like I was looking at a picture of the Greek statue of *David* I'd seen in Art History class. The top of his blue boxers rested below his belly button, a fine line of dark hair running downward...well...sighhh.

Brig was already at work setting up a tripod over the fire pit to cook lobster and steamers for dinner. He saved me from an embarrassing demonstration of teenage lust. "Help me out here, will ya' Sunshine?"

I dragged my eyes away from Alex who had stopped long enough to notice me gawking and send me a satisfied nod. He continued chopping, making the splitting of logs appear effortless--not to mention incredibly sexy.

Focus on something else. Breathe.
Distraction—you need a distraction.

"What can I do for you, Gramp?" Brig hated it when I called him that.

He furrowed his brows, "Don't get on my bad side, Young Lady." He handed me the lobster pot. "Go fill it up about a third of the way with water." Then he turned to watch Alex attacking another log. "That should be enough there, Son. Why don't you head down to the showers before supper? You worked hard enough for today." It seemed Brig was conspiring for us to have some time alone.

"Oorah, Sir," Alex planted the axe deep into an uncut log and pulled a grubby tee-shirt over his head. He grabbed a change of clothes, a small shaving bag, and a towel. We headed down the gravel road towards the showers, Alex even more quiet than usual, his sweaty scent driving me mad in a good way I couldn't define.

"Do you want me to help you re-bandage your leg after your shower?"

"No, I got it." He was quiet for a moment. "You don't have to take care of me, Jordie. I'm really doing all right." He flashed the brilliant smile that made my heart jump.

"So you and Brig are spending a lot of time together. Is he helping you? You do seem better the last few days...I mean...sorry to butt in...it's not really my business..."

"No...it's okay. Yeah, the General has been very helpful," he said with certainty, giving my hope button a solid push.

"I'm glad." I waited for him to add to his declaration, but he changed the subject.

"I had a really good time last night," he said.

He glanced my way and I gave in to the grin that crept over my lips. "Me, too."

His color had returned to a deep shade of golden brown and the afternoon light gleamed across his sun-bleached hair through the trees. Now was as good a time as any to talk about what our plans might be. I had less than a week to get back to my school life and I still needed to decide about college. I had no idea where Alex fit into those plans or how I fit into his. As of yet, I didn't think he had a plan and that made me more nervous than anything else. "Have you thought about what you'll do next?" I asked.

Alex face lost all expression. He walked solidly beside me, his prosthesis not even noticeable. After a minute, he took a breath and exhaled slowly. "I'm starting to figure it out, but I need more time. I need you to be patient."

I stopped him and pulled him around to face me. A couple of kids on bikes passed, forcing me to step closer to Alex. I wanted to tell him I wasn't going anywhere, but I couldn't say so for sure with all of the decisions I had coming up about college. Instead, I said what he most needed to hear, and what I knew to be true. "Whatever you decide, I'll always be here for you."

He smiled a little sadly. "I hope so, Jordie. But I don't want you to change your plans and I don't expect you to wait around for me." He reached out and touched my cheek, his expression slipping into the intense look of hunger I'd often seen on his face when he thought I didn't notice. Right now, that look was all for me. "I can't make you any promises. I think we should wait and see how the next few months play out." He kissed my forehead, turned away, and disappeared into the showers before I could respond.

He was the most infuriating person I'd ever met. He couldn't answer a question straight if I tied him to a chair and interrogated him with torture—a thought that seemed appealing on many levels.

I fumed and took deep breaths while he was in the shower. I filled the lobster pot with water and set it on a boulder, pacing back and forth trying to decipher what he'd said. Of course I would always be here for him. Was he questioning my loyalty after all we'd been through together? Wait around for him to what? And what did he have to figure out? Could he be any more cryptic?

And what promise did he think I wanted? I wasn't looking to get married at eighteen, but I wanted to have an idea if his feelings for me went beyond a friendship with benefits before I thought about leaving for eight years of college. Trying to get him to tell me how he felt was obviously a losing battle. Now he was asking me to do the one thing I was worst at—be patient.

Chapter 27

All of my anger and annoyance fell to my feet, making my knees wobble when he walked out of the showers. Clean shaven and smelling wonderful from six feet away, he flashed me a one sided dimple and tossed his wet towel over his shoulder. Shoulders exposed by a white tank top which looked amazing against his tan, and a pair of fatigues that hung loose and comfortable over his muscular legs. His hair was combed down and off to the side, still short, but not military cut and spiky like it had been.

He really was too handsome for his own good. Or mine, I thought with a desire so intense it startled me and I couldn't think beyond it. More than the physical need that swirled around my insides like a cyclone, I knew I loved him with every part of my heart. He was my best friend--the sweetest, smartest, coolest guy I'd ever known—and when I was with him, I felt full of life--like I wasn't quite complete or whole without him. A surge of determination welled up inside me. If I had to be patient to make him mine, I could do it.

He wrapped an arm around my shoulder and pulled me close, scattering my thoughts. "Thanks for waiting for me." He kissed the side of my head and then released me and grabbed the pot of water. "Let's get back. Brig's probably ready to get those steamers going."

I let it go and didn't pursue my earlier line of questioning. *Patience, huh? How did one go about exercising patience?* We talked about mundane topics like fishing and how lucky we were to have had such good weather. I mulled over our progress toward a relationship, concluding I didn't know anymore where it was going than I had a week ago. My jaw clenched with tension. Being patient was going to be even harder than I thought.

When we reached the site, Brig and my mother had an intense conversation going on--one that stopped when we approached. Mom was tearing lettuce for a salad as if it had insulted her somehow and she was taking her revenge. Brig had the fire banked into red hot coals, ready for cooking.

"It's about time," he said, taking the pot from Alex and exchanging an imperceptible nod. He hung the pot on the tripod and put the lid on.

The rest of the evening went exceptionally well once the mood shifted to food and a mean game of set-back. The lobster and steamers were amazing, dripping in butter and served with baked potatoes and salad. Somehow food always tasted better cooked on an open flame. It also had the power to overcome any angst or stubborn attitude, of which there were several in the group, not the least of which was mine. Brig and I played against Mom and Alex, beating the pants off of them five games to two. Finally, we settled down around the fire, slumped into folding chairs, marshmallows on sticks at Mom's insistence.

"It's not camping without Smores." She handed me a square of graham cracker and a piece of dark chocolate to melt with my marshmallow which burst into flame at that very moment.

I quickly blew it out, leaving one half charred. I slipped it between the crackers. "Perfect."

Alex chuckled, his marshmallow a foot above the fire and toasting a light brown on all sides. Everyone laughed as I bit into the gooey treat, making a mess all over my cheeks and fingers, and shamelessly licking it off.

"Levi would have loved this--all of us camping together again." Mom smiled sadly, her eyes glistening in the firelight.

It got quiet for a while after that. I guess I wasn't the only one who noticed his absence. It felt like we were all missing some integral piece of ourselves, and I empathized with Alex on a new level. Levi was part of me that remained like a phantom limb--there but not.

I lay awake for a long time listening to the night sounds, Mom's deep slow breathing, and the rain drops pattering on the tent overhead. My heart ached. I missed reading Levi's letters. Mom was right, he would have loved the idea of us all camping—one last chance to lounge around or find an adventure before school started. I wondered again about what he would have thought of me and Alex being together. It would have been so weird for all of us. I found myself glad in some small way that I wouldn't have to face him about it. A tear ran down into my ear and I rolled over, tucking the sleeping bag under my chin.

Knowing what I knew now about what had happened to him, I didn't know if we could have talked about his abuse and gotten past it—if I would have seen him the same way anymore. I'd always accepted him, protected him when I could, and loved him no matter what. I knew there was a deep part of him that was broken—that needed protection and unconditional love and something I couldn't even give him—peace. I drifted into sleep remembering the summer he nearly succeeded in taking his life, reliving that day for the thousandth time.

He was fifteen and I was twelve. It was the end of summer and he had spent it fishing, hiking, and working in the wood shop with Brig, his every waking hour monitored by our grandfather. Until

the day Brig got called away on some emergency
trip and Levi found the opportunity he'd been
waiting for. Brig's presence had kept him from
cutting himself for weeks, all summer in fact.

I had been with Vic all day at the gym, my
prescribed punishment for smoking pot with Levi at
the beginning of the summer--my first and only
attempt at living on the wild side. I got home
around three and Mom was still at work. I looked
everywhere for Levi and finally checked the barn.
The door to the work shop was locked but I knew
where the key was. My heart exploded in my chest
as I unlocked the door, already afraid of what I
would find inside. There he was, the razor knife
clutched in his hand.

I walked into the work room just as he ran
the blade over his wrist, cutting deeper than he ever
had before. It was like he'd stored up the urge for
months and when he finally gave in, he wanted it to
count. I never understood his fascination with pain
or his lust to see himself bleed, but finding him that
day, I knew that he was screaming for help.

He needed stitches, but refused to go to the
hospital. So we stopped the bleeding and I patched
him up. He made me promise not to tell. Maybe if
I'd told someone…everything would have been
different. No one ever knew. He wore long sleeves
or wrist bands to cover the evidence. I could see
how awful he felt that I had found him that way. He

never said he was sorry, but I saw it in his eyes.
Regret and sorrow deeper than any kid should have
to feel. He trusted me to keep his secret. Maybe
that's why it was so important for me to know the
truth about what happened to him in Iraq. There'd
been enough secrets between us and I felt partly
responsible since I hadn't told my mother what was
really going on.

Mom had been distraught, depressed,
anxious—seeing a counselor and taking medication.
I couldn't tell her. Brig was busy—disappearing on
trips for weeks at a time. Levi recovered, acted as if
it had never happened, and promised it would never
happen again. He continued to walk the edge,
getting into trouble and dragging Alex down with
him. He wanted to protect me, so he pushed me
away, telling me he was too old to hang around with
his little sister anymore. As much as it hurt to be
excluded, I left him and Alex alone. Part of me
wanted to help him, but something between us had
shifted.

After that day, I learned to insulate myself. I
ran, I learned to fight, and I dove into my books,
determined to be smarter, stronger, faster…because
if I stopped…I could be just like him. I could
become someone who tried to use the pain in my
flesh to wash away the scars inside, too wounded to
live, too broken to recover from the death of my
father, the loss of my mother's stability. But I

wasn't like Levi. I hadn't suffered the way he did. I had a chance to live a normal, happy life. For whatever reason, the universe had skipped over me in a gene pool that included depression. I wouldn't waste that gift feeling guilty for surviving. Maybe it was time to let go of the past, of keeping secrets and of holding on to a moment I couldn't change.

When I woke in the morning, wet from our leaky tent, I sucked in the cool, clean morning air, and felt grateful to be alive. I followed the scent of coffee.

"Did you sleep well, Sunshine?" Brig had the fire crackling and coffee percolating on the camp stove.

"Not really." I zipped my hoodie and headed for the outhouse nearby. The clean bathrooms were too far of a walk this early. When I got back, Brig had a coffee cup full for me and was stacking pancakes on a griddle. He had the lobster pot washed out and filled with hot water.

"Wash up here if you like." He handed me a bar of soap and a wash cloth. "I figured I'd let Alex sleep in this morning since it's our last day. He's a hard worker. I like that about him." He eyed me over his mug. "He's also mighty fond of my granddaughter."

"Did he say that?" My head popped up as I scrubbed my face and hands.

Brig grinned. "He didn't have to. I know what's going on between you two. It doesn't take a poet to know romantic feelings when I see them."

My cheeks heated. "I wish he would just tell me how he feels." I dried my face and hands with a towel, and sat down at the picnic table. I sipped hot, creamy coffee, letting the first jolt of caffeine ease my nerves and wake me up at the same time.

"He's got to straighten out this mess on his own, first. And you have to let him—even if it means letting him go, Jordan." He gave me the sympathetic but stern look that made me sit up and pay attention.

"But we're so close right now," I said. "I like seeing him every day. I like spending time with him…I like where our time together is going…" I closed my mouth, feeling like I had said too much.

Brig shook his head, "Ahhh—young love. So foolish, so demanding…so untamed." His brow lifted and his ears turned pink as he flipped the pancakes. "I understand where you're coming from, Sunshine. I really do. But you are setting yourself up for disappointment if you are depending on Alex to make you happy or think that somehow you can fix whatever is wrong with him. The simple truth is that you can't depend on anyone else for your happiness without placing the burden of it on their shoulders. Trust me; a sure fire way for any relationship to fail is to expect someone to change for you. It's too much pressure. You have to let people be who they are."

I thought about what he said for a long time, pouring a ton of syrup on the short stack of pancakes he put in front of me, and cutting them into small squares. Was that what I was doing? Making Alex responsible for my happiness? Trying to fix him so he would be exactly who I thought he should be? That didn't sound much like love to me. My understanding of love was that you accepted people for who they were and loved them unconditionally. The way I'd loved my dad…and Levi. Had I been putting conditions on my feelings for Alex? Was I trying to change him?

"I hear you, Brig. You're probably right as usual." I rolled my eyes at him over my fork full of pancake. "I know how much you love to hear me say that." I stuffed my mouth and chewed, the sweet sponginess exploding in my mouth.

"I'm glad to hear it," he said, his bushy eyebrows arching. "Let Alex make the choices he needs to make for himself, and you do the same. Have a little faith. Things will end up just the way they're meant to without you trying to steer the ship."

"You sound like Vic. You know what she would say right about now?" I asked.

Brig's eyes crinkling at the corners at the mention of her name. "No, what's that?"

"She'd say, '*Kid, don't push the river.*' I never knew what she meant by that, but I think I get it now."

Chapter 28

Alex and Brig broke camp in half the time it took me and Mom to pack up our one tent, tarp and our few amenities, including a small gas grill and the kitchen box Dad had made for their honeymoon when they first started camping together. It had his initials--JD--carved in the side. I slid the large wooden container further back into the CU-V to make room for the beach chairs, wondering how my life would be different if he was still here. I shrugged off the familiar pang of sadness that came with those 'what if' musings.

"Did you pack the Frisbee?" I asked.

Mom slid the last sandwich into a baggie and popped it into the cooler. "I put it in the bag with the chips."

"And that makes sense...why?" I rummaged through the bags.

"I knew you would want it at the beach and I figured we'd be packing sandwiches, and what are sandwiches without chips?" She smiled, satisfied her logic was sound.

"Okay...right."

Brig interrupted. "You ladies all packed up?" He eyed the back of the CU-V, shaking his head. "You didn't leave room for the cooler."

I lifted the beach chairs and stuffed them up on top of the tent. "There. Now there's room." I grinned at him, knowing how much order meant to him. Just as he knew how much I needed to be able to be me. I think he understood—sometimes better than Mom.

He gave a low "Hmmph." Then he flashed a crinkle of his eye. "Okay, Sunshine. Do it your way. Alex and I are gonna' meet you at the beach. We're itchin' to drop our lines off the breach way. You never know when you might catch an eel or two."

"Just don't ask me to clean and cook them," Mom said.

"Wouldn't dream of it." Brig smirked at me and turned his back, waving over his shoulder. "See ya' there."

Mom and I finally got the CU-V loaded, stuffed to the gills with sleeping bags and blankets tucked in between the stove, the lantern, and the kitchen box so nothing would break. I said good-bye to the campsite and felt a little sad. This would probably be the last summer campout I would share with my family. I couldn't imagine fitting in family outings once I started college and found a real job. Having time for anything else didn't seem likely.

My world was about to change. I could feel it in the way animals know when there is going to be an earthquake or a thunder storm. My thoughts went to Alex. How could a relationship with him ever possibly work? I pushed the thought aside, remembering his lips on mine, the smell of his skin and hair. I closed my eyes, resting my cheek on the cool glass of the window.

As we neared the beach, the smell of salt air hit me, faint at first--that subtle moisture in the air, the tang of salt and sea life on my tongue. I rolled down my window the rest of the way and soaked in the sun, my arm hanging out and my face stretched to the sky--the perfect beach day, eighty degrees and sunny.

We parked the car and I went to unload the beach chairs. When I lifted the back hatch, out tumbled the cooler. Crap! My face flushed with anger, aggravation, annoyance, and then humility. "Brig was right again."

Mom looked around my shoulder. "Isn't he always?"

The old mom would have freaked about the mess. Instead, we both started laughing and picked up the sandwiches, drinks and scattered ice cubes. We spent the next twenty minutes re-arranging the back of the truck.

I wondered what was different about her. She seemed calmer, more at peace the last few days. Maybe it was just being on vacation, but she was starting to let go--of me, of Levi, of the past. I suppose being forced to start over at forty was

bound to affect a person. If all you've known is
being a mother and a provider, how do you figure
out who you are now? I felt sad for my mom.
Would she be one of those empty nest mothers who
wandered the house crying? Or would she use this
time to go back to school and get a degree and start
living her own life. I found myself desperately
hoping for the second to be true. We loaded our
arms with chairs, blanket, umbrella and cooler,
struggling with everything between the two of us.

When we finally crested the dunes, the view
was beautiful accept for the million or so other
people on the beach. Waves rolled into the shore,
one after the other, splashing up over sand castles
and dragging pebbles out into the sea. Mom and I
claimed a spot and laid out our blanket and chairs.
We dosed up on sun block and Mom put up the
umbrella. Grateful for the shade, I pulled my
baseball cap over my forehead, protecting my face
which was just beginning to feel better. I sat looking
out over the waves, Mom settling into a reclining
position on the beach chair.

The sky was filled with patches of cottony
white clouds with bright blue spaces between them.
The misty shape of Block Island sat on the horizon,
reminding me of a giant turtle shell. Huge ships
appeared as small as toys and barely moved in the
distance. As much as I hated to admit it, the view
would only be made better by Alex sitting beside

me. Common sense told me that no matter what, I needed to be okay without him. But my hormones made my skin itch with the desire to be close to him. Before I had the chance to wonder how he and Brig would find us on the beach, the two of them were winding their way through the hordes of people sprawled across the sand.

"Well, I'll be..." Brig tipped his fishing hat back and rubbed his jaw, setting his tackle box and fishing pole onto the sand.

"I told you I could find them." Alex had the latest techno-gadget in his hand, showing Brig the screen. "It's simply a matter of triangulating the GPS signal from her phone." He eyed me smugly.

"That's a pretty handy talent you have there, Son." Brig examined the device, enthralled by the possibilities no doubt.

I glared at both of them. "I suppose my civil liberties are of no concern to either of you?"

The smile left Alex's face and he handed the unit to Brig. "Sorry. I just wanted to try it out." Then he flashed a broad grin. "I *did* find you, though."

"And you're going to show me later how to deactivate the GPS in my cell phone, right?"

After lunch, we spent the rest of the afternoon walking on the beach, playing Frisbee, and swimming in the ocean. This late in the season, the water was tolerable, though still nippy. I hardly noticed. I felt so happy and relaxed riding the waves with Alex, laughing together as we dove under the curling tunnels before they could crash on us.

When we were out beyond the breakwater, the two of us bobbed up and down like corks on the swells that rolled toward shore. After my near drowning, I felt a little apprehensive going into deep water, but within minutes my attention was drawn completely to Alex. There appeared to be no limits to his adaptability with his leg. He stood shoulder deep a few feet away, his hair wet and spiky, his face lit with a confidence and peace I hadn't seen since before he'd left for Iraq. It warmed my heart. Back on the beach, both Brig and Mom were sprawled out and napping under the umbrella. I took the opportunity to close in on Alex.

He didn't resist when I wrapped my arms around his neck. Instead, he pulled me close, his hands at my waist sending a swirl of warmth to my belly. "It's been a great vacation, Coop."

His face changed to a look of concern. "It definitely has…but I have to tell you something and you aren't going to like it," he said.

"What do you mean?" My heart rate doubled and I pulled back, my arms unwilling to let go completely. I rested them on his shoulders, the feel of muscles bunching under my hands making it hard to focus on what he'd said.

"I have to go away for a while."

I snapped to full attention. "For how long?"

"I don't know."

"Where are you…?

He pressed his lips to mine, holding me tight and stealing my question. After a long, breathless kiss, he broke away, the two of us hopping together to jump the next wave.

"I can't give you any details, Jordie. I know you want more, but…I can't." His face had a stubborn, hard expression, and I figured it was useless to argue.

Instead, I narrowed my eyes, Brig's words coming back to me about Alex not being responsible for my happiness and him needing to find his own way. "I get it," I said, "you have to go and you can't tell me where or why." My teeth began to chatter, fear creeping into my chest. "Just promise me you'll come back," I said softly, a gull overhead casting a shadow as it flew past.

He rested his forehead on mine and we closed our eyes, the water holding us buoyant as we pushed off the bottom at the same time. His face was so close I felt the warmth of his breath, his hard body encompassing mine. The safety I had always felt with him seemed tenuous, like something huge was about to come along and pull us apart.

Alex held me in a tight embrace. I wrapped my legs around his waist, and there I clung, the heat between us infused with an intensity that made me want to both laugh and cry. He jumped one more wave and when he set down he said, "I can only promise to do my best." His eyes filled with a certainty that sent all my fears scattering. "I have every reason in the world to want to come back...right here in my arms." He kissed me sweet and slow, the ebbing waves holding us together and lifting our bodies with the rhythm of the sea, my heart in danger of being swept away on the tide.

Chapter 29

Later, after we'd unloaded the car, had dinner, and said goodnight with a quick kiss on the front porch (Mom gawking out the window every two minutes), I sat in my room, contemplating my first day at school tomorrow and wondering when Alex planned to leave. I hoped it wouldn't be for a few days. We'd just started to really connect—like we were finally on the same page and going in the same direction with our relationship. It was killing me not to know exactly where he was going or when he would be back. No amount of pestering could drag any more info out of him and Alex reminded me that we shouldn't spend our limited time together arguing. Since kissing seemed preferable to butting my head against a brick wall, I let it go.

I had a feeling the trip had something to do with Brig, but I knew if that was the case, Brig would be no more help in finding out what was going on than Alex was. I'd said my goodnights to both of them at the door, leaving them with a scowl of frustration on my face to show my disapproval. Not that it seemed to matter to either of them. They had their heads together mumbling something about

Brig showing him the workshop before he left. I headed to my room, exhausted from the trip.

I pulled the box from under my bed, anxious to read Levi's letter again before I could sleep. I had missed my ritual and I needed the reminder that he approved of me and Alex, a notion I planned to share with Alex the next time I saw him.

Voices drifted up to my window from the direction of the barn. I turned out my light and looked out into the darkness, noticing a dark SUV parked in the antique shop's parking lot, and four people standing in a small circle by the barn doors. The motion sensor light over the parking lot illuminated the shadows, though I couldn't see any faces. I could clearly make out Brigs robust frame and Alex's long legged, if slightly lopsided stance. The other two men I couldn't identify from here, but I thought they were some of Brig's poker buddies. In hushed voices I couldn't decipher, they seemed to conclude their business quickly and disperse. I watched Alex shake Brig's hand and climb into the vehicle with the two men. My stomach twisted and I suddenly had a very bad feeling. He wouldn't leave without saying good-by, would he? And why would he leave with Brig's friends?

I waited at the top of the stairs.

"He's gone, isn't he?" I asked, startling Brig as he locked the door behind him and shut off the porch light.

He looked up at me, an expression that flashed from sympathetic to stern much too quickly. "You should get some sleep. You've got a big day tomorrow."

"Is what he's doing dangerous?"

Brig stared for a long minute. "He'll be okay. You have to let go, Jordan. Focus on yourself--school, track, the gym. Keep yourself busy and he'll be back in no time." He smiled, but it didn't quite reach his eyes and I saw the worry underneath. "He's in God's hands—there's nothing you can do but keep him in your prayers."

An hour later, when the house was silent, I lay down on my bed and studied the pages of Levi's letter, reading in the dark about how he knew Alex and I would be together someday. I just hoped Alex and God could be so sure.

I woke for school the next morning and headed for the shower. I stared in the mirror. Crap. My forehead and nose were peeling. So here I was starting my first day of senior year, having to face all of my friends and classmates, who would no doubt identify me as the girl whose brother died in Iraq, and I had to do it looking like a lizard. Alex was off to parts unknown and I had no idea if and when he might return. The thought sent another heaving lurch to my stomach.

I did the best I could with makeup and a new pair of jeans, a flowery top and a pair of open healed Merrell's that fit like slippers. At least my feet would be happy. I pulled my layers of wild curls back into a clip, and ran a lip gloss over my mouth. Not too bad. I looked nice, but not like I was trying too hard. I heard Mom downstairs fixing herself breakfast. It seemed strange to be back to the same old routine. Only nothing felt like it did the last time I left for school, back in June. It hit me how much had changed in just a few short months.

We exchanged pleasantries and Mom handed me ten dollars for a week's worth of lunches. "Good luck, Sweetheart. Have a nice day." She grabbed her lunch bag and headed out the door, a travel mug of coffee in her hand. Brig was conspicuously absent from the breakfast table as I downed a bowl of cereal and re-checked my notebooks and folders in my bag. "Here goes nothing," I said to the silent kitchen as I closed the door behind me.

It was a ten minute drive to Somerville High from Thompson Lake. I met Penny and Sami in the parking lot, hugged them, and asked about Katie.

The two girls gave each other knowing glances and Sami, her hair streaked a God-awful blue, smirked. "Her parents transferred her to a private school. I think they were trying to get her away from us." I could understand their concerns about their very prim and proper Catholic daughter hanging with the likes of Sami. She liked to party and had a reputation as somewhat of a flirt, but she was harmless once you got to know her. But Penny was as straight an arrow as they came. Figure skater, straight-A student, and devoted to taking care of her mother through a terminal case of cancer. I had the feeling Penny's perfect façade was crashing in around her. She looked worn out.

"How's your mom, Penny?"

We walked into the building, the crowd filing in through the double front doors, shoulder to shoulder and chattering like a flock of geese, everyone nodding and smiling to catch up after a not-long-enough summer break.

Penny smiled sadly, her perky dark hair and brown eyes unable to cover the pain she was going through. She'd lost weight over the summer and the dark circles under her eyes made her look too old and tired for a high school student. "She doesn't have much longer," she said.

"I'm sorry, Pen. That's awful." I couldn't think of anything to say that would make her feel any better. I of all people knew that sometimes words were not enough. "If you need anything, let me know." I gave her a hug and was relieved to see her smile, though I was immediately shocked by the feel of her bones beneath her baggy tee shirt.

She and Sami peeled off and went to their respective homerooms and I walked into mine, the whole class turning to stare. The noise dissipated and the silence caused a wave of heat to rush to my face. I could see that my day wasn't likely to improve. It was only 7:40 in the morning on my first day of school and I was already dreading the rest of the semester.

I only needed five credits to graduate, but I had a full course load, heavily weighted toward the sciences since I'd been planning on medical school since I was seven. Calculus and Physics would be my big challenges this semester. Latin, English and PE would be the cake-walks. I had my work cut out for me for the next few months. The spring semester would definitely be less grueling academically, though track season would be super busy with all the meets. I couldn't imagine what I would do if Alex was gone longer than that. Would he be away for a week, a month, three months, six months? My stomach curdled at the thought, an irrational anger rising in my chest. Maybe Brig was right. If I stayed busy, the time would go by faster.

The days dragged on, my thoughts repeatedly wandering to my concerns about Alex and when I might see him again. He hadn't given me the chance to argue about him leaving and had avoided a painful good-bye scene by simply disappearing, a dirty tactic that had part of me fuming. But in all honesty, I don't think I could have handled good-bye. Maybe it was better this way. Caught up in daydreams of our summer together, the times we'd kissed and how those kisses had gone from him trying to shut me up, to teaching me a lesson, and then to mutual and undeniable passion. I ached with hunger for him to touch me and kiss me again and I could think of little else.

My day-dreaming presented a problem on several levels. My teachers sounded like Charlie Brown teachers, their voices droning on and making little sense. I tried to concentrate, but heard only half of what was said, until the final bell of the day released me from my chair, my legs burning to escape. I ran the track after school, my time slower than at the end of last season. Probably due to my lack of practice and focus these last months, when I'd only run intermittently while trying to help Alex with his rehab. My life had taken a back seat to him and I realized how much of myself I'd given up without knowing it.

After track practice, I went home to work the antique shop, Brig offering no more information and avoiding any discussion of Alex's where-a-bouts. Then I ate dinner and exchanged small talk with Mom about school. I spent evenings on homework, desperately trying to keep my mind on the task at hand. I couldn't let this obsession with Alex derail my life completely. School had to be a priority and I had some decisions to make about my own future. Whether that future included Alex or not, I needed to do what was best for me.

Days turned into weeks, each one a lesson in mental focus and what Brig might call intestinal fortitude. I stayed tough, studied hard, kept up with grades, work, doing girl stuff with my friends on the weekends, all the time pretending my heart wasn't aching and my mind wasn't consumed with confused emotions I fought to control. And each day, as fall blew in with blustery intensity, my heart grew a little colder.

On a late October afternoon while I was at the gym, I ran into Vic, who was just coming out of the women's self-defense class. I hadn't seen much of her the last month or two with school and everything. She wrapped her arms around me and tugged me in for a sweaty hug. "Hey Kid, I haven't seen you in ages. Come with me and we'll get caught up."

Before I knew it I was slamming the heavy bag and spilling my guts. "Not even a good-bye!" Six weeks and three days and I obviously wasn't over it. I kicked the bag harder and followed up with several tight punches to its mid-section. "Not one freakin' word since he left!"

"Sounds like a man on a mission to me. Don't take it personally."

I grabbed the bag in mid-swing and glared at her, breathing heavily. "Not personal? He kissed me senseless and then left me. That's as personal as it gets," I snapped, and slammed the bag again before turning away and heading for the water cooler.

Vic followed and studied me in silence until I sat down and looked at her. "Are you calm now?" She didn't wait for me to respond. "Good. Now listen to me. Alex did not leave you. Wherever he went and for whatever reason, you have to believe he was doing what was right for him. If you really care about him the way you say you do, you will respect that and trust him."

"But he didn't even say…"

"Stop whining. Accept that he had his reasons, and move on. You take care of you and let him take care of himself. If you two are meant to happen, you will. Be patient. It's a virtue, I hear." Seeing my expression of dejection at the hopelessness of that pursuit, her face softened and she smiled. "You've heard it all before, huh? Here's the bottom line. You can either live with the secrets or you can't. Are you willing to let him live his life and go on living yours, even if it means time apart? If you want to be with Alex, you need to decide if you can handle being on your own."

I rested my chin on my hands, elbows on my knees. "Of course I can, but..." I leaned against the wall and let out a long breath. "All I know is that being without him sucks." My brain was tired of thinking about it. A new thought came to mind. "Is that why you and Brig aren't together?"

Her face went instantly blank. "I don't know what you're talking about?"

"Right. So was it the secrets, or the traveling, or that he wouldn't let you in on the action?"

Her blank face shifted to an amused sneer. "You think you're so smart." After a thoughtful moment, she said, "Brig and I are complicated, but let's just say we both agreed our friendship was too important to ruin by getting overly involved." She turned to walk away, clearly done with her half of the conversation. "You might want to consider the same option for you and Alex."

"Yeah, like being alone has made you so happy," I called after her, not willing to let the last word be hers.

Chapter 30

My eighteenth birthday fell on the second Saturday of November with a cold rain pouring down in buckets. I wanted to be excited and happy about such a major milestone, but my mood was as foul as the weather. Penny had buried her mom two weeks ago. We hadn't talked much, but she seemed lighter in some ways, maybe relieved that her mom was no longer suffering. For me, the funeral brought back memories of Levi in another flood of unexpected grief that made my chest ache. I missed my brother more with each passing day.

I'd stopped thinking I would hear from Alex again until he was good and ready to show his face or pick up a phone. Not even a text—the jerk. I'd also given up reading Levi's letter at night, having tucked it into the bottom of the box and sworn it off limits. But I knew myself well enough to know that as hurt and angry as I was with Alex, I was more worried than anything else. What if something had happened to him? I couldn't bear the thought of losing him, too.

Brig had gone on a trip a week ago and left us a note that he had closed up the antique shop for the season and was headed to Miami to visit his sister for a few weeks. At least *he'd* left a note.

Mom was trying to get me into the party mood, but I refused her repeated attempts to woo me into having a bash for my birthday. It didn't feel right celebrating when my closest friends were so solemn. Besides, with my worries about Alex, I wanted nothing to do with a party. In fact I was thrilled to be home alone in my room.

I sent Mom off to the store for a couple of pints of Ben & Jerry's (Cherry Garcia for her, Chunky Monkey for me.) We planned a night of ice cream and horror flicks. With Halloween just passed, there was a monster movie marathon on TV. Mom and I loved the really old movies with Lon Chaney and Boris Karloff. Something about the black and white picture and gothic clothes made them creepy in a cool way.

I'd just finished returning e-mails from study partners when a clap of thunder drew my attention to the rain outside. I looked out my window to see a flash of lightening followed by a second rolling burst of thunder. My heart jumped. Had I seen someone out by the barn? Maybe my eyes were playing tricks since I was here alone on a stormy night in a big creepy old farm house thinking about vampires and monsters. I turned off my light and went to the window, staring out into the darkness made thicker by the downpour. Another lightning bolt illuminated the night and I caught sight of a shadowy figure slipping through the barn door. My pulse rate doubled. Crap!

Who could it be? I immediately thought about calling the police. Maybe it was a burglar, but that made no sense on a night like this. I scanned the grounds and saw the parking lot was empty. Unless he meant to walk off with his loot, he appeared to be out of luck. Whoever it was had either come on foot or was dropped off. My brain spun with the possibilities. Maybe it was one of Brig's buddies looking for him. Or it could be some stranger whose car broke down and they were just looking for a place to get out of the rain. Whoever it was, I didn't want the whole police force coming to my rescue for something silly. If it was any of the local kids just out having fun, I could handle them, and I didn't want to be known for ratting them out.

I tugged on my boots and grabbed a sweater since I only had on a tank top with my sweats. I slipped down stairs silently, my heart thundering against my ribs. I found the big black military issue flashlight from the closet and threw on my rain coat. If I had to defend myself, the flashlight was as good a weapon as any. I snuck out the kitchen door and made my way quickly around the house and across the yard, determined not to be spotted. The flashlight remained in my hand but I kept it turned off. I knew the property well enough to make my way in the dark. The rain soaked my sweats and made them cling to my legs as I ran through wet grass and puddles to reach the barn.

When I eased the door open a crack I stood still, listening. I heard someone rummaging through papers on Brig's desk in the office he'd built at the back of the building. The door was half open but only a pen light glow illuminated the room. I needed to get closer to see who it was. I took a slow breath and held it, stepping as quietly as I could through the antique furnishings. White sheets covered them in ghostly shapes. I slithered between aisles trying not to bump into anything and give myself away. My head knocked a lantern hanging on a hook. I caught it and silenced the creek immediately, holding my breath again. A chill ran up my arms. I shivered and froze in place when the pen light went out.

A long moment of silent darkness passed before the man started walking out of the office. Now was my only chance to catch him off guard. As he moved past me in the shadows I jumped him from behind, my height, weight, and velocity enough to tackle him to the ground. I swung as he rolled onto his back and my fist connected with his jaw.

"OW!" We both yelled--me from my aching hand and him from the rattling of his teeth.

Before I could wind up and hit him again his voice stopped me in mid-motion. "Jordie, it's me, Coop!"

"Coop? Oh, my god. You scared me half to death! What are you doing here?" I had him pinned on his back, my knees securing his biceps to the floor.

"If you let me up, I'll tell you," he said, clearly annoyed I'd gotten the upper hand. I couldn't believe he was here. I suddenly realized that he really *was* here, and my heart gave a shout of happiness. I moved my knees but stayed straddled on top of him, resisting the urge to smother him with kisses or punch him again.

"I'd like an explanation," I said. "Here is as good a place as any for you to answer me." I smiled down at him in the darkness, enjoying my seat on top of him. Awareness ran through me like a freight train and all I wanted to do was kiss him and feel him hold me. But I sat there waiting, my breath coming in shallow gulps.

His hands came to my waist and he pulled me down on top of him. Our noses only inches apart, he held me still, and studied my face. A flash of lightning lit the small space between us. "I'll tell you everything you want to know. But first, I want to wish you a happy birthday." His fingers brushed across my lips and then his hand went to the back of my head and his lips were pressed against mine in a warm and wonderful kiss that melted my anger and made me forget all of my questions.

We burst into the kitchen, both of us laughing and dripping wet. I tossed Alex a clean dish towel and hung my rain coat in the mud room, kicking off my boots and trying to get a grip on my emotions. Part of me was so ecstatic Alex was here, I wanted to squeal. But the other part of me—the part that had been crushed and fuming for the last seven weeks—wanted to give him a swift kick. At the very least, I didn't want him to see how much his absence had affected me.

"Not that I'm not glad to see you, but what were you doing breaking and entering into Brig's private office?" I stood barefoot in soggy sweatpants in the kitchen and peeled off my sweater, self-conscious that I was wearing only a damp and clinging tank top. I watched Alex dry his face and rub the small towel over his wet hair, not taking his eyes off of me for a second.

"He asked me to get some information and fax it to him." Cutting me off before I could ask the next question, he said, "How else would I have access to his office?" My voice caught in my throat as he pulled his wet tee-shirt off over his head. "Have you got a dry shirt I could wear?" I stared at his bare, muscled chest, my mouth going dry.

I found him one of Brig's flannel shirts and turned my back, putting the hot water on to boil for tea. My hands trembled. From the chill of the rain, the taste of his kiss that lingered on my lips, or the sight of him shirtless in my kitchen, I couldn't be sure. Before I could decide, my mother burst through the kitchen door, a sopping grocery bag in her arms.

"It's awful out there…" She stopped when she saw Alex. She stared, eyes wide, darting suspicious glances between us.

I suppose it didn't look good, Alex buttoning the third button of the flannel shirt and looking much like the Brawny paper towel guy standing in our kitchen, me half-dressed and looking like I'd just rolled in the dirt with him, which technically, I had. I said all I could think of to say.

"Mom…look…Alex is home."

Chapter 31

"So I see. Hello, Alex." She set the groceries on the counter and surprised us both when she hugged him. "Welcome back." She sent me a sly smile. "We missed you." Then her face fell. "Jordie, you're a mess. Go get cleaned up and I'll fix us a snack. Then Alex can tell us all about his trip."

Leave it to Mom to cut to the chase and still be polite. Alex nodded and took a seat obediently, his face a calm mask I couldn't decipher. I retreated upstairs, changed into flannel pajama bottoms and a dry tee-shirt and washed up in the bathroom. My hair was a wild mess that would take me fifteen minutes to get a brush through, so I pulled it back in a frizzy bunch, stuffed my feet into warm slippers and dashed back down stairs. Mom was putting the final touches on giant ice cream sundaes and serving tea.

The three of us sat at the kitchen table, my mother and I sitting across from Alex like a tribunal ready to interrogate a witness. Although it was hard to look threatening while eating a spoonful of gooey hot fudge and Chunky Monkey ice cream with heaps of whipped cream. Alex took a few hungry mouthfuls before starting.

"First, let me say that I'm sorry I haven't been in touch." He paused, setting his spoon down and straightening his shoulders like he was preparing for me to blow up. "An opportunity came up and I had to go. There wasn't time to say good-bye."

"We understand," Mom said, and she laid her hand over mine, stifling the sarcastic remark that sprang to the tip of my tongue. Her fingers felt warm and reassuring and I figured for now, we would do it her way.

Alex seemed to appreciate her efforts, because all of his attention went to my mother. His face lost the mask and the Alex I knew appeared, strong, confident, and sincere. "I've been in Iraq, Ma'am. Something Jordie said made me start to remember bits and pieces of what happened and I had to go back and see if I could put it all together. I thought if I could explain exactly what happened on our last mission, it might help you put Lee to rest." He glanced my way, a flash of a sad smile curving his lips.

He went on. "I interviewed several locals who I'd made contact with while I was stationed there. It took some digging, but I eventually found a boy who admitted he was in the house that night. When the shooting started, he hid and watched from behind a couch, but he confirmed your suspicions, Jordie."

A pounding started in my ears. "What do you mean?"

"I told you that the men in the house were human traffickers. Apparently, they had taken the boy from his aunt and uncle who thought he would be shipped to America to live with an adopted family who could give him a better life. They were paid a sum of money and told to keep quiet."

"That's awful," Mom said. "Is the boy still living with his aunt and uncle? It must be terrible for him to believe his family would sell him off to total strangers."

"He knows they were doing what they thought was best. Things are difficult for the people in Iraq. Many of them live in horrible conditions, they have no work, and the infrastructure will take decades to recover. Their only hope is that America and the UN will continue their efforts to stabilize the country."

"So what did you find out from the boy?" I asked, my patience dwindling as my Sunday melted in the dish. I'd suddenly lost my appetite.

Alex hesitated. "Lee must have saw or heard them through the window. The boy said he was being beaten for trying to run away. Lee rushed in and hit the man with the butt of his gun, and didn't see the other man come into the room with an AK47. He fired and Lee dropped." Alex paused, his expression filled with emotion. "I still don't remember all of the details myself, but I guess that's when I came in and took out the second guy." His face paled and he swallowed hard before continuing. "He must have got off a couple rounds because I went down. If I had come in a few seconds sooner…"

Mom reached across the table. "You were trying to be a good soldier *and* a good friend. Sometimes it's hard to be both at the same time. No one blames you, Alex." She had tears in her eyes, but I could tell she was being sincere. "Thank you for telling us. I'm very proud of you. I'm proud of both of you boys." By now, I had tears in my eyes and Alex looked extremely uncomfortable facing two crying females with his own emotions clearly so close to the surface.

"Well, thank you, Ma'am." He took his hand from beneath hers and leaned back. His shoulders slumped as he said in a low, tight, voice, "I was team leader on the mission. However it went down, I'm still responsible and I have to live with the choices I made." Alex looked to me solemnly. "I'm going to do my best to put the past behind me and move forward." He cleared his throat and shifted his gaze to my mother. "The boy also gave me these." Alex produced a few folded sheets of paper and handed them to my mother. "Before the other Marines in our unit busted in the back, the boy took those out of Levi's flack-jacket and escaped out the door. He thought there might be money in the envelope, but it was just letters."

Mom opened the pages slowly and her hand went to her mouth, stifling a gasp. She read through the top letter and handed it to me, her hand shaking and her shoulders heaving, overcome with emotion. She caught her breath. "…if you'll excuse me…I can't…" she left the papers scattered on the table and hurried upstairs.

I stared at Levi's left handed scrawl, the words blurry through my tears.

Dear Mom,

If you're reading this, I didn't make it home. I'm sorry for everything I put you thru, but I want you to know that I died doing something important with my life. I only regret that I didn't get a chance to show you what I could be. I know I disappointed and hurt you sometimes. I'm sorry about that.

If I could go back, I would have done things differently, fought harder to be strong. I just didn't know how. I spent so much energy trying to escape the pain I was in, that I lost myself to it. I can't explain it really, but I want you to know it wasn't your fault. You did the best you could with me. Now you need to forgive yourself and be happy.

You know Dad will take good care of me. I love you…always.

Lee

I gathered the other pages and laid the second letter on top. I wiped my tears away and looked up at Alex, whose face was serious, his eyes glassy as he watched me. I took a breath and read…

Jordie,

Take care of the Rabbit for me. I know it's a piece of junk, but me and Coop had some good times in it. Maybe when you get a new car, Coop can keep the Rabbit alive for me.

I'm sorry I'm not there to see you turn eighteen, to graduate, go to college, get married and have kids. I would have been a good uncle. You have an awesome future ahead of you. If I can from where I'm going, I'll be watching over you for all of it. I bet you'll kick ass in college and try for straight A's, but don't forget to enjoy the ride. Life's too short to waste time and too long not to have any fun.

You have been the very best part of my life and I can't thank you enough for looking out for me growing up. I wish I'd been a better brother. You deserve all the best life has to offer. You and Coop take care of each other. I love you guys,

Lee

There was a third letter for Brig, but I didn't read it. I folded the papers together and laid them on the table, tears streaming down my cheeks. Alex laid a large warm hand on my arm. "I think he would want us to let him go."

I dropped my face into my hands, his words sinking in, finally. "I fought so hard to discover the reason for my brother's death, and now that I know, it doesn't really change anything, does it? Lee is still gone, and we have to go on without him."

Alex stood and pulled me to my feet, wrapping his arms around me in a firm embrace. He whispered against my ear. "Trust me, knowing the truth changes everything. If you hadn't believed in me and pushed me so hard to keep looking for answers, I never would have faced what happened, and I...don't know where I would be, Jordie." He stepped back and brushed the tears off my cheek, his eyes intent on mine. "You saved me in ways I can't begin to explain, and even though Lee is gone, he will always be with us." A tear drop slid down Alex's face, his voice hoarse with emotion. "Please, believe me when I say, the truth makes a difference."

Chapter 32

Mom and I rode to church the next morning in relative silence, each lost in our own reflections about the letters Levi had written. Up until now, I hadn't realized I'd felt so cheated out of an opportunity to say good-bye. I read the letter over and over, each time feeling a renewed sense of loss and a precarious sense of closure at the same time.

Alex's words played in my mind, comforting me with the knowledge that in some small way, I had helped him heal. It also helped me to know that my brother had died for some noble cause, and that my keeping his secret might have somehow led to his redemption. I would never know for sure. All I knew was that there was no going back, and no point in regrets. I sat through church feeling a little more connected to the faith I'd been raised with, a sudden unexplainable peace washing over me at the thought of Levi looking down on us, our father at his side.

At least now, my mother could let go of any residual worries that Levi's soul wasn't at rest. She seemed lighter and more at ease than I'd seen her in a long time at church. Her face had lost the pleading look she got when she stared up at Jesus. The lines at the corners of her eyes turned up now and she sang the hymns with a little more enthusiasm.

On the ride home, I decided it was time to tell her about another letter--three to be exact. I had received them one a t a time a few weeks after school started and I had avoided telling her. I didn't feel bad about it. I'd needed the time to make up my mind.

"Mom, I got accepted to Stanford...and Columbia...and Harvard..."

"You what?" she squealed. The CU-V swerved and she regained control. "When? Why didn't you tell..."

"Calm down and listen to me. And watch the road, for God's sake!" She swerved again, this time avoiding running over a squirrel. "I didn't tell you because I'm not going."

"What do you mean, you aren't going?" Her brows furrowed, her grip on the steering wheel visibly tightening.

"I've thought a lot about why I wanted to go to medical school and I came to the conclusion that it was your dream...you and Dad's...not mine. I've given it a lot of thought and I want to stay in Connecticut and go to the University here. They have a great Physical Therapy program and I can specialize in rehabilitation of Veterans. I really think I can make a difference. After helping Alex through his rehab, I realized how much I've learned from Vic all these years. The martial arts, the yoga, the aquatic therapy, the meditation--it's what I want to do..."

Mom was silent for a few minutes, her face softening. "I've only ever wanted you to be happy, Jordan. Your father would be very proud of you. I know I am...if you're sure it's what you want..."

A lump formed in my throat, "So you won't mind if I live at home--at least the first year? Maybe next year I'll live in a dorm on campus out in Storrs, but right now...I'm not ready to move away." I looked out the window, embarrassed to admit my fear of leaving home. Maybe I just needed a little more time to get used to the idea of how much had changed in my life in such a short time.

Mom glanced my way, her eyes bright. "I would love to have you stay close to home, Sweetie." Then her smile dimmed. "I just hope you aren't doing this because of Alex."

I thought about it for a minute and answered honestly. "I made this decision while Alex was away and I had no idea when or *if* he would come back. I realize I can't plan my life around what he is or isn't going to do. This is what I want. I'm sure of it."

We pulled into the driveway and my heart did a quick backflip. Alex was sitting on the porch. He stood to meet me, a happy grin making his handsome face glow. My belly quivered. I really had missed his smile. He greeted me with a hug and Mom shuffled past us, giving me a knowing raise of her brow.

"I'll see you two later. Jordan, don't forget to invite Alex and his mom to Thanksgiving dinner." She disappeared into the house leaving us staring after her.

"I guess your mom is cool with everything, huh?" he asked.

"She's coming around," I said, hugging him back and looking beyond him to the house. A feeling of relief and gratitude filled my heart. I stepped out of his embrace, the chill in the air making me sorry I hadn't worn a heavier jacket. The day was sunny, but the dampness from last night's storm hung in the air, making it feel raw.

"Let's walk. I need to talk to you," he said. He took my hand and our fingers wove together in that perfect fitting way, my pinky resting between his ring and middle finger. His warmth gave me a shiver against the cool air. "Here, take my jacket." He handed me his jean jacket, not appearing any worse for having just a hoodie on to keep him warm.

I slipped the jacket over my sweater and inhaled the scent of him, a smile curving my lips. He took my hand again and pulled me along. My heart did a fluttery dance, filling me with warmth and excitement. We walked past the remnants of

Brig's garden, a huge plot that had grown every year until it consumed most of the yard. A few last tomatoes hung on the vines and a row of cabbages and brussell sprouts remained left to harvest along with the root vegetables that would stay in and winter over.

"What did you want to talk about?" I asked, a nervous knot forming in my stomach. I hated the thought of his leaving again.

"I wanted to apologize again for starters. I know how mad you must have been that I left without saying good-bye." He glanced down at me, studying my reaction.

"I'll admit I was hurt. And yes, I was mad for a while, but I was more worried than anything. You could have called, texted, e-mailed...something."

"I really couldn't...but I thought about you every day. I can't explain..." he let out a frustrated breath. "It's protocol on a mission to have no contact with family or friends. They don't want us to be distracted..."

"Who are they?" I asked, my heart rate jumping a notch.

He smirked, "I can't tell you that, either. Let's just say, my trip to Iraq was like a job interview."

"Do you have to go back again—to Iraq?" I felt my eyes widen. "Did you re-enlist?" My palm had started sweating in his and I let go, turning to face him, fear and anger colliding.

"No. My discharge was official and final. The Marine's has no place for a soldier who can't function at full capacity in battle." He looked down at his leg, knocking on the hard composite material with his knuckles. "Thanks to my new hardware, I'm not fit for full duty." He wrapped an arm around my shoulder and pulled me along to keep me warm and keep us moving forward. "I'm not really sure what's going to happen next. That's why I wanted to talk to you."

Alex led me to a sunny spot on the side of the barn, the building blocking the breeze and the suns' rays reflecting warmly off the red wood. We climbed up on the fence rail and sat side by side like we had on a summer's day long ago. It dawned on me this was the first place we had kissed. I didn't think he'd brought me here by accident. "The thing is Jordie...I can't make any promises right now. My future is pretty uncertain and I don't want you changing your plans and waiting around for me."

I didn't know what to say. I felt hurt and angry and sad all at the same time. I wanted to tell him I'd already decided to stay home for college, but I didn't want him to feel pressured into making a decision about his future based on what my plans were. It wouldn't be any more fair, than me changing for him. "Coop...what do you want me to say? You have to do what's right for you. If taking the job and traveling around is what you want, then do it. I won't stop you." My heart ached even as I said the words.

"You really mean that?" He asked, surprised.

I took a slow breath in and out, taking in the changing leaves, yellow and orange like the trees were on fire. "I want you to be happy, Coop. I would never stand in your way."

"And I would never stand in yours." He hopped down from the fence and stood in front of me, his hands coming to my waist. He pulled me close and I laid my head on his shoulder, his mouth resting close to my ear. "You're amazing, you know that?" He kissed my temple, sending my thoughts spinning. "You're smart, strong, funny..." he lifted my chin to meet his gaze, "...and beautiful." My cheeks grew warm as I looked into those green eyes filled with intensity.

"Will you at least promise to never leave again without saying good-bye?" My throat burned and I fought tears that pushed to the surface.

He tucked a stray curl back from my face and stared down at my mouth, like he wanted to kiss me and distract me from the question. I kept my gaze locked on his eyes, drawing his attention back up. "I can only promise you, I'll try."

"So, will you be here for Thanksgiving?" I pressed.

"I wouldn't miss it." He grinned at me, his eyes full of mischief. "And if you'll let me, I'd like to take you to the prom."

"Seriously? You would do that?" I hadn't even thought about the prom, but I really did want to go. "That would be great. I didn't think you would want to." I bit my lower lip to hide my excitement. "What made you ask?"

"I thought if I waited too long, someone else might ask you. As much as I hoped you would say no if they did, you are too pretty to go without a date, and I don't want you to miss out. So I'm all yours." He chuckled, "Besides, I can't wait to see Principal Griffin's face when he sees me again."

We both laughed--a comfortable sound I could so get used to. But part of me was still afraid. Afraid I would lose him--afraid that what we had would be lost to time apart and the uncertainty of the future. I fell into his eyes, my expression no doubt revealing my insecurity. Then he closed in for a kiss and I let him, my heart bursting with emotions too many to name. If I could freeze the moment, I would have, because all I ever wanted was right there in his arms—in his kiss—and I knew there were no guarantees in life. All we had was now, and I could never be sure that he would ever really be mine.

Chapter 33

"Good morning, Sunshine!"

I woke to the light flickering on and off and Brig standing in the doorway, like he hadn't been gone for two weeks without a word. I stuffed my head under the pillow. "Welcome back!" I called in a muffled voice.

"Aren't you going to get up and help us with Thanksgiving dinner? Your Mom could use some help with the pies."

I lifted the pillow and looked at the clock. "God, Brig, its six-thirty in the morning—on a day off from school." I rolled onto my back, groaned, and stretched.

"All right, suit yourself." He shut out the light and turned in the doorway, "I guess you don't want to hear about where I've been." He shut the door.

I bolted upright, "Hey…wait a minute."

The door opened and he poked his head in. "See you down stairs at 0700."

Twenty minutes later, having peed, dressed, brushed my teeth, and pulled my hair into a massive nest of tangles; I stood in the kitchen doorway and stared out into the driveway.

"It's mine?" I asked, not believing my eyes. "Are you serious?" A red Honda Civic sat next to Mom's CU-V.

"Well, it's not new. My sister Felicia was getting a new car so I bought this one from her." He wrapped an arm around my shoulder and kissed my head. "Consider it an early graduation present."

I threw my arms around his neck. "Oh man, it's awesome Brig." I kissed his cheek and dashed out the door. He followed behind and tossed me the keys. I sat in the front seat and checked out the console, the hands free blue tooth, the stereo with five disk CD changer, and a great set of speakers. The interior was tan leather with bucket seats. Great Aunt Felicia rode in style. I'd never met her, but often wondered who would name their children Alistair and Felicia? I really knew nothing about Brig's family and by extension, my father's--the man I'd tried to please my whole life and hardly knew. I could see him giving me my first car and being at my graduation, but his face always turned back to Brig's, the only real father I remembered.

I hugged him again, tears spilling over, "Thanks, Brig. You're the best."

"Awww, c'mon. Quit you're crying and come help me with the turkey. You can make the stuffing."

And so I did--after an hour of putting myself together with one of my nicer pair of jeans, a bohemian blousy kind of top, and my black low heeled boots, and spending far too much time straightening my hair. I made stuffing, peeled potatoes and turnips, and cored a thousand apples for Mom's pies. By noon, the house was filled with luscious smells that made my stomach grumble. I was just filling up celery sticks with peanut butter when the doorbell rang.

"I'll get it!" I ran to the door expecting Alex and his mom, but instead, found... "Dr. Stevens?"

My mother came up behind me. "Hello, Roger. Please, come in." She wiped her hands on her apron and blushed.

I opened the door and let the man pass, my jaw a little slack and a, *what the heck is going on,* look toward my mother. She ushered him into the living room. Before I could follow, a knock on the door drew me back. I opened the door to Alex and his mother. "Hi Mrs. Cooper—Alex." I smiled politely and let them in. I was just about to close the door when the sound of another car pulling into the driveway stopped me. Could the day bring any more surprises? A moment later, Vic stepped out of her Jeep Wrangler. She shrugged and gave me a squeeze when she hit the porch, her short blond hair combed neatly back and a curious sparkle in her brown eyes. "Brig invited me." She looked at me quizzically as she passed through the door—as if I knew what was going on.

Introductions had made the rounds and everyone was chatting amiably around the dining table we only used for holidays and special occasions, Brig and I having put two extra sections in to be able to seat seven. Mom did a fantastic job on setting the table with Grandma Josie's old china, the food smelled like heaven, and I was sitting across from Alex, feeling a warm glow I hadn't imagined I could feel without Levi here, celebrating our first holiday without him. His absence was palpable, but more like the hum of a bee and less like the blaring of a horn that once announced our loss on a daily basis.

Brig laid the platter of turkey in the middle of the table to a round of *oohs* and *ahhs*, compliments to the chef making him turn an interesting shade of crimson. He sat at the head of the table, me on his left, Alex on his right. Mrs. Cooper sat on the other side of Alex, and Vic remained guarded at the far end of the table across from Brig, eyeing the turkey like it was some diabolical weapon Brig could use to soften her up. From the look on her face, I'd say it was working. She exchanged a smirk of resignation met by a satisfied twinkle in Brig's eyes.

Mom and Dr. Stevens sat to my left, and I couldn't help but notice the warm vibes she was putting off towards her boss and our family doctor. How had I not known this was going on? Had I

301

been that self-absorbed? I remember Mom telling me his wife died a year or so ago. I felt a single flash of anger over her betrayal to my father and then it was gone. I wanted her to be happy and if Roger Stevens could keep that dopey grin on her face, I was all for it. I'm sure my dad would have agreed.

Brig cleared his throat, quieting all the conversations that went on around the table. "I'd like to say grace and offer up a toast. He bowed his head, and we all followed. "Lord, we thank you for this bountiful feast, for family and friends, for freedom, and for the rising sun of another day. Amen."

We opened our eyes and Brig stood up, a glass of wine in his hand. I raised my glass of ginger ale and waited for the toast, determined to hold back the tears I could already feel coming. Brigs voice rang out strong and clear. "I want to make a toast." He raised his glass. "To those fallen soldiers who have gone before us…and to Levi and Alex, who in death, and in life, embody the principles of duty, honor and code." He turned to Alex, "It's been too long coming Son, but on behalf of a grateful nation and the United States Marines, I'd like to thank you for your service to this country and the sacrifice you've made."

"To Alex." We all chimed in and sipped our drinks, the mood solemn, and all eyes gazing proudly at the guy I was hopelessly and madly in love with. We smiled through tears and clinked our glasses together.

"To Levi," Alex said, downing his glass, his eyes watery.

"To Levi," everyone agreed. Mom wiped her eyes with her napkin. Dr. Stevens laid a hand over hers and she smiled, her cheeks turning a happy shade of pink.

Brig reached into his pocket and slid a box across the table to Alex. "For meritorious conduct in battle...you've earned this, Corporal."

Alex slowly lifted the lid on the box and stared for a long time. "It's a Silver Star," he said softly.

Mrs. Cooper covered her mouth to hold back the emotions her expression couldn't hide. She touched Alex's shoulder. "The General is right, honey. You deserve it."

Alex swallowed hard, stood, and faced Brig, his shoulders assuming the rigid military posture that came as second nature to him. He lifted his hand in a salute, "Thank you, Sir."

Brig saluted him back and shook his hand. "I'm just sorry it took so long for the Marine's to acknowledge your service." He cleared his throat. "Now, let's sit down and eat this bird before it gets cold."

Chapter 34

Brig passed the potatoes to Alex who heaped a considerable pile onto his plate before handing it to his mom. "Everything looks great, Mrs. D," he said.

"Yes, everything smells wonderful," Mrs. Cooper added.

"Thanks for thinking of me, Brig." Vic flashed a quick smile down the table at Brig, whose eyes lit with affection.

"Thanksgiving is a time for family and friends. No one should be alone on the holidays." His ears turned pink and he cleared his throat. "We're glad you all could come." He glanced between Mom and Dr. Stevens sitting on my left, his welcoming expression an acknowledgement I knew Mom appreciated. Brig turned back to Alex, passing a bowl of green bean casserole over and grinning when Alex piled the veggies on top of his potatoes. "I wanted to also welcome young Alex here to *Something Old, Something New Antiques and Fine Furniture.* I'm too busy filling furniture orders these days to run the place all by myself. Alex has agreed to be my new partner."

Alex spoke after swallowing a mouthful of turkey, "Brig is going to teach me to make rocking chairs and dressers." He sucked down half his water, taking in my expression as if waiting for me to object.

Brig glanced across the table at Vic, a conspiratorial look in his eye. "All my traveling is getting old. I think I'm ready to stick closer to home and Alex here has convinced me I need to update my filing system. He's going to get the whole thing set up on the computer for me."

Mom and I looked from Brig to Alex and back. I spoke first. "I've been telling you that for years." I raised a brow to Alex, "How did you convince Brig he needed to jump into the twenty-first century?"

"It wasn't so hard once I showed him the advantages." He shot a quick glance at Brig, who grinned at each of us.

"Oh, stop you two. I'm just being practical. No use resisting change." Brig looked proudly at Alex. "Besides, I could use a man with your skills, and I have every confidence you'll take good care of something I love so very much. You know this antique shop has been around for about a hundred years. It would be nice to have it looked after when I'm gone."

His quick glance toward me was no doubt to make sure Alex knew he wasn't just talking about the antique shop. "And, with Jordan here going off to college next year, I figured I would need somebody to pick up the slack." He eyed me nervously. "I thought maybe you could help train Alex to replace you…" he patted my hand looking a little panicked like he thought my feelings might be hurt. "Not that anyone could ever replace you, Sunshine. You're not mad, are you? I know you and I have been partners, but you're going away and…"

I looked at my mother, "Oh, didn't Mom tell you?" My heart beat fast. Brig had always pushed me towards medical school, just like my mom. I hated the idea of him being disappointed in me. I sucked in a breath. "I'm staying home. I've applied to go to the University of Connecticut."

His face fell and my stomach dropped, the turkey and mashed potatoes coming to a lurching halt in my digestive system. Before he had a chance to say anything I was spouting off about my plan to go into the PT program and how it was a doctorate program and that I wanted to work with vets and…he finally cut me off.

"Jordan!" I stopped, recovering my breath as he continued. "That sounds like a fine idea. I'm happy for you. Besides, I'll feel much better knowing you aren't all the way across the country where I can't keep my eye on you." He glanced at Alex. "Everything will work out just fine."

Alex in the meantime, had been staring at me and taking in my tirade, his eyes boring into me with an intensity I could sense without looking. But when I did look, my heart melted and I felt an overwhelming urge to be closer to him—to touch him. His eyes were soft, like a huge weight had been lifted from his shoulders. I bit my lower lip and reached my foot toward his beneath the table until our feet touched and a small smile curved his mouth.

As soon as dinner was over and the table cleared, I insisted on taking Alex for a ride in my new car. We were excused from dish duty and the 'grown ups' were having coffee when we made our escape and buckled into my cool new wheels. I drove around the lake and headed toward Wolf Den Falls. A walk would do us good, and I felt like we both needed to be close to Levi today.

"I'm stuffed," Alex said, tilting his seat back to a reclining positing and resting his hands over his stomach.

"You ate half the turkey all on your own," I laughed.

"I'm a growing boy, what can I say?" he grinned back, a charming smile that could have easily derailed me from the real reason I wanted to get him alone.

"That is such great news about Brig and you being partners," I said, a topic both of us needed to discuss. We had several issues to talk about that I wasn't sure would go smoothly.

"You aren't upset about Brig making his decision without talking to you first?"

"Of course not; why would he have to talk to me about it?" It didn't feel at all intrusive to have brought Alex in—I was quite happy about it actually. Running the antique shop wasn't something I wanted to do for life, so it made me happy to know it would be in good hands. I also had a tremendous sense of relief that Alex had a plan— and that it included sticking around.

"I just thought…" Alex said, pulling his seat upright and facing front.

"It's fine, really, Alex." I smiled and glanced over at him reassuringly. "I'll have lots of fun teaching you the ropes and we'll have loads of time together. It's going to be great. Don't you think?"

A note of doubt rose in his voice, sending a shard of apprehension into my gut. "The job might include a lot of traveling," he said. "Brig asked me to take over his auction and estate sale trips."

The air grew tense between us. He wasn't telling me something. The knot in my stomach tightened. I had a suspicion that Alex's talents were going to be used beyond running an antique and fine furniture business. I wasn't sure if I was ready to accept a life of secrets and spy missions, but I knew if I loved Alex it would mean loving all of him—for exactly who he was. For now, I would play along, but at some point, Brig and Alex would tell me the truth. I would pester them both until they did.

That thought cheered me. "It's okay. I'll be busy with school and track. I hear UCONN has an amazing track coach. Besides, it'll be nice not to have to worry about helping Brig at the antique shop as much."

"I'm glad you aren't upset." I felt his shoulders relax beside me. The conversation wasn't over by a long shot. Hopefully, I could learn to live with worrying about what danger he was in when he went away. Maybe it would be easier to keep thinking he was at some antique dealer's convention rather than putting himself in harm's way. I guess I had no choice but to trust him and Brig, and live my own life to the fullest. I owed it to Levi—and to myself.

I pulled into the parking area of Wolf Den Falls and Alex and I hiked down the trail following the sound of cascading water. It turned out to be a beautiful day, the sky a mass of white clouds, patches of blue poking through. The trees were half bare, a few red, orange and yellow leaves hanging on in the autumn breeze. Alex and I made slow progress, the trail slick with wet leaves and both of us silently mindful of his prosthesis. I noticed it less and less, but I suspected there wouldn't be one minute of his life that he wasn't aware of it. We reached our destination, the ledge of rocky outcroppings that lay below the falls.

It was unseasonably balmy and the scent of earth and moss and moisture filled the air. We stood quietly taking in the beauty and majesty of the forty foot wall of rushing water, the sound drowning out the beating of my heart. Alex turned me to face him, moisture clinging to our skin and making me shiver. He wrapped his arms around me and his eyes found mine.

"Are you sure you don't want to go away to school? Stanford or Harvard would have been awesome opportunities."

I finally said what I'd wanted to say for months, but had been too afraid. Afraid he didn't feel the same way, or that my brother would always stand between us, or maybe just because I was afraid I could lose Alex, too. No matter the consequences, I needed to say it now. "Everything and everyone I love is here, Coop." I wrapped my arms around his neck and leaned up to kiss him, our eyes following each other's lips until they met in a sweet, slow kiss.

When we opened our eyes, Alex smiled shyly and said, "I'm glad to hear it." He hesitated and added softly, "I've loved you forever, you know. I think it happened when I helped you up after you fell off your bike the first time we met. You were only six years old, and even through your tears, you kicked the bike. You were so cute. I knew then, I was a goner."

My heart sang with contentment. Then I was instantly angry. "Wait! If you really felt that way, why didn't you say something?" I punched him in the arm.

"Ow! I tell you I love you and you punch me." He laughed, which served to make me feel foolish and madder all at the same time. "And you wonder why I never told you before," he said, mock indignation in his voice.

"You know what I mean. Why didn't you tell me?"

He waited before responding, a sheepish look taking over his face. "I made a promise to Lee that I would wait until you were eighteen before I...said or did anything about it." He was holding me in his arms again, our bodies pressed together and the sound of the falls loud in the air beside us, the mist making my hair frizz into curls around my face.

"I can't believe he would ask you to make such a stupid promise." Anger seeped into my words. If only Alex had told me. At least then I would have understood. Or maybe I would have tried to convince him that my age shouldn't matter. Maybe Levi had known something we didn't.

"Lee wanted to protect you, Jordie. He loved you. He only wanted what was best for you." His voice grew softer as he tucked a curl behind my ear. "I think he would be okay with us being together."

I had forgotten to tell him about the letter, but it didn't seem to matter anymore. "I think you're right. Lee would have been happy for us."

He ran a finger down my cheek and then gently kissed my forehead, his lips warm on my cool skin. "Everything's going to be all right, now."

As I did when I was little, I believed him. I didn't know what the future held for us and part of me was terrified, but I looked up to the top of the falls and said, "If Lee were here, I think he would say, '*Just jump*'."

Epilogue

Winter passed and spring burst with color, a warm breeze, and the scent of lilacs thick in the air. As promised, Alex was home to take me to the prom. I had only imagined how great he would look in a tux, and man, I wasn't disappointed. In classic black and white, we made an entrance that rivaled Prince William and Kate Middleton. All eyes, including the glaring Principal Griffin, followed us onto the dance floor where Alex proved to be a surprisingly graceful partner—at least for slow dances.

"When do you leave on your next trip?" I asked, making a point not to ask for details on location or how long he might be gone this time. So far, his trips had only been for a few days or a week at most.

"I'm not sure," He said, his green eyes dark and mysterious in the dim light as he turned me in slow circles. "But I promise you'll be the first to know."

His smile never failed to send warm tingles to my insides and I found it impossible to stay mad or upset with him for long. Being best friends had its advantages. I'd decided that I could forgive him just about anything knowing we would always be

there for each other—even when we were apart.
Being able to each stand on our own made our time
together less about what we were missing and more
about what we shared in common.

The pay-off was that after a week of being
apart, the welcome home included a lot of kissing.
The kissing had led to more and we were struggling
to find our way in unfamiliar territory. Neither of us
wanted to do anything that would compromise our
friendship or our futures, but we were heading to an
inevitable moment of pushing beyond the tentative
boundary that lay between us.

If it were totally up to me, I would have
booked a hotel room that night and made things
'official.' As usual, Alex was determined to do the
right thing. He didn't want the prom night cliché.
He'd said, when the time was right, he wanted it to
be special. I didn't argue. More than anything else, I
was learning to trust him and let things happen in
their own time.. When the time came, I knew it
would be perfect. He already had my whole heart. It
was just a matter of time before we shared body and
soul and I couldn't wait for that day. *No pushing the
river,* as Vic liked to remind me. Alex seemed to
understand this concept much better than I did,
except when it came to his own recovery from his
PTSD symptoms.

He was still in counseling and working
through the residual nightmares that brought him

back to the moment when my brother's eyes went empty and he lost his best friend. Sometimes we would talk about it, but mostly we tried to put it all behind us. I would wait until that memory no longer stood between us, no matter how long it took.

Grief is a weird and powerful force. It creeps in when you least expect it and colors your memories, smoothing out the rough edges and softening the scars. Time truly does heal all wounds, even if the scars that are left behind break open once in a while to remind us how fragile life can be. I had come to realize that the wounds you couldn't see were the ones that took the longest to heal. My family would heal in time, adapting to our new state of being without Levi, each of us carrying our own regrets about how we could have loved him more—or at least differently.

Mom and Roger were engaged on Valentine's Day, which I thought was a little fast, but Mom reminded me that life was too short to waste time, a quote from Levi's last letter which she knew I would understand. The friction between us had dissipated considerably with this new philosophy we'd adopted about accepting each other's differences and flaws, and respecting each other's choices. Mom was finally letting go and letting me grow up.

Brig still played poker with the guys on the last Friday of the month, but he now included Alex

in his circle of comrades. I could see Alex
becoming more confident and relaxed in his new
role as Brig's business partner more every day, and
I had no doubt he would be a great asset to the
team. I tried not to worry and to leave Alex in the
hands of God or the Universe or whoever was in
control up there, because it was now clear to me
that I had no control over anything in life besides
myself and my own choices.

Levi's last letter to Brig, the one I hadn't
been able to read the night Alex brought it home
from Iraq, remained folded on top of my stack in
the shoe box under my bed. Brig had given a copy
to me and Mom and I took it out to read it again.

Dear Brig,

*I'm sorry I didn't make it back like I
promised you I would. I want you to know I did my
best over here to make you proud. You've done so
much for me. I hope you know how much I
appreciate it. And thanks for keeping me and Coop
together. It's meant a lot having a friend here.*

*I know you'll take care of Jordie and Mom,
but could you look after Coop too? He's been
without a dad for a long time. We had that in
common. I guess it's why we're so tight. I think he'll
treat Jordie right. It's pretty obvious those two were
meant to be together. And don't let Mom get
between them. You know how overprotective she*

can be. I wish she could just lighten up and not be so hard on herself and everybody else. I don't think God would expect her to be perfect or to be right all the time. Heaven would be a lonely place if we all had to earn our way in. From what I've seen, I think it comes down to good and evil, and it seems like nobody is all one or the other. I guess only God can judge who goes where.

It stands to reason there must be a heaven— a place we go where there's no more pain and suffering. After the things I've seen, I'm thinking hell is right here on earth since there is so much ugliness in this world. It makes me wonder what happens to the people who hurt those who are innocent—is there any justice?

All I know is I've seen a lot of good people who have died in this war--people who fought for those who can't fight for themselves--guys who fought even when they were scared. Those guys are the real heroes. Maybe Mom was right about one thing. Maybe heaven is for heroes. I only hope there's room for me.

Lee

I folded the letter and returned it to the top of the pile. Then I wiped my tears, smiled, and closed the lid on the box, most certain of exactly where my brother was.

PJ Sharon is author of several soon to be released, independently published, contemporary young adult novels, including HEAVEN IS FOR HEROES. Her stories have garnered several contest finals, including two awards for her up-coming book ON THIN ICE, due out in December, and a place in the prestigious Valley Forge Romance writer's contest for SAVAGE CINDERELLA coming out in the spring of 2012.

On the road to publication, PJ decided that indie-publishing was the best fit for her books. Although the themes are mature, evoking plenty of drama and teen angst, PJ writes with a positive outlook and promises a hopefully ever after end to all of her books. She believes in strong heroines empowered by learning valuable life lessons. Because of this, readers of all ages will be captivated by the emotional and romantic journeys of her characters.

Writing romantic fiction for the past six years, and following her destiny to write Extraordinary stories of an average teenage life, PJ is mother to two grown sons and lives with her husband and her dog in the Berkshire Hills of Western MA.